A
Garland Series

VICTORIAN

FICTION

NOVELS OF FAITH
AND DOUBT

A collection of 121 novels
in 92 volumes, selected by
Professor Robert Lee Wolff,
Harvard University,
with a separate introductory volume
written by him
especially for this series.

WILLIAM BLAKE

William Edward Heygate

Garland Publishing, Inc., New York & London

1975

———

Bibliographical note:

this facsimile has been made from a copy in the
British Museum
(1362.g.11)

———

Library of Congress Cataloging in Publication Data

Heygate, William Edward.
    William Blake.

    (Victorian fiction : Novels of faith and doubt ;
27)
    Reprint of the 1848 ed. published by J. Masters,
London.
    I. Series.
PZ3.H5154Wi7 [PR4789.H48] 823'.7   75-473
ISBN 0-8240-1551-7

Printed in the United States of America

WILLIAM BLAKE.

Page 4.

WILLIAM BLAKE:

OR,

The English Farmer.

BY

THE REV. W. E. HEYGATE, M.A.,

AUTHOR OF

PROBATIO CLERICA, GODFREY DAVENANT, ETC.

LONDON:

JOSEPH MASTERS,

ALDERSGATE STREET, AND NEW BOND STREET.

——

1848.

TO HER UNDER WHOSE ROOF

THE FIRST YEARS OF HIS MINISTRY WERE PASSED,

AND WHOSE ADVICE WAS

NOT LESS VALUABLE THAN HER KINDNESS,

This little Fruit of Rural Parochial Work

IS GRATEFULLY AND AFFECTIONATELY

INSCRIBED BY

THE AUTHOR.

PREFACE.

THE Author of this tale cannot happily commit it to his readers without begging them not to allow the lighter portions to hinder thoughtfulness in reading the more serious. The transition from the mirthful to the grave is perhaps unusually sudden; and this may be more startling because authors generally divide narratives of this description into solemn and cheerful chapters. But it is difficult to see what they gain by this method; for such works are not read by chapters, but by large portions, or straight through: so that, whatever objection attaches to the quicker transitions of this tale belongs equally to all books of the same class. And, indeed, the tendency which they have to mix up different states of feeling, and to lead persons to regard grave subjects with some degree of levity, might well induce the clergy to abandon this style of writing but for

peculiar and counterbalancing advantages. Those
advantages are that, just as catechising enables
the teacher to mention many things, and to use
modes of speech which are precluded in preaching;
so here, it is easy to enter into details, and into
lesser faults or virtues, or greater, as they manifest themselves in common-place life, and so to
give advice where it would not otherwise be possible. Again, a narrative partakes of the uses
of biography. It pictures and makes vivid; it
realises, and to all appearance renders possible,
and even probable, virtues which would generally
seem difficult, and almost unattainable.

Besides, it is well known that many persons
can be induced to read an amusing book, who
will not look at one which is grave and closely
reasoned, though twice as improving. And we
must add, that, after all, this sharp transition is
truer and more faithful, more like our real daily
life, and therefore not only safe but profitable, if
rightly contemplated. Each day of a Christian
man is made up of hopes and disappointments,
of worldly business and pleasures, constantly
seasoned and broken in upon by devotional acts
and thoughts. To a thoughtful man, indeed,
pleasures and pains, labour and rest, and everything around him, are constantly suggesting some

spiritual meditation, so that all the day, from morning till evening, is a succession, and quick succession of ideas, grave and light, spiritual and worldly; and a man is never safe, and never happy, until he is able readily, and as it were naturally, to pass out of one state of feeling into another, or rather until he is so fixed and formed in religion, that those things which are not of it pass as it were through his mind, leaving him always the same; just as the blue heavens are crossed and re-crossed by the clouds, but remain in their own unchanging clearness.

It remains, therefore, with the reader to go with the transitions of this tale as with the transitions of his life. The Author can secure him from risk neither in the one case nor in the other; but a serious intention to do right, and to improve, will go far to insure its object, and will leave the mind free to pluck a few flowers of amusement by the way.

The Author, then, commends this little volume to his readers, in the belief that the farmers of England are an important class, and one hardly recognising its privileges, power, and consequent responsibility; believing, too, that hard times are coming, and that habits of exertion, simplicity of life, a more scientific and thorough education, with the self-discipline and quietness of spirit which our Church, when followed, so eminently produces, are necessary to meet the trials and difficulties of the day.

Would that he might also believe that, under God's blessing, these pages will assist some of those for whom they are written in the course before them; and help to make the English farmer that blessing to himself, and to those under and around him, which he may and ought to be.

CONTENTS.

CONTENTS.

WILLIAM BLAKE.

————◆————

CHAPTER I.

A Sunday Unimproved.

" Look to thy actions well :
For churches are either our heaven or hell."

GEORGE HERBERT.

THE population of Great Staunton amounted to
six hundred persons; but, on the bright July Sunday
which commences our story, the congregation
attending divine service at the parish church consisted of some thirty persons, besides the school
children.

In the reading-desk might have been seen a fine
hearty-looking gentleman, about sixty years of age,
whose life seemed to have been passed in the fields,
more than in the study, the cottage, or the church.
Small trace was there of thought, either upon his
features, or in his manner; and the clear, manly
style in which he read the general confession seemed
to express an approval and confidence in the truth

B

and excellence of what he was saying, rather than any humiliation of spirit, or any deep sense of the sins and spiritual necessities of himself and his flock.

Whilst the rector was thus occupied, those of his parishioners who were present might have been seen in various postures and situations, through the church. A few labourers stood leaning over the high pew sides with their heads upon their arms; the women sat, quietly listening; and the farmers sat, or stood, as they liked best. One thing only was certain, that no one knelt but the clergyman; and that no one responded, except the clerk and the school children. And so the service proceeded, until the Psalms, during which some stood, and some sat, gradually composing themselves after their churchward walk, for the Lessons, during which, owing to the work of Saturday, and the heat of Sunday, as they would have maintained, a large proportion of this small proportion of the people of Great Staunton were asleep.

At the close of the Litany, a twang and moan sounded from the gallery, upon which, some of the men rose, and, turning their backs upon the Communion Table and the clergyman, gazed vacantly up whilst the band, by means of violin, bassoon, and hautboy, went over and over some verses of the old version. The poor thought it very fine, but received no benefit from it, and took no interest in it: the farmers' daughters occasionally smiled, and looked at each other; and the only entirely imperturbed and imperturbable persons seemed the clergyman and the farmers.

At last came the sermon, and in it there was nothing to blame, and nothing to praise. Any heathen philosopher might have used it after cutting out a few names and allusions; and, as far as Church doctrine was concerned, any dissenter might have preached it.

Then, after the peace of God had been pronounced upon those whose consciences were altogether untroubled, and whose cares were those upon which that peace does not descend, the congregation departed, and in two minutes the church was empty.

The most important farmers in the place, however, stayed behind a minute or two in the porch, in order to greet each other, and their rector. They had not to wait long for Mr. Eccles—he was with them in a trice; and "Good day, Mr. ———,"—"How d'ye do, Mr. So-and-so?"—"Fine-morning!"—"Famous weather for the wheat!" and similar observations, formed the staple of the conversation which took place on the way between the porch and the churchyard-gate.

One family, in particular, occupied Mr. Eccles' attention. An elderly man, with his wife and two fine lads, nearly of an age, waited for a respectable, but somewhat heavy phaeton; and, meantime, seemed occupied in pointing out various objects to a pale, thin youth, who had evidently come from London, on a visit.

"Hey day, Mr. Blake! you have brought us down a Londoner to spy out the land," said the good-natured rector. "And what do you think, Sir, of our country? You don't see such crops everywhere, do you? Come down to my house whilst you're here, and I shall show you a few beasts that you'll have, one of these days, at Smithfield."

"He don't know much about beasts, Sir," replied Mr. Blake; "I don't think he can tell wheat from oats, till they are threshed out. But, perhaps, he'll learn a thing or two, before he returns, to astonish the cockneys with." "Well, but you have not told me who your friend is, Mr. Blake. But here's your carriage, so I won't keep you any longer."

"A cockney nephew, Sir! a cockney nephew!" shouted Mr. Blake, as he turned his steady old horse away from the church.

It was a sweet drive to the old Moat House; for the landlord would not suffer the trees to be lopped or thinned in his boundary hedges, and the elms feathered down over the bank, and threw shadows on the turf sides of the lane, which moved gently to and fro, and made the sunlight play along the ground.

The Moat House was an old pile of timbers and plaster, quaintly figured with scrolls, medallions, and various patterns. Some of the mullioned windows remained, and some were gone. It had, evidently, seen better days, but it was a house to interest and please any man of taste or education.

But the rick-yard, not empty even in July, and the new farm buildings of red brick and blue slate roofs, which harmonised badly enough with the old house, for they were of his own planning and building, were the pride of the present tenant; and, indeed, he might well be pardoned for liking their good arrangements, and substantial workmanship, if he had not been so blind to the merits of his forefathers. Men must not expect the sympathy which they refuse to others.

As soon as the phaeton arrived, the whole party dismounted, and strolled off into various parts of the premises. Mrs. Blake went to see whether the dinner looked prosperous; Mr. Blake sauntered in the garden; and the three youths went into the orchard, towards the cherry-trees. The two Blakes differed little in age or character. They were both fine, good-tempered lads, and, if they had enjoyed a good education, would have made useful and happy men. Yet Mr. Blake had not been at all stingy in their education. He had spent as much upon them as his neighbours did, and much more than had been spent upon himself. They had been to a large school at the county town, kept in a large house, entitled, in very large letters, "Classical and Commercial Academy;" at which they had learned absolutely nothing of classics, and only a smattering of ordinary subjects. The history of their country, the habits of other nations, and, which was worse, many of the doctrines of their Church, and their position, privileges, and duties, through her, towards God and man, were practically unknown to them. And on these points, they heard little in the pulpit, and nothing in private, from Mr. Eccles. He was a good shot, and a good farmer, and a good dining companion ; yes, and he was a kind neighbour, and a ready giver to the poor ; but he was not a teacher— he knew but little, and he taught still less.

It was curious enough, then, to see these lads, who had never received any deep sense of religion, nor thought of it as an affection and a principle which could and would make a person deviate from the usual ways of men, and think, and read, and give up a pursuit; but who, on the other hand, were rigid adherents to the Church, and despised dissenters ; it was curious enough to see them brought into contact with their London cousin, who was, in many respects, the very reverse of all this.

John and William Blake were Churchmen without any piety. Edward Jones, their mother's nephew, was pious without any regard to the Church, and he was not satisfied, either with his cousins or himself, as he followed them into the orchard and fell to some extent into the light conversation of his companions. But dinner was soon ready, and all parties agreed in being equally glad of the news, and ready for the good fare of the farmer's hospitable board.

We need not pause to describe the dishes, nor the process of their removal. By the time the meal was over, what with the heat of the weather, and the dinner, a sort of languor stole over Mr. Blake, and his chin gradually pressed the collar of his waistcoat into his shirt, until, the balance being lost, too great a nod roused him to the acknowledgment of his being rather drowsy.

It was immediately proposed to take the wine into an arbour in the garden; and in a few minutes all the party was comfortably seated under its shade on benches or chairs; and Mr. Blake's pipe and the lads' cigars disturbed the gnats and other insects from their accustomed shelter.

Young Jones gave a momentary turn to the conversation, by asking whether it was not time for church; and, on being assured that it was only a quarter-of-an-hour's walk across the fields, they began again upon the anecdotes of a fair which was just over.

The next time Edward looked at his watch he found that it wanted only five minutes of three, the time for service; and jumping up he said, "We must not lose a minute, it's almost three. Look here!" he exclaimed, as he held up his watch before his cousins.

"*We*, indeed!" cried William. "I'm not going again, this piping day, I can tell you."

"Not going again on Sunday! Will you, then, John?"

"Not I," replied John, with a yawn, as he knocked off the ashes of his cigar into his cousin's hat.

"Come, come, youngster," interposed the host; "sit down and make yourself comfortable. We've all been to church, haven't we? And our parson never expects us to go again."

"I certainly shall go," said Edward, colouring up. "I wish you had told me at first that you did not mean to go."

"Then you'll just lose your way, and be there when it's half over. Our rector is never more than half-an-hour in the afternoon, and has begun by this time."

Edward gave up; but he resolved, in his own mind, to go to the meeting-house in the evening which he had seen on his return from church. He went accordingly, and found it filled. The sermon was good; and he naturally concluded that it was a much more useful place to the village than the church, and he told his cousins so at tea. They were highly indignant at him, both for going, and for saying such a thing; but he bore all their ridicule and reproach pretty well, and at length got them to argue the matter over instead of abusing him and the dissenters.

When they came to discuss the question, Edward had the best of the argument, for he was right in all he said upon the duty of keeping the Lord's day; and the Blakes' objections to dissent were those of prejudice and not of principle. They thought it enough to sanctify the *morning* of the Lord's *day*, to give *two hours* of God's *day* to Him; a poor *day*,

if it had been worked upon their farm, by plough-
man or by shepherd; a poor day this, if it had
been a shooting day for themselves! whilst Edward
considered that *any* means of hallowing the Sabbath
were justifiable and acceptable to God. If they
had been consistent Churchmen, they would have
dedicated the whole day to God; and then, and then
only, could they have honestly reproved dissenting
worship. If Edward had been as well instructed as
he was sincere, he would have known that, to read
the Church service to himself, with a sermon or book
of devotion, would have been not only his plain
duty under such circumstances; but would have
strengthened his soul far more than the loose doctrinal statements and unformed prayers of a meeting, whose very assemblage is a violation of that
unity to the observance of which the promises of
our Lord's presence are attached.

But though vanquished in argument, the Blakes
remained unconvinced; and, as they were tired of
the subject, they proposed a turn into the home
close before supper.

William and Edward went on, and John soon
caught them with a gun in his hand. Edward re-
monstrated; but John said, that he had seen a cat
about lately, and he would not have the rabbits
which he had turned out killed for anything, so
that, Sunday or no Sunday, he would shoot it if he
could. In a few minutes something white showed
itself behind a filbert hedge which skirted the

orchard; and John crept slowly up with his gun raised, ready to fire upon the least movement. At length he paused at thirty yards and listened. All he heard was a gentle crackling, like the crushing of bones, and this determined him. He fired; a long howl was the answer. It was his favourite pointer; and it lived but a few minutes.

Supper passed off gloomily enough. Mr. Blake was displeased; John was ashamed and vexed; and all retired earlier than usual, dissatisfied and unimproved after an ill-spent Sunday. There was no day in all the week in which they had earned sleep so little—no day so wasted as the day of all days; and they went to their slumbers without a thought of the likeness between sleep and death, and of the warning which each night conveys; for neither had they remembered the resurrection when they rose at morn, nor thought even once of heaven as an object of search and longing, although the whole day was the memorial of the eternal Sabbath, the witness of the resurrection of Christ and the foreshowing of their own.

CHAPTER II.

Cockneys and Countryfolk.

"The cockney sneers when country bumpkins stare
Along the stones, and jostle all they meet.
Nor less the bumpkin jeers when cockneys dare
His miry roads with dainty-booted feet."—CRITIC.

NEXT day the three lads rose early for eel-spearing. Each carried his many-pronged weapon, and a lad bore a great basket after them. Many and many a ditch was searched, but nowhere did they find the small breathing-hole, which betrays its simple inhabitant, nor did random dibbings and dashings serve to place a single fish in the basket.

"I say, Jem," exclaimed William to the boy, "they must have been working this pretty well lately. Have you heard anything about it?"

"Noa, I don't knoa anything about it," replied the lad. "May be the Welford chaps ha' been down here again."

"No; these are not Welford shoes," cried Edward as he pointed out to his cousins the short hob-nailed impression of a country boot stamped again and again into the edge of the ditch.

"No; that they are not, that's clear," he replied. "But I don't know any more for that."

Edward looked hard into the boy's face, then at his boots, and then again in his face. The boy looked uncomfortable. Edward was suspicious; but said nothing. By this time they had reached some wider and deeper ditches; and they grew merrier as their hopes rose. Their merriment was chiefly at Edward's expense. They quizzed his shoes, which were not fit for the country. (They ought to have lent him some.) They laughed at his coat. (They ought to have given him a shooting-jacket.) Not that they were generally forgetful of him, or inattentive to his comfort; but they thought more of themselves, and could not, any how, refrain from quizzing. Unfortunately, farmers have, like other people, a greater sense of the faults of others than of their own. They are not conscious of their own want of education and of their own awkwardness in many things; and yet often entertain a most profound contempt for townspeople. It would be better if they piqued themselves upon their real merits and position rather than on their being able to do a few things which, living as they do in the country, they cannot avoid understanding. They really have a *position* and a *character* to maintain and be proud of. The English farmer is a member of a class, and that a most important class of society. Living in the country, and in the enjoyment of sun, and air, and fields, and trees, without the wearing routine of labour, which too often blinds the peasant to all these blessings, and makes him walk amongst them as if they were not; removed from all the excitement of city life; enjoying a distinctly marked position, free from the temptation of moving up into a higher grade, and so losing happiness and fortune, and all which makes life sweet and honourable; living in old manor-houses, occupied often from father to son for centuries, with their quiet country church, and honest, invigorating recreations, *the English farmer has the means of being one of the most sober-minded, sensible, independent, and happy men in the realm.* If he is not this, it is his own fault, or the fault of parents, or clergyman, or of some external circumstance. He might be an anchor and a principle of *stedfastness* to his country, and more useful, by far, in his quiet circle, than many bustling men in larger spheres and of greater pretensions.

But to return. Our party found the new waters very much more promising; and soon filled their baskets with the finest eels. During their sport, they had frequently to cross the dykes, and, to do this, they placed the handle of the spear upon the near bank, and used it as a leaping-pole, to throw themselves across. The Blakes were naturally much more expert at this than Edward; and he was several times very nearly in.

At last they came to a broad ditch, which had not more than two feet of water, and they found it impossible, owing to a steep back behind, to get run enough for their usual method. Edward thought he would now redeem his character—as well for skill as boldness, and, placing his spear in the centre of the ditch, he threw himself boldly forward, expecting easily just to reach the opposite side; but alas! he did not know the nature of the bottom. Four feet of mud absorbed in a minute the greatest part of the spear; and Edward and it were standing upright in the middle. How to get out was no simple question. In less than two minutes Edward had sunk in the mud up to his waistcoat, and the water reached his chin. However, he was hauled out by his cousin's spear, and landed, reeking with black mud, and smelling of the very essence of ditch-water and fetid pools.

The Blakes roared and roared again, and Edward's good nature at last gave way. He fell sullenly into the rear of the party, and walked on with heavy and sour looks, wishing himself in Fenchurch Street again, or anywhere rather than with such rough bumpkins as his then companions.

In a little while the Blakes paused and examined the ground where they were standing.

"Here's been another sheep killed here," said John, "as sure as I am alive."

"What do you mean?" exclaimed Edward.

"Why, they've been carrying off another of our ewes, that's all."

"We'd better go up to the house at once, then," said William, leaving the spot.

"Stop a minute," called Edward, who had followed a sort of roughness in the grass into the hedge and found some of the offal lying there. They came up, and examined the spot, but found no clue. As they were leaving the field, however, John found a knife lying near the plank which crossed the ditch. He opened it, and handed it round.

"This is a rum knife," he said, as he handed it to William. "Did you ever see such a thing?"

"It's precious like the old woman's which had three new blades, and two new handles. I say, Jem, do you know this knife?"

"I never seed it afore, Sir," replied the boy; "it ai'n't like any of our hands'."

After a few minutes the boy volunteered another remark.

"I doant think none of our people would have left their knives here, Sir."

"Why, you fool," said William, "you don't think they left it here on purpose?"

"Don't knoa, Sir, but I am sure it ai'n't none of our hands' "

Edward's attention was again aroused. He looked at the boy hard, and his eye quailed before him. As he moved on, he saw a cottage two fields up, and asked the boy whose it was.

"Mick Thompson's, Sir."

"I shall go there, and get a wash, before I go up to the house."

"It ai'n't no use, Sir. He's not at home."

"Why, it's only five now; he'll be about, surely."

"Noa, you won't find him, I'm asure."

"How do you know that?" said Edward, looking at the boy again, who made no answer.

They now approached the cottage, and found no one, just as the boy had said. Edward looked at the windows, and saw that the house was empty. As he went round the garden, however, he observed a drop of blood upon the bricks under the pump, and pointed it out to his cousins. They assured him the cottage should be searched. "No time like the present," he replied, as he groped about, and looked everywhere. Time was now wearing on, and they were impatient to leave.

"One minute more and I will be with you," said Edward, pointing to a little open window in the gable close under the thatch. "I must just look in there."

"But how are you to get up?"

"Oh, give me your shoulder. There, that will do. Stand steady. Yes, here it is; keep quiet. Now, let me down, and get up yourself." So saying, he helped William into the same position, and they now ascertained that the stolen sheep was hanging under the roof above.

"Look, look, here's Thompson coming!" called John.

"Then we had better be off," answered William, "before he sees us."

Edward was wiser however. "It's too late now," he spoke in a lower tone, watching the boy, "you must catch him now or never."

The boy began whistling, and Thompson paused. "Hold your tongue, you young rascal," said Edward, shaking his fist over him, "or I won't leave a bone in your body. Take him behind John, and William and I will secure the fellow." Edward now went forward, and calling out boldly for water, showed his muddy hands and feet. Thompson came on without suspicion, and put his key in the door. It opened, and they followed him in. He stooped down for a bucket. Edward pushed him over, and in a minute the two lads had secured him with the well-rope.

"Keep that boy, John," said Edward, "I'm sure he's concerned. You'd better take him up, you and William, and I will wait here till you come."

"But how will you manage if he gets away?" they answered, pointing to Thompson.

"Oh, trust me for that; I'll give him some of his own knife if he stirs a peg. Do you know this knife, Thompson? It is not any of our hands', boy, is it?"

The boy's wits were no greater than his honesty.

c

He could say nothing.   He pulled his hat over his eyes, and quietly followed the Blakes.

Old Blake was delighted.   He praised Edward to the skies; and said, that "the cockneys were sharp enough, any how;" and his nephew's superior cleverness and decision in this matter completely silenced his cousins, so that the eel-spearing was forgotten in the capture.

Mrs. Blake found fresh clothes; and an excellent breakfast, begun and concluded with old English ale, set everything straight; so that very soon all parties were ready to proceed with their prisoner to Squire Althorp's, the nearest magistrate.

Mr. Althorp was at home; and, at the other end of the library was a middle-aged man, in black, busily occupied with books and papers. The case for committal was made out; and the man and boy were soon handed over into the hands of the constable for safe custody. Before they left the room, however, the magistrate inquired whether either of them could read or write, and, being answered in the negative, he was about to dismiss the party when the visitor, at the other end of the room, requested leave to ask Mr. Blake a few questions after the prisoners were removed.   Mr. Althorp at once assented; and Mr. Blake felt himself under the searching eye of a man evidently accustomed to read the characters of those with whom he had to deal.

"May I ask you, Sir," was the first question,

" whether you have any other hands on your farm whom you think connected with the prisoners?"

" I really can't say, Sir. Can't prove it."

" Do you think it likely?"

" Why, yes, like enough. There are several of them would not mind helping."

" Have you many men whom you would trust in your granary?"

Mr. Blake stared.

" Are there many of your men, Sir, who would not take your corn if they could get an opportunity?"

" No; that there ar'n't."

" How many do you employ?"

" About thirty hands altogether, Sir."

" And how many of them would you trust?"

" I can't say."

" Twenty?"

" No, nor half that."

" Ten?"

" No."

" Five?"

" No."

" Thank you, Sir. May I ask you also how many of your men can read? Do you suppose half of them?"

" May be about half."

" Can they read well enough to read their Bibles?"

" I really can't say, Sir; but I should think not."

" Are you churchwarden, Sir?"

"Yes: I have been that these twenty years."

"How many people attend church in the morning?"

"About thirty or forty, I should say."

"In the afternoon?"

"Can't say; but I think about eighty."

"Why can't you say? Perhaps you do not attend in the afternoon?"

"Why, no; I can't say I do, Sir."

"May I ask whether the public-houses are full on the Sunday?"

"Yes, pretty well for that, Sir."

"And is there much shopping in the morning?"

"The butchers, Sir, and bakers, and grocers, do a good deal of business."

"When do you pay your wages?"

"Every Saturday, as regular as possible."

"Have you a weekly school in the place?"

"No: none."

"Thank you, Sir," concluded the interrogator with a deep sigh; and Mr. Blake felt much relieved, but he was not safe off yet. The stranger requested permission to ask another question or two of the prisoners.

"Certainly, my Lord," replied Mr. Althorp.

"My Lord!" Mr. Blake opened his eyes, and was beginning to understand that this could be no other person than their new Bishop, when Thompson and his companion were brought in again.

"Thompson," said the Bishop, in a deep, clear

voice, " I am going to ask you some questions. It will do you no good to tell me a lie, and it may do you some good to tell me the truth. Now attend. Have you always been a labourer?"

"Noa; I kept the beasts once."

"You mean you fed them, and kept them when they were feeding?"

"Yes, Sir, that's what I meaned."

"I know what you had to do very well. You were with the beasts always, were you not?"

"Yes, Sir."

"Night and day?"

"Yes, Sir."

"And how long did this work last,—about six months?"

"Yes, about that, I fancy."

"Did you ever go to church during that time?"

"Noa."

"Could you if you wished?"

"Noa, Sir."

"Is that true, Mr. Blake?"

"Why, I believe it is. They can't leave the beasts, Sir, that is, my Lord, I ask pardon, on any account."

"And why did you leave off your feeding trade; for you had better wages in that, I think?"

"I turned him off," interrupted Mr. Blake, "for selling some of the cake."

"Have you ever been confirmed, Thompson?" pursued the Bishop.

"Noa, my Loard."

"Did your clergyman ever ask you to be?"

"Noa, my Loard."

"Why not?"

"May be I was out in the fields of a day."

"Has he ever talked to you about your soul?"

"Noa, my Loard."

"Do you know you have one?"

"Why, yes, my Loard," said the man with a stupid grin.

"And do you know what will become of it?"

"Noa; I ain't 'ad no time to think o' the like of that."

"That will do. Thank you, Mr. Althorp;" and the Bishop leaned back in his chair, and put his hand across his face.

Mr. Blake was leaving.

"One minute more, Mr. Blake. I have a word to say to you as your bishop. You do not know me now; but, I trust, you will do one day, if we are both spared. I would not have given you so much trouble, nor have taken up Mr. Althorp's and your time without good reason. I think you will see that I have not. You have told me, Sir, that in your parish you have no school; that your men are paid on Saturday—so that their shopping and their chief temptation to drinking both fall upon the Sunday morning; I learn besides that not half your people can read their Bibles; that one, at least, is kept from church, for months, by the arrangement of his work; that the thief has never been confirmed, nor even invited to confirmation; and that he has never been personally warned or exhorted in private as to the state of his soul.   How can I wonder, then, that, out of six hundred souls, only thirty are found at church in the morning, and only eighty in the evening? and how can you or I wonder at the fearful fact that you cannot trust your men, or at the crime of the prisoner?

"I thank God, I am not a judge to condemn that man.   They used to pardon men for their possession of knowledge; but far more do they deserve pity when want of instruction leads them into crimes like these.

"Do not think me harsh, Sir.   I speak strongly, for I feel strongly.   I feel for the undying souls committed to me.   I do not blame you, Sir, in particular.   The blame may be transferred from you to others, and from them onwards; but surely *the greatest blame and peril rests on us somewhere. It must rest.*   To see Englishmen so degraded into dishonesty; to see Christians living below even the rules of heathen sages, must teach us this, that there is a grievous sin at the door of some of us, and a grievous danger impending over all.   What would become of us if there were a famine?   Our labourers would pillage our houses and murder our families.   What would become of us in a war for our religion or our liberties?   We could not get a handful of them to side with us.   What will become of us at the Last Day, when we have such crimes to answer for as that of to-day, which it may be we might have prevented, and have not? Let me beg of you to think over these things most earnestly, to consider what you can do; and to pray God to pardon and to save us even now."

The Bishop bowed to his hearers; and they left the room in total silence. But discussion soon succeeded thought, and his words had little effect on Mr. Blake, who had never seen any better-ordered parish than his own. William thought of them, and forgot to remember them at a future time; and Edward Jones came to the conclusion that a bishop might, after all, be more useful than he had been brought up to imagine—something more than a hospitable gentleman and a preacher of charity sermons.

The prisoner was removed to the county gaol after the ensuing magistrates' meeting, and in less than two years was at Norfolk Island; an Englishman—a Christian—consigned to the miseries and wretchedness of that dreadful place, without a hope, either here or hereafter.

CHAPTER III.

Market Day.

" Joy not in malice; that is a mortal sin;
  Man is perceywed by language and doctrine;
  Better is to lose than wrongfully to winne;
  He loveth wisedome which loveth discipline."

ALEXANDER DE BARKLAY.   Ob. 1552.

Two days after these events came the market.
Mr. Blake rode, and the three young men drove a
spirited colt in a sort of dog-cart, which carried
them along at nine miles an hour, through the green
lanes, until they came into the crowded little town
of Belborough.   The place was full of carts, and
gigs, and horses, and all manner of cattle.   Women
with butter-baskets and eggs; and men driving pigs,
which bolted in every direction but the right, and
tall fellows bearing crockery on their heads.   The
drover, with his slouched hat and shaggy dog, hollo-
ing and shaking his short greasy-looking ash stick;
young farmers, with cut-away coats and bright, brass,
buttons, and gay stocks; and the generation before
them in yellow waistcoats drab breeches and very
yellow tops; butchers hanging out their meat; gay
wives and gayer daughters, threading in and out of

the edges of this living mass, presented a scene for a painter's admiration; but not for Edward's, who found as much to laugh at in the dress and ways of the crowd, as his cousins had seen in his manner and want of skill in rural sports and works.

Mr. Blake arrived about twenty minutes later, and started off to sell some wheat amongst a knot of millers who stood in one corner of the old market-house. John was ordered to part with a cow for from £12 to £8. The three proceeded accordingly to find the cow, and John and William began at once to talk with the people who came to see her. She was a very fine-looking animal, but, for some cause or other, gave little or no milk. Under these circumstances she should have been sold to a butcher, not to any one who wanted a cow. This, however, did not suit Mr. Blake's views. He desired the highest price he could get, and, after much bargaining, she went for £10 to a man who kept a dairy-farm higher up the country. The money was paid, and all was settled.

As soon as this transaction was completed, the three lads, chuckling over their success, adjourned to the Saracen's Head for a glass of ale.

"I am as dry as the old cow," said William; "I vote we go in and get a glass of Mother Matson's ale."

"I don't mind if we do," replied John; "we can afford it out of our bargain, though we do pay for it."

"That's what old Nichols must do for milk if he wants any, I fancy."

This remark produced a good deal of laughter, and the three men proceeded to drink the purchaser's health, and to wish that the grass of Newleigh might prove more successful than the meadows of Staunton in filling the milk-pail.

Strangely enough, some of our readers will think, not even Edward Jones saw the dishonest and unchristian character of the job. But it is not strange to those who know what Bishop Butler calls the dishonest ways which had crept into business even in his time, and which have borne fruit an hundredfold since then. It is not strange to those who know how vague, unpractical, and unreal, is the popular religion with which Edward had been imbued, how generally it stops short, and reaches no height nor depth, satisfied with an acknowledgment of *one* doctrine, justification by faith, and with a few prescriptive acts, such as public worship on Sunday, and family prayer, and does not insist upon those duties that devolve upon us as members of one family, as all equally dear to Christ, partners in His death, life, gifts, and promises.

The business was over by three o'clock, and at that hour they who wished sat down to excellent dinners at their respective inns. Our party were, as we have seen, at the Saracen's Head, and thither repaired most of the persons from Staunton and the adjoining parishes. The crops, the weather, the members for the county, the board of guardians, were the general subjects of discussion, and we are sorry to add that they were mentioned often with that querulousness which is too often justly charged upon the farmer. It seems as if nothing was right, and nothing could please him. If the prices are high, the crops are short. If the crops are fine, prices are too low to remunerate the grower. If it be dry weather, the turnips fail ; if wet, the wheat. Yet farmers have sense enough to acknowledge generally that they could not arrange things better than they are, even if they had power over seasons, and storms, and showers. Why do they not then *act* on this conviction? If all is really well, why is not everything an occasion of content and thankfulness? If all things are wisely ordered, why are they not received cheerfully and gratefully? Indeed, men sadly forget the force of their example, the influence of the anxious face and the discontented speech to make men's hearts around them gloomy and worldly, and to prevent obedience to the precept, " Rejoice evermore." Indeed, they also sadly forget that a cheerful voice and thankful bearing are better praise than hymns and psalms, and that the reverse of them is the contradiction of all their worship, an obscuring instead of setting forth of God's glory.

After dinner, it was evident that Mr. Mann, whose farm adjoined the Moat farm, had taken more than he should have done. He became quarrelsome, and began to vent his old spleen and jealousies against Mr. Blake. First he spoke of certain stray cattle, then of a pauper case, and finally attacked him for

using the road scrapings which adjoined his land,
because he had intended to buy the whole scrapings
of the parish himself.

"Well, all I can say," he grunted out, "is, that
next vestry I shall propose the scrapings are sold
every year."

"And you're quite welcome," replied Mr. Blake;
"I'll bid against you any day."

"You don't bid so high generally, so you needn't
tell o 'that."

"As high as you at any rate, Mr. Mann; and now
I think o't, I should like to mention that bit you've
taken in by the pound there. I can hardly get a
waggon now past another at that ugly corner you've
made."

"That's the real width o' the land, I had it
measured myself."

"May be you did, but it strikes me you took the
centre of the road in the wrong place."

"How d'ye mean, Blake?"

"Why, you took a middle on my side, and
measured from that, so that all the common fell to
you, and none to me. That's all you did."

"I'll appeal to the commissioners any day. It's
all the same to me. Fair is fair all the world over,
and my name's Mann."

"And a very rum sort of man you are, neighbour,
in my humble opinion."

"No worse than my neighbours, I take it. To
think of a man scraping the parish roads in that

way! That's the way to scrape money together, indeed. Road scraping, money scraping. They'll call you Road-scraper Blake, I fancy, soon in our parish. Well, you are in a scrape anyhow, ah! ah! in a regular scrape, you old road-scraper!"

Blake could stand this no longer. He rose up and looked about him wildly. His neighbours begged him to sit down, but he would not. He walked up to his enemy, and took him in his left hand by the collar, and said, "I say, my neighbour Mann, you and I aren't over cool, and I think a little fresh air would do you good; so come along."

Mann struggled in vain against Blake's great strength. In a few minutes he was being carried towards the window by the nape of the neck and his corduroys, and every one made way for him, for he was very unpopular, and, as it was a fall of only three feet, they thought more fun than harm would come of it. Unfortunately, Mann's corderoys were none of the best. They gave way, and down he came with very little breeches remaining. For a moment, Blake's intention seemed to change, but a grim smile came over him, and he took Mann up in a lump, and huddled him out with the remark, "You can't sit down with us very comfortably now, so you may as well make a start of it, and get a new pair of breeches."

"They're sure to be *smalls*," exclaimed one, alluding to Mann's size.

"He's no more seat to his breeches than he has in

his saddle," cried another; and so Mr. Mann vanished away.

After this the wine flowed more freely, and many coarse jokes and unseemly tales were bandied about. Merriment mixed with oaths in repeating stories, as if an oath in jest were more innocent than an oath in anger; flushed faces, and obstreperous clamour, all showed that they who were there, if they were Christians at all, were very bad ones, were wholly forgetful of the strict commands against "all foolish jesting and talking," "banquetings, revellings, and such like."

Alas! if any one there present had obeyed the precept, "If any be merry let him sing psalms," what mockery would it have seemed! what profanity would it have been to introduce the words of David into the congregation of sinners! The thing would have condemned itself, not merely as out of place, but as blasphemous. But if so, what a profanation was it of the Christian's body, that it, the temple of God, should have been unfit to sound His praises! Yet so it was. And if death had cut short any of that party at that moment, it would not have found them ready, but rather eating and drinking with the drunken, worthy to be cut in sunder, and to have their portion with the hypocrites, where shall be wailing and gnashing of teeth.

As was the beginning so was the ending. In the hearts of both Blake and Mann there had long been lurking a jealousy and bitter feeling, wholly contrary to the command, "*as I have loved you*, that ye also should love one another."   Things had been professedly forgiven, but not forgotten, and so there had been no real forgiveness at all.   Parish feuds and private clashings had gradually caused a settled rupture between two fellow-Christians living close to each other, who flattered themselves that they were not guilty of uncharitableness, in quietly disliking and thwarting each other at every turn.   If God had *so* loved them, where would they have been ?

No soft anger turned away wrath, but, directly contrary to God's word, they had exchanged railing for railing, and not, contrariwise, blessing. Hence, feelings led to words, and words to deeds, and both were all along, to use God's own words, "in danger of the judgment."   A flushed triumph followed, drinking, 'wherein is excess,' and an ungodly clouding over God's glorious gifts of reason succeeded an ungodly despisal of God's blessed grace of charity, and Satan entirely triumphed.   And, if spiritual things could be seen as earthly things are, the spirit of evil might there have been distinguished as glorying in his victory of sin and wrath, and folly and punishment to come.   "For because of these things cometh the wrath of God upon the children of disobedience," and no custom, no numbers, will turn it aside.   "Though hand join in hand, the wicked shall not go unpunished."

At nine o'clock the party broke up.   Indeed, that was unusually late ; some stayed later, but Mr. Blake and the more respectable guests bade each other good evening, and left. Edward Jones was heartily sick of the whole evening, and was not well satisfied either with himself or his cousins. He had not checked them : nay, he had even joined in many things which his conscience forbade. John drove home, and they started at a pace even greater than that at which they came. Posts and rails seemed to whizz by them in the half darkness, and the objects of the way-side, trees, and gates, and bushes, appeared to form one straight stream, rushing past them with great rapidity. But John drove well, and kept the colt under command, and they had broken the neck of their drive before the least inconvenience or danger occurred. But in turning a sharp corner, the cart received a shock which nearly jolted its occupants from their seats. The horse was frightened, and dashed off at full speed, going wildly from side to side. In a few minutes the right wheel passed over a heap of the fatal road-scrapings which had been the occasion of contention ; the Blakes were jerked out on one side, and Jones on the other, and horse and cart went on as fast or faster than ever.

They scrambled up, and felt rather hurt. Their faces were wet, and they rightly concluded that it was with blood. In a few minutes one kicked against the whip, and further on Edward stumbled over one of the lamps. It seemed as if this was an omen of the destruction of the whole cart, and they expected every minute to find it in the ditch, or to pass it without seeing it. On and on, however, they went, and saw no more until they arrived at the welcome gate of the old house. There stood horse and cart, uninjured and quiet, and all the damage caused was to their own clothes and noses, none of which looked any better for some time, the former not until the tailor had seen them, the latter not until Mrs. Blake's management and some days' quiet had dispersed the rainbow colours of their bruises, and restored the pristine red and white.

So ended Belborough market-day, neither honourably nor prosperously; and when Edward went to bed, he felt somewhat like the country mouse transposed. He thought he got into plenty of scrapes at Staunton, and perhaps would have been safer and better in Fenchurch Street in the warehouse. However, a few days set all right. He and his cousins became better friends; he got into their ways, and they ceased to be struck with his. He determined to stay out the harvest, and then, for so his father's last letter told him, he was to go out to Chili for some years, to be under a correspondent of his father's house, in that distant country. His heart sank within him, but it was to sink still more before he bade adieu to England.

CHAPTER IV.

Harbest Home; or, the Last Load.

"Meanwhile the Farmer quits his elbow chair,
His cool brick-floor, his pitcher, and his ease,
And braves the sultry beams, and gladly sees
His gates thrown open, and his team abroad,
The ready group attendant on his word,
To turn the swarth, the quivering load to rear,
Or ply the busy rake, the land to clear."

BLOOMFIELD'S FARMER'S BOY.

July was spent, and half of August. The wheat and the oats were gathered in, and a field of barley alone remained before the "Harvest Home;" and all this time the cousins had been enjoying themselves in the fields by day, and at home and at their neighbours' houses by night; so that Edward had no reason to complain of the dulness of the country, or that the ancient hospitality was diminished. All were good friends—and full of fun and frolic.

There was, however, one circumstance which added greatly to John and Edward's merriment. There was a pretty Miss Hilton in the next parish, who had recently returned from a long visit in a distant county; and the youngest Blake was decidedly taken with her. It was useless to deny it, or turn the subject, or make any shift whatsoever; there was no convincing them to the contrary; for every reply, accompanied, as it was, by blush, or hesitation, or some awkwardness or other, confirmed the imputation. Nor, to say the truth, was the surmise unfounded.

Ellen Hilton was a simple, warm-hearted girl, who, without being beautiful, expressed so much good-nature and cheerfulness in blue eyes and on smiling lips, that any one might well think she would make a good wife, unless there chanced to be some unseen and unsuspected drawback. Such drawbacks it is not very kind to suspect; and, in the case of young men, not very natural. So William became fairly taken; and, fortunately for him, not mistaken. Still there was much to be done. Neither Mr. Hilton nor Mr. Blake had been asked; and, if this had been all settled, it did not yet appear what the lady herself would say. Then if three yesses combined, still he had no capital and she had no capital; so the affair was, at present, confined to a very small compass, namely, William Blake's wishes and intentions; and there we must leave it for the present.

There was, however, one good result of this fancy of William's, that John was thrown a great deal into Edward's sole company and influence; and although young Jones was by no means in possession of complete and sound religious principles and practice, yet, being earnest and sincere, he was the first young man whom John had ever found really interested in religious duty, and ready to give up anything for it. The effect of his society was, therefore, so far, good ; and even to the making John's private prayers more real instead of the mere form and show which they had been. In fact, he began both to think and to pray.

It was one of the hottest days of a hot August when the barley was to be carried. The horses were faint, and the men were fagged ; but the young men would not give in, and they worked in the field with hearty good-will until the end. Edward Jones had afforded a fund of amusement all the day, although of a good-natured kind. The mistakes he had made, and the difficulties he got into, excited continual merriment with his companions.

First, he took so much up on his fork, that it overbalanced him, and he fell quite over ; then he pitched it into the waggon, with the fork turned towards him, so that it would not come off the prongs, and all came down again. After awhile he tried the iron rakes, and often was pulled up quite sharp by getting their teeth in the ground. His driving was not much better. He could not keep the horses straight ; and nearly jolted his cousins off by running against a gate-post. The last load of all, however, was managed differently. The two Blakes loaded, and Edward was on the top. All went on well except that the load was not very well packed, and was higher and wider in one part

than in another.   Still Edward considered it a
triumph of genius ; and as he struck his foot into
the last lump that was pitched up to him,   he
dropped his fork, and, pulling off his hat, began to
cheer heartily, for the last load of the harvest.

He went on cheering, without looking down or
seeing how that beneath him the voice of joy was
changed into sadness.   William was holding his
brother's head, as he lay senseless on the ground.
Beside them was the fork which had been dropped
from Edward's hands, and which had fallen heavily
upon the head of his cousin.   It was, indeed, the
last load, the " Harvest Home," in which another
soul had been gathered in, and a pilgrim, at the
very outset, had reached what is called his last,
long home.

We shall not attempt to describe what was said or
felt at the Moat House.   It is enough to say, that
Edward was not blamed ; but he could not stay.
He knew the very sight of him would be bitter to
the parents of the dead—and he left them.

Mr. Eccles came down as soon as he heard of the
accident.   He did his best ; but it was little.   There
are two things which make a man a comforter—a
practical acquaintance with suffering, and thoughtful devotion.   When a man has mourned deeply
himself and received comfort, he does not readily
forget the thoughts or the words, which, in the hour
of his trial, assuaged or sharpened his sufferings ; but
even without this, he who has lived in the study of

God's word, and has suffered by love and the power of sympathy with prophets and martyrs, and, above all, with our blessed Saviour, knows many a thought and saying, many a promise and circumstance, which is able to give peace and to instil consolation—where and when the soul of the mourner is able to receive it. But neither of these, neither sorrow nor meditation had ever exercised their blessed influence upon Mr. Eccles. Life had run smoothly with him. His fortune was ample; his health and circumstances propitious; and his parish had never given him any trouble; and so he had learned nothing from life, and had nothing to teach. The kind sympathy which he felt was little different from that which Mr. Blake received from his neighbours in general. It was friendly, and little more.

With all his kindness, he was a most unfit and neglectful clergyman; and it was no wonder that the Blakes had so little religion among them, and the cottagers were in the state before described, for nothing had been done for either one or the other. And this Mr. Eccles felt in later life. Before he died, his omissions were brought before him by illness and by the advice of a faithful clergyman, who was his neighbour and friend; and very bitter were his regrets—very sincere his repentance. "Where is the flock that I gave thee, my beautiful flock?" were words often upon his lips, and in his heart; and he testified his changed feelings, by warning his younger brother, with free confession of his own neglect, and by giving much property for different good purposes to the parish of Great Staunton after he had left it. He will not, however, appear again in this short narrative, for within a few months he came into the estate and title of his brother, Sir Reginald, and immediately left the neighbourhood, greatly to the joy of the Bishop, who knew his incompetency and the difficulty—the almost impossibility—of changing a man of his age and character.

His successor was a man of a wholly different stamp. Learned and studious, yet a most active visitant of school and cottage; gentle, and affectionate, and devout; but firm and decided, Mr. Lee was admirably calculated to restore a parish; and he set about his work most prudently, earnestly, and prayerfully. He had much to discourage him; but he was not the man to be discouraged, because he had faith and patience. His church was almost a ruin. He had no schools but a Sunday-school. Out of six hundred people, but ten were communicants. He was poor, and people were prejudiced against him, simply because they did not know their own Church; and when they saw Her obeyed, and represented as She desires, they found Her so different from what She had been, that they thought it must be Popery to change from their long-used ways. Alas! they did not know what Popery is—neither did they know what our Church is; and if they were to blame for pronouncing on things of which they knew so little, on whom did the fault lie that they were so ill-informed ?

It must not be supposed, however, that Mr. Lee began at once with a thorough change to what is right. No; he was too wise, too kind, for that. It was rather the reputation with which he came, and his personal observance of solemn seasons, which could not but at once be evident, which occasioned the first prejudice against him.

The death of his brother at first prevented William from seeing Ellen Hilton, or thinking much of the matter. He was obliged to be with his father continually, who could not get over the shock ; and this, and the work of the farm, left him little opportunity for going to Gillingham. But as time went on, and as his feelings became less acute, the want of that society and constant brotherly intercourse which he had once enjoyed, made William very desolate ; and turned his affection almost unconsciously towards her, who, if she could be his, would, he thought, be more than even a brother to him. This lonely and desolate condition, and desertedness, led him, therefore, the more rapidly to urge his suit ; and, before Christmas, he was accepted by Ellen Hilton, with the approval of both families.

But this was only one step out of many. The engagement was to be a long one. The young people promised to do nothing rashly ; and William was to save out of an allowance made him by his father. The end of the engagement could not be calculated ;

but to them it seemed very near as often as they pictured their future arrangements and happiness. Wait how long soever they might, they were sure that time could never diminish, but would rather confirm their attachment; a conviction not un- common, and true or false, according to the cha- racter of those who entertain it.

CHAPTER V.

The Vestry.

"The church's guardian takes care to keep
  Her buildings always in repair,
Unwilling that any decay should creep
  In them, before he is aware.
          Nothing defaced,
          Nothing displaced,
He likes."

THE CHURCHWARDEN.

A VESTRY was called at Great Staunton to consider
a notice of repair which the Archdeacon had sent.
Nothing substantial had been done to the church for
many years. The last great expenditure had been in
substituting pews for oak benches, wooden mullions
for stone, painting the oak roof white, and plastering
the outside. But all these magnificent measures
failed to keep out the wet. The rain had come in
year after year, and the rafters were quite decayed
close to the wall, so that the whole roof threatened
to come in with one crash upon the congregation.
The whitewash was indeed irreproachably white, but
it could not avail against such trials as this. How
long will it take to convince men that a triennial
colouring of paper thickness is not walls, nor but-
tresses, nor oak, nor lead, nor anything which will

protect the strong works of our forefathers, or the soft heads of their posterity?

At last the day was come when repair could be deferred no longer, and the only question was what that repair should be. Mr. Lee had done everything in his power to meet the emergency; he had procured a gratuitous plan and estimate, and had obtained promises of help from various friends, should a judicious and complete restoration be adopted.

The vestry consisted of some farmers, amongst whom were Mr. Blake and Mr. Mann, two publicans, and a grocer, and the chair was, of course, taken by the Rector. The Archdeacon's letter was read, and Mr. Lee addressed the meeting in the following manner.

"I am exceedingly sorry that so expensive and troublesome a repair should have been found necessary so soon after my arrival among you. It seems as if I had only just come, and had begun already to trouble you. But, my neighbours, I believe you will not look on the matter in this light. Necessary as these repairs are, you will see that I did not propose them. They are suggested, or rather enjoined upon us, by a higher authority, and that not without an absolute necessity. You will see by the report of the architect, which I lay before you, that the roof cannot be expected to hold up more than a few months, and that meantime we sit in imminent peril of our lives. Under these circumstances, it is not only a duty but a great kindness on the part of the Archdeacon, to call our attention to this danger in time. In order to save as much expense as possible, I have procured a gratuitous survey, plan, and estimate, which I lay on the table; and I am happy to add that, should these plans be adopted, I have the promise of pecuniary aid from various friends. However, here they are, and I hope you will be good enough to go into them with me."

The papers were then opened, and the entire alterations were found to amount to £800, amongst which was the reseating the church with open sittings, in oak. After some objections, to which Mr. Lee said, if they would pass over these for the present, he would reply afterwards, the plan was approved, and, deducting £150 for the sittings, was considered very reasonable, as the payment of £650 was to be extended over three years, and the sum reduced by promised subscriptions, and, perhaps, by some grants from Societies.

Mr. Stubbs, the grocer, however, rose to speak. "He had a friend an architect, he might say a very good architect; he had built the Wesleyan chapel at Belborough, and a very pretty thing it was, and he begged to submit his friend's plans and estimate to the vestry."

They were these—to cut off the rotten ends of the rafters, and thus lower the pitch of the roof very considerably; to cut the old pews into slips, using up the old material; to recolour the interior and exterior altogether for £350.

This was a bonus. Mr. Blake looked brighter, and Mr. Mann looked brighter, and a very dull day was suddenly quite sunshiny. A rise in Mark Lane could scarcely have produced a happier effect.

But Mr. Lee now rose, and entered on his promised explanations. "You have now," he said, "two plans before you. One, three hundred pounds cheaper than another. I must allow this is very tempting; but let us look a little into the matter. In the dear estimate, I find very substantial repairs done; in the cheap, very trifling alterations. The old wood is used, the old pews, the old everything, so that I really think if we decide on Mr. Stubbs' plan, it ought to be done for much less. But let us examine again. Mr. Stone proposes to put us up a roof like this. Mr. Plaster cuts it down two feet. Now, I do not think you would like to see your old parish church lowered in this way. Should you?"

"It'd be all the warmer," said Mr. Mann.

"It's quite warm enough now," replied Mr. Blake, because Mr. Mann had said the reverse.

"Warm enough for such hot-headed folk," grumbled Mann, and then there was a silence.

"Well," said Mr. Lee, "suppose we go on, and we will come back again to this question, by-and-by.

"You are all aware that this church is made of good, hard stone, and yet it is plastered all over, outside as well as in, and now this plaster is coming off. Mr. Stone proposes to take it off, entirely.

Mr. Plaster is, naturally enough, for keeping it on."
(A general laugh.) "Well, now I think you all see
how much better the church would look when the
stonework is clean; and although it costs more to
clean the walls than to patch up the plaster just
now, you must remember that we shall not want
any more wash inside, nor plastering outside. That
expense will be saved for ever."

"That's true enough," said Mr. Blake, "but it
will look very rough and queer, I fancy."

"Have you ever seen a church finished in this
way?"

"No, I never have."

"Well then I have, and I can assure you it looks
exceedingly well."

"I dare say it would," said the amiable Mann, to
plague Mr. Blake.

"Aye, but about those pews, Mr. Lee," said
another. "It isn't only the expense I object to,
but I must say I like a pew. My wife and family
like a pew, and I won't stand by and see our church
altered in this way."

"I am coming to the pews directly, Mr. Hodgson, but we can only do one thing at a time. Let
me put this question first. Shall we have the plan
which lowers our roof, and patches up this old
plaster, or one which keeps the church as it was,
and restores the walls to a nice even face of good
hard stone? But, before I ask you to decide, let me
mention one thing, that my friends' money is given,

only on condition of Mr. Stone's plan being adopted. They have no interest in this parish you know, and they give it to restore a fine old church to what it should be, so that I cannot ask them to subscribe to an alteration that they would not approve of. The case stands thus, putting aside the pew question.

"Mr. Stone's estimate	.	.	£650
Deduct subscriptions	.	.	200
			450
Mr. Plaster	. .	. .	350
		Difference	100

"So you see my plan costs more than the other, but the dearest plan is the best. It puts you in new timbers and does everything in a most workmanlike manner. Which will you have?"

There was a pause.

At last Mr. Stubbs said, "We ought to give a neighbour a job if we can, and not employ those Lonnoners."

"Mr. Plaster is not much of a neighbour, I take it; he charged us enough for that pound he built," said Mr. Blake.

"He is a very good workman, I count," replied Mann.

"Regular sticking-plaster," said Blake.

A laugh ensued, and, after some similar witticisms, the vestry fell into a good humour, and this first proposition was adopted.

Mr. Lee rose now to explain the alterations which had been passed over until the main question was settled; and he did so pretty much in these words:

"My dear parishioners, we are now come to a part of the subject in which I feel I must speak to you as your clergyman, rather than as your chairman. You have all been used to sit with your families in particular pews, and have attached yourselves to them, and have found that they screened you in, gathering around you without interruption those whom you would have more nearly associated with you, in public worship. All this I know, and feel; I know that I am asking you to make a sacrifice, and I would gladly not have had to ask it, so soon after my coming amongst you.

"But necessity and our safety, as I said before, have brought on these measures, and by them I am compelled to make a great request of you, without having had the opportunity of showing how earnestly I desire your happiness, and how unwilling I am to do anything which can give you pain. As it is, I have no other course than to bring the subject before you, and to request your kind and patient attention to it. I will mention several reasons for which, I trust, you will adopt the plan I propose.

"We are all, my brethren, by far too much disposed to rest upon our wealth, or our degrees of wealth, as that which makes us superior to others. Now one of the great objects for which we come to church is, that we may learn to feel that we are *not* superior to others, that we are all equal in God's sight, who is no respecter of persons. But, if the more wealthy have their pews, and the poorer are crowded here and there, as it may be, the richer members of the congregation find the church itself a means of perpetuating and increasing that trust in riches, that feeling of inequality which they come here intending, I trust, to shake off.

" I urge you, therefore, for your own sakes, to sit with your poorer brethren without having better, more honourable, or private seats.

" Another reason is, that the church is a *parish* church. Now, what do we mean by a parish church? What do we mean by a parish? A parish is a district of people. This church is the church of those people, of the people of that district: and, therefore, for any man to say, ' This is mine,' ' That is not yours,' is to say, this is not a parish church; and I am sure you will never wish to say this.

" Again, we all know that the lot of the labourers is a much harder lot than our own. They work day after day; and in sickness, or old age, banishment from home, friends, and old scenes, is too often their portion. Almost everything is unequal and is against them. They have less to eat, and less rest, and less knowledge, and less help, in sickness and old age : and to what are they to look, to cheer them in all this ? It is my blessed office, and it is your comfort to know it, if that office is fulfilled—it is my blessed office to tell them that the next world is their riches, their rest, their security. And where do they learn this ? Is it not here—here, where they are baptized and confirmed ; here, where they pray and receive the means of grace, and finally are carried to the grave ? If they come here, then, where they learn of heaven, here, where there is an example and faint pattern of heaven, and find this inequality still going on, all things still against them, how shall they receive the words of comfort which it is mine to give, and which you anxiously wish them to receive ? how shall they realise the equality of heaven in regard to all earthly distinctions, if they find in the very courts of God and the gate of heaven the very same exclusion and difference which they behold in the world ?

" I could mention many other reasons,—the necessity of banishing from our minds the exclusive selfish feelings of mine and thine as often as we can, and especially in the presence of God ; the tendency which pews have to keep part of the church occupied and useless, whilst the poor and strangers find no place ; the difficulty of really joining in public worship, and of meaning the whole church when we say 'we,' 'us,' instead of ourselves and our families only, which difficulty is much increased by that which cuts us off from our fellow-worshippers, forms us into separate parties, and renders our service more like family prayer than public worship. I could dwell on these, and other like facts, but I will not weary you. For these reasons which I have stated, and on these, for your own sakes, and the sake of the poor, and that this church may be truly a *parish* church once again, I *beg* and *entreat* you to make a sacrifice, and allow the adoption of the plan which I have laid before you."

After this there was a long pause, which was broken, at last, by Mr. Stubbs, who said, " I don't see why I should give up my pew to any one. You never hear of such things except at some Catholic place or other, like Addington new church, where they have a cross on the roof, and all those sort of things."

" I feared," replied Mr. Lee, " that some persons might fancy that there is something Popish in the alterations I proposed; and, fortunately, there is that in this church which will in a moment allay such a suspicion. May I request you to come with me into the church?"

When the party arrived in the nave, Mr. Lee pointed out some old benches which had been left, and said, at the same time, " Now, these benches are too large, and by no means handsome, but they were made at the end of Queen Elizabeth's reign, after the Reformation, so that there can be no Romanism about them."

He looked at his audience, to see what effect his

words produced. He soon perceived that they had absolutely none, and that the vestry knew no more about the Reformation than they did about the Copernican system.

He was not, however, a man to be foiled, and he briefly told them when Popery was abolished in the land, and that open benches had been usual for a very long period after its abolition. The explanation was satisfactory; but the personal objections, which were the strongest, and the *real* hindrance, the objections of dislike, and not of principle, remained. However, they were not put forward again, under their own colours. The pretext made was, that the extra £150 was a sum which they could not think it right to lay upon the parish, in addition to the necessary burden of repair. Mr. Lee fought his battle as well as he could, but he found that his enemies were entrenched behind interest, and a professed principle, and were, therefore, invincible. He paused, and sat silent for some time: at length he rose, and said—

" My dear brethren, I am a poor man, and I do not say this to increase the value of the offer I am about to make, but to show you how very important I consider the step which I urge. I am ready to pay out of my own pocket the cost of the alteration, or whatever Mr. Stone's plan costs more than Mr. Plaster's in respect of the seats—I will pay the difference."

" Perhaps you'll give the same sum towards the repairs, Sir?" said Stubbs.

"No, Mr. Stubbs, I *will not*. It is the plain duty of the parish, as a parish, to make them ; and I am not called upon to sacrifice so much for such a purpose. In the pew question, I am asking a sacrifice of people who scarcely know me, and, therefore, I am ready to make one myself, in order to show them what I mean, and feel, and am."

"Well, what do you say, Mr. Blake?" said Mr. Hodgson. "I think we might do what Mr. Lee wishes."

"Why, yes, I think we might. It is a very handsome offer, and I am sure I will not be one to oppose him."

"Then I will!" exclaimed Mann; "I call it nothing but regular Catholic Popery, as Stubbs says, and I'll have nothing to do with it. I'll vote against it to the last, that I will."

"Well, you may do as you like," said Mr. Blake; "I fancy it does not make much difference which way you vote. You are not such a great man as all .that."

So the resolution passed. Open seats were resolved upon, and Mr. Lee was to pay for them. This was no more than he expected ; and, indeed, the whole meeting was quite as satisfactory as he had anticipated : but what grieved him was the bitter spirit which showed itself between Mr. Mann and Mr. Blake. Whatever one approved, the other was sure to oppose.

"Alas!" thought Mr. Lee, "there are too many

Blakes and Manns in the world ; and what I have witnessed to-day, is, I fear, of very frequent occurrence. Rivalry and spite influence useful or mischievous plans alike, raise a subscription, or withhold an alms, just in order that the very principle on which all alms are founded, and by which alone they are acceptable, may be destroyed, that ill-will may have its way instead of love."

Another thought also weighed heavily on Mr. Lee's mind, as he returned home. Before business began, and at intervals, Mr. Mann had been full of gossip as to what his landlord, to whom he had been, did and said. Sir John said this, and Sir John said that. No flattery, no obsequiousness seemed too great for Mr. Mann, in the presence of his landlord. With him he had not only no independence, but no principle ; but out of his sight he was the great man, and lorded it over the poor, and even bullied his parson. Thus Mann was a true coward; and yet no uncommon character, for bravery and independence of character go hand in hand with moderation and forbearance.

Whilst the coward bullies and oppresses those beneath him, the true independent Christian is gentle in the exercise of power, and is the same under all circumstances, remembering that God is above him, and the grave below him, and that he is no farther from either in the presence of a lord, than in the cottage of a peasant.

CHAPTER VI.

Affliction.

" Glory to Thee, who hast bestowed
  No settled home below,
No perfect good, no sure abode,
  No pleasures safe from woe;
Peace to our wandering feet Thou hast not given,
Nor to unerring souls their fulness out of heaven."

GRESWELL'S EXPOSITION OF THE PARABLES.

MONTHS wore away: Mr. Lee was making progress with his people, that is, with his poor; but little enough with farmers or tradesmen. These were only to be gained by time. He had few opportunities of being kind to them, and still fewer of advising them, with any hope of that advice being gladly received; whereas the cottage had always need, and always, therefore, offered means of approach to its affections; and the poor, who were conscious that they knew nothing, received counsel gratefully, and often acted upon it.

At last it came to William Blake to need comfort and support; and he at once received them. The spring had been a long and cold one; and what was at first an indisposition in Ellen Hilton, became, it was feared, a consumption. This was a sore trial, and the weight of it became more oppressive and overwhelming when it was determined that she should be removed to a distant county, in order to try a different air and scene. Parting was very painful, and scarcely cheered at all by Christianity, for although Ellen often felt religiously disposed, her mind had never been disciplined or instructed; she did not know herself, nor had treasured up any of those truths and principles which alone are able to endure in the day of adversity. Unlike the wise householder, the truths which she had she knew not how to bring forth; and her comforts were few and failing.

After the separation, an utter desolateness came over poor William. His brother was gone; and now she whom he loved more than brother or parent, who had more than filled up the void of his heart, seemed about to follow him. He was unused to read. True religion he had not. His farming occupations seemed insipid and useless, for what could property serve him, if she for whom he sought it was to be his no longer? The love of money had not seized upon one of his age; neither did he find enough to make him happy in the routine of his calling. He had not as yet been reduced into the bondage and dull apathy of mere work. He was, therefore, most unsettled and desponding. He wandered through the fields, scarcely looking at them. His heart and mind were utterly unhinged.

It was in this state of feeling that Mr. Lee found

him on a hot June day, leaning over a stile far from his house, and resting as if he had been ill. He rejoiced at his opportunity, and, by kind inquiry after Ellen, and manifest interest in William's sorrow, drew him on to open much of the hidden sickness of his soul. Having gained this point, he turned the conversation for a time, and asked:

"Does this oppressive heat remind you of anything as you sit here, weary and listless, and feeling scarcely able to move?"

"No, Sir; I don't understand what you mean."

"Even thus, with this same feeling of weariness, with sorrow and faintness, sat our blessed Saviour. Do you not remember the words? 'Jesus, therefore, being wearied with his journey, sat thus on the well; and it was about the sixth hour,' that is, about noon. These words have never struck you, for you have been well and strong, and real weariness has never befallen you until now; but they have given comfort to others. A living poet has entered into them, and writes thus:—

> 'Thou, who didst sit on Jacob's well,
>   The weary hour of noon:
> The languid pulses thou canst tell,
>   The nerveless spirit tune.
>   *   *   *
> From darkness here and dreariness
>   We ask not full repose;
> Only be Thou at hand to bless
>   Our trial-hour of woes.'

"You have never felt comforted by these reflections, and was it not because you have not habitually thought of your Saviour? If you had been accustomed to meditate upon His sufferings, you would have thought of His weariness and sorrow; and if you had thought of them, they would have lightened yours. Let me beg of you to reflect, with prayer, upon this subject. You will find it more than a consolation."

William Blake was much struck with what Mr. Lee said, and still more by his kindness. Hitherto he had considered that a farmer had one course and a parson another, and he had no notion how the two were connected with, or had anything to do with, each other. He felt no interest in Mr. Lee, and was amazed and won by Mr. Lee's interest in himself.

Shortly after this, Mr. Lee preached on the relation between pastor and people; and in his sermon begged his parishioners to avail themselves of his services as often as they needed them; and to come to him at any hour, and on any matter in which they felt that he could be of use to them. William thought much of this invitation, and had very nearly resolved to go to the Rectory; but a false shame and the unhappy novelty of such a step held him back.

But Mr. Lee was not satisfied with mere invitation. He asked men to come to him; but if they would not, he went to them. He called at the Moat House again and again, but never found William at home. At last, somewhat hopeless, he left a copy of the

"Holy Living and Dying," as a gift, thinking that this must bring him to the Rectory, were it only to acknowledge the present. The plan succeeded, and one day William was announced.

As he entered, he was much struck with the different aspect of the house. He had known it in Mr. Eccles' time. It was then handsomely furnished. Good carpets, and sporting pictures, and guns, and antlers, gave the house the appearance of a very comfortable bachelor's residence. But now, although Mr. Lee was married, things were widely different. There was nothing good in the house except some sacred engravings, some old oak chairs, and bookshelves, and the valuable library which filled them. The drawing-room was little better than any other apartment. It contained nothing which would have excited the wonder of the poor, or made them afraid to sit down in their clergyman's house. It was just dinner-time, and William Blake was still more astonished at the coarseness of the table-cloth, and the great homeliness of the fare. The meal was soon despatched, and the conversation was so cheerful and natural, that he felt at ease and quite relieved, both from shyness and from the pressure of his anxieties.

After dinner was over, Mr. Lee and his guest adjourned to the study, and soon entered into conversation.

"You seemed," began the Rector, with a smile, "rather astonished at my furniture; but you are too polite to say anything, whereas some of my friends are positively angry about it. My wish is to spend as little on luxuries as possible, not only for my own moral good, and to save that great means of usefulness, money; but to show my parishioners that they may be very happy without them; and that their clergyman is not like a 'squire, but a real hard-working, hard-living man, who tries to act up to what he preaches. It would never do for me to preach content upon humble fare whilst I lived luxuriously; or to reprove, as I am fond of doing, the tendency of this age to multiply comforts, and to push up into the habits of richer and greater people, whilst I was yielding to the temptation myself. And so, though some think me over strict, and some fanciful, and some censorious, and nearly all wrong; I adhere, and intend to adhere, to this system, and, I trust, it will be useful. Have you ever seen ' George Herbert's life?' "

" No ; never."

" I hardly thought you would. But I will lend it you some day. However, I think that other books should come first. How do you like the ' Holy Living?' "

" I have not read much, Sir; but I thought it very good ; but ——"

" But what ?"

" Why, Sir, I thought it very strict. It seemed to order a great many things which are very hard, and which I had never thought of."

"That may be, that may be; and yet Bishop Taylor be right, you know. If you remember, the other day you had never thought of our Lord's weariness until I mentioned it; and you will find many other things of the same sort, and rules, and duties, and privileges, which have never yet struck you."

"Yes, Sir, I know; but I thought our religion was so simple, Sir, that any one could understand it."

Mr. Lee was rather astonished at William's objection, for he had found so little thought amongst the young farmers of his present and former parish: but he did not pause a moment in his answer.

"Our religion is, indeed, very simple. It is all in two rules:—'Thou shalt love the Lord thy God with all thy heart and with all thy mind; and thy neighbour as thyself. It is all in this, William; but do you require no help to find out the numberless ways in which you can show your love to God, and your love to man?"

"O yes, Sir; certainly."

"Let me be your Bishop Taylor for a minute. We are to love our neighbour as ourselves. Well, then, we must consider how we love ourselves, and who is our neighbour? Now our Lord showed by the parable of the good Samaritan, that Christian love never stops to ask who is a neighbour? but as soon as it sees any man in distress immediately relieves him, if possible. So we are to do all the good we can. But, on the other hand, if we have only a certain amount of time, money, and strength, we must find out, not a limit to our good offices, but rather a beginning; we must ask who are to be served first; who have the first claim on us, and thus we find that parents and near relations, servants, fellow-parishioners, fellow-christians, and others come in order, just as one circle lies outside another. Well, then, you owe all the good you can do to those whose wants call upon you, but first and chiefly to those whose wants call loudest; those nearest to and around you. Now look at your practice, and whilst I suggest some heads of self-examination to you, do not think me unkind or harsh. I am trying to show you the use of such books as I gave you, and how much more you have to do than persons of your calling are accustomed to think.

"We start, then, from this point, that you are bound to do all the good you can to your servants and labourers, as being next to you, and having, after your near relations, the greatest claim upon your time, and care, and kindness.

"Now, I will ask you to inquire how much you give away to them?

"Do you see to their saving money?

"Do you try and make their cottages comfortable?

"Do you endeavour to cheer and encourage the industrious and good?

"Do you induce them to send their children to school?

"Do you try to arrange that they are not kept away from church through you?

"Do you urge them to go there?

"Do you reprove drunkenness and swearing?

"Are you so cautious of what you say and do that you would not appear inconsistent and hypocritical if you were to fulfil all these obligations?

"Do you feel that you and they are connected together; that they are not mere tools which you may use as you like, and part with when worn out, or when you can get better, but living men of your very nature, and of that nature which your Lord and Saviour took upon Him, and lived, and died, and ascended in?"

William was silent. Mr. Lee said, "I fear I am as bad as the 'Holy Living.' But I trust I have not hurt you."

"O no, Sir. I was thinking of what you said, and I hope I shall not forget it."

"Shall I write it down for you?"

"I should like it very much; but I fear it will be too much trouble for you."

"My duty, William, ought to be no trouble— what I have been saying to you applies doubly to me. You have still more claim on me, and a claim which I wish you would exercise."

Mr. Lee then wrote for some minutes, and gave William the paper, adding, "All that I have been saying may appear very poor comfort. You came here partly for solace, and I fear you go away to self-reproach. But do not despond. Your duties have not, perhaps, been placed before you, so that in some sense they are new : do not despond! if you will hereafter perform them consistently, all may be well, and they will be your consolation. I can suggest to you many thoughts of joy, many comforting truths; but I cannot make your heart lastingly quiet and peaceful, except in the path of duty. If God leads you to see that the highest happiness is to do His will, that if you are really serving Him from the heart, He is watching over, and blessing, and strengthening you, then you can never be entirely cast down. Friends may fail; but in your daily work you will find God, and He cannot fail. Hopes, plans, joys, may recede, and go farther and farther away, but *duty remains,* and in the *performance of that duty to God, and in God*, He draws nearer and nearer unto you, and you to Him. This is your happiness, your sure happiness, and you never can be safely or long at peace without it. Neither rich, nor strong, nor blessed with the tenderest and firmest human love in you, and to you, can you be really happy without this root of all happiness. Consider, and convince yourself of this, and then remember, 'If ye know these things, HAPPY ARE YE if ye do them.'"

William left the Rectory with a heavy heart. He was, as yet, stupified, and knew not whither to turn, when to begin, or how to begin a better life. Mr. Lee's kindness, and his anxiety about Ellen, were the great hold upon him. He had, at present, little higher principle.

Two days after the conversation described, he had occasion to go down to the village at night, to see for the farrier. It was half-past eleven, yet the noise and light showed that there was drinking at the Anchor. He could not find the farrier, and, as a last hope, he resolved to peep in through a chink in the stuff curtains which lined the bay window of the public house. He saw there about fifteen men, at different tables ; some playing at cards, all drinking, and smoking.

The card-players were full of "anger and clamour," but the rest seemed stupified and dull, with the liquor, and heat of the room. Amongst them, William Blake recognised several of his own men, as well as the farrier. He at once gave up all notion of calling in the latter to the horse which was ill, and was turning away, thinking of Mr. Lee's words, when he became conscious that another person had been engaged in the same work of observation as himself. It was the Rector, who, laying his finger on his lips, beckoned to William Blake to follow him. When they were clear of the house, he took William's arm, and said, in a kind voice,

"Do you not see that I was right in my questions the other day ?"

" Yes, indeed I do, Sir, and I feel that I am much to blame."

" Do you know the men that were inside?"

" Yes, I know them all; they are all of our village."

" Was not Baxter there?"

" Yes, Sir."

" He was the man, I think, that took the horses' corn?"

" Yes, Sir, he was the man."

" And Lennett was there, whose wife came up about the rent. He works for your father, I think?"

" Yes, Sir, he is one of our hands."

" You see how it is, William; these men should have been reformed, or turned off, and men like Rivers and Holmes taken on."

" Yes indeed, Sir, it's all too true; I quite feel it all."

" And now, William, you must be my witness, for I shall summon the landlord next Thursday."

" Wouldn't you give him warning, Sir? It will make you so exceedingly unpopular."

" I have warned him twice, and only a week back, so that I must run the risk of the unpopularity."

They walked on a few yards in silence; at last William Blake said—

" If you'll allow me, Sir, I think I'll inform. I think it will be best."

" I don't think your father will like it, William; and you are younger to bear obloquy than I am."

" I don't think my father will mind it; and he'll
be so angry now, because Will Jemson is too drunk
to come to our horse, that he'll be rather pleased
than not."

" Well; but then there's yourself, everybody will
laugh at you next market."

" I won't mind that, for I think it is the right
thing to do."

"You shall do as you like then; but remember
people may say it is very inconsistent of you, for, if
report says true, your club, William, has not always
conducted itself very respectably."

" Yes, I know it, Sir; but I must make a beginning to do right, and perhaps it is well to begin in
this way."

" I will not try to dissuade you any more, for I
am sure you are right, but I wished you to count
the cost first; for then you will not only be less
likely to regret the step afterwards, but, knowing
your difficulties, will more easily surmount them."

So it was fixed. The information was laid, the
man convicted, and fined, with the admonition that
a second offence would forfeit his license.

Mr. Lee did not escape the obloquy, for his former
warnings, and his being called on as witness, made
this impossible, but William Blake intended that
he should, and made his first stand, an event of
infinite importance in his future history. A single
step in right or wrong is often the turning point
in a man's whole life, leading on to similar steps,

and so commencing a course of action which fixes the character, becomes identified with the feelings and principles of man, and daily makes it more difficult to turn back.

The laughter and obloquy which William brought upon himself, will be readily imagined. He bore them all firmly, though he felt them more than he need have done; but his conscience supported him, and Mr. Lee's kind intercourse, which was gradually increasing as it became better appreciated, and more useful, rendered him more independent of his old associates. A better account, too, from Ellen Hilton, made him happier, and inspired him with hope that he might still not only be a more useful man, but also eventually obtain the object of his fondest wishes.

CHAPTER VII.

First Steps.

" My child, the counsels high attend
    Of thine Eternal Friend.
  When longings pure, when holy prayers,
  When self-denying thoughts and cares
      Room in thy heart would win,
  Stay not too long to count them o'er;
  Rise in His name; throw wide the door,
      Let the good Angels in."

LYRA INNOCENTIUM.

THE improvement which God's grace, acting very
much through His minister, was effecting day by day
in William Blake, was not confined (as, indeed, good
never is) to the person in whom it commenced.
That which Mr. Lee said to William was faithfully
reported to Ellen, and exercised an equal influence
upon her. It was a most happy circumstance for
both of them, that Mr. Lee was not only kind and
zealous, but also very judicious. He made a point
of seeing as much of his young friend as was necessary to guide and encourage him, but not so much
as would render him dependent, and prevent him
from meeting and surmounting his first difficulties,
or withdraw him from his plain duties to his father
and his calling. Still, in spite of this reserve, William Blake saw so much of his Rector, as to make

quite a confidant of him, and to be able to consult him about Ellen Hilton, as well as himself. Ellen had, indeed, written on one subject with the evident intention that her question should be communicated. She was puzzled at William's report of Mr. Lee's earnest exhortation to kneel in prayer, and seemed disposed to regard it as a mere form, not knowing that forms are the handmaids of spirit, its support, and means of action.

"My reasons," replied the Rector, in answer to William's question as to what he should say, "are very simple. I will state them as clearly as may be. First, when we come into the presence of our superiors, we always use a posture of respect. How much more, then, should we do this, when we come before the mercy-seat of God!"

"But, Sir," said William, "is it not a mark of respect to stand in the presence of a superior?"

"True, the posture of standing is generally, though not always, the understood posture of respect to the great of the earth, and therefore it is as generally observed. For the same reason, then, or rather for much stronger reasons, whatever is the *understood* posture suited to God's presence should be most rigidly and carefully adhered to. It may be one posture, or it may be another; but whatever it be, it should be strictly kept. The understood posture of prayer, now, is kneeling. It was, once, standing at certain seasons—it is, now, kneeling always; and because it is the generally acknowledged posture, as well as because the Church orders it, it should be observed whether we regard it as more or less suitable. But we will consider its suitableness. It is, certainly, a posture of humility. You cannot but feel that it is this. It is a stooping down, and lowering the proud erect bearing of a man, and approaching the dust whence he was made, and to which he must return. I am sure no one doubts that it is a posture of humility; and, if so, then just as walking makes the recovered sick man rejoice in his strength, or as sitting down refreshes the mind as well as the body of the weary, so kneeling really does humble the kneeler, and really puts him into a frame of mind more fit for addressing our most Holy God. I say, then, without hesitation, that a Christian of our age, who really wishes to feel aright in prayer, will be found on his knees; and his kneeling, or not kneeling, will generally test his state of mind.

"The third reason is the example and authority found in Holy Scripture, in which we are invited to fall on our knees before God's footstool; in which we see the Lord bowing down at Gethsemane, and St. Stephen and St. Paul setting us examples for our imitation.

"But I wish to say something more on the common fear of forms. Forms are outward things, intended to express things inward. They may express them, or they may not express them, but such is their object. When you come into my house I shake hands with

you; that is the form by which I express a welcome. If I did not like you, and yet gave you
a hearty welcome, I should be a hypocrite, and
my form would be justly hateful to you. But if
I did like you, and was forbidden to show it by
any outward act, you and I would both be very
uncomfortable. The constraint would be unnatural,
and painful ; and generally, in the world, if outward
tokens of regard were discontinued, people would
become more rude and selfish, and inward regard
would be diminished also. You see, then, that
forms are useful to express and keep alive inward
feeling ; they are natural and necessary, and only
mischievous when people never had the inward feeling, or, thinking the form enough, and, resting on it,
gradually let it die away. So, when you come to
church, you are surrounded on each side by two
dangers. If you neglect forms, you act unnaturally ;
you cannot show your regard to God ; you forego a
constant memento of Him, and a summons to those
feelings which are proper when you are before Him.
If, on the other hand, you observe them, and gradually forget their meaning, then you become a
formalist, and, to some extent, a hypocrite.; you
worship God with your lips, whilst your heart is far
from Him. You must watch and pray earnestly
against both of these dangers. When you kneel,
kneel in heart. When you sing, be joyful and
thankful. When you turn to the east, think of the
Sun of Righteousness, and turn in heart towards

Him. When you bow at our Lord's Name, bow your spirit before Him in gratitude and awe. These forms should never be mere forms, and never be separated from spirit. Whenever this is unhappily the case, they are like a corpse from which life has fled! and spirit also, without forms, is as unnatural and powerless, in this world, as a soul without a body."

This explanation led William on to consult Mr. Lee upon a practical question connected with the same subject. He had been in the habit of attending the fairs with his father, and often at such busy times the bed-rooms of the inns were crowded, and many persons slept in the same apartment. Whenever this was the case, whatever was their usual practice at home, the farmers retired to their beds without kneeling down in prayer. This was a great difficulty. William had too lately turned to better ways for it to be wise to draw attention to himself; and besides, his father would have been annoyed and reproved had his son differed from him in this matter. On the other hand, it seemed a want of courage, and a yielding to the fear of man, to kneel at home, and, seemingly, to be prayerless in public. He therefore consulted Mr. Lee, who advised him to go up-stairs before the others, and so to escape notice; remarking, at the same time, that as he grew older, and more fixed in principle, the difficulty would disappear, and that then he would be bound, and able to act simply as he was accustomed to do at home.

The harvest now came on, and William was fully occupied. He saw less of Mr. Lee; but he did not on that account fall back. He prayed more and more earnestly; and was able, without display, to check much evil in the harvest fields. At length, the anniversary of his brother's death approached. He felt it deeply; and saw that both his father and mother did not know how to bear it. He resolved to go down to Mr. Lee, and consult him how he and his might pass that trying day with comfort and profit.

It was an evening in which a singular freshness and stillness succeeded to the heat and toil of a burning harvest-day, and seemed to give a new life to those who enjoyed it. A thin, grey mist became more and more distinct above the meadows. The beetle hummed through the air; the partridge called from field to field; and here and there a sound of voices came over from the village. William lingered in every field, and at every turn; and, unthoughtful as his life had been, even he could not help thinking of his brother's state, and how that sweet nightfall was a type of rest after the turmoil of life. He gave himself to the scene, and let it influence his feelings as it would : and well were it for those who live in the country if more frequently they surrendered themselves to its influence, and let the rising sun rouse, the setting sun compose their thoughts, and the sounds and sights of nature tell them of another and more lasting order than that of their own careful plans and anxious forecasting arrangements.

It was dark by the time that William reached the Rectory. The light of evening had failed, and the moon was not up. He paused at the door, and heard through the open windows, which looked out round an angle of the house, the voice of prayer. It was Even Song, which Mr. Lee was reading to his family. The Psalms were chanted; and the sound passing through the trees came softened to the listener, and seemed, in such a scene, unearthly. William waited until the service was concluded; and then, after a few minutes' hesitation, rang the bell. He was received at once, and taken into the study, to which the Rector had retired, and soon declared the object of his walk. Mr. Lee heard him out, and said : " I have a sketch by me of a kind of service drawn up by a friend suffering under circumstances somewhat similar to yours. There are lessons, and prayers, and psalms in a succession. I will just look it through, and will give it to you if it seems to suit."

After about ten minutes, Mr. Lee, having made some trifling alterations in the paper, put it into William's hands, adding, that he should be very glad to walk up to the Moat House in the course of the day if he could be of any service. "Perhaps," he said, " your father and mother would have liked me to read a sermon to them. You must see about this, and as you find, so you can tell me. And now let me say a word to yourself. How long do you contemplate waiting before you become a communicant? You must have thought over the subject lately; tell me what you have felt."

"I never thought of it, Sir, until Ellen's illness, and since then you have been so good to me that I felt sure you would tell me when you thought best."

"That is just what I feared. Take Bishop Wilson's book home with you, and examine yourself by the 'Holy Living,' and I will talk to you again. I have much to say, and much to explain; but I will only add this one word now, that although you are *already* pledged to an entire renunciation of sin and to a life devoted to God, so that the Lord's Supper cannot, in this respect, increase your obligations; yet that, to fall away after such grace and such privileges as it confers, and to give such an occasion of scandal as you would do by recurring to a worldly life, are all such very fearful things, that I would have you examine yourself *well* now, and *see to it,* that your present impressions and resolutions are not the result of anxiety only, and such as will pass away should that anxiety be removed. Do your best to secure yourself against relapse, for the sake of others and for the sake of yourself."

The moon was up when William returned, and the owls were calling with their clear, cool cry along the lanes. Everything was the same, and yet how different! The same scene was a morning, or mid-day, or evening, or moonlight landscape, just as the light which fell upon it was various. So William viewed his pursuits, his present and future prospects, and his whole life, just as selfish anxieties, or a lively gratitude, or the world, or Mr. Lee's counsels, and his Bible, and prayers, and thoughts, gave the tone to his mind for the time being. Not that he was more inconstant than most men; he was, perhaps, even less so.

Mr. Lee's written suggestions, as well as his offer, were both accepted at that hour of sorrow; and thenceforth the anniversary of John's death was a solemn and hallowed time to the family—a day kept in a religious spirit—and a centre round which holy resolutions and heavenly desires gathered and clung.

Mr. Lee proceeded carefully to prepare William for the reception of the Holy Communion. He catechised him twice a week; lent him books of various sorts; made him understand the service; and did all that a good parish priest could do. But, with all this, William had many difficulties. He had so long been indifferent and careless in prayer, that he found it very hard to keep his attention fixed in devotional thought: he had given license to his tongue and his imagination; and, therefore, impure thoughts intruded themselves continually into his mind even when they were most grievously offensive. These and other difficulties beset him constantly; and with all his efforts and with the help of Mr. Lee's counsel, he could not overcome them at once, for we are creatures of time; days and moments make us what we are, and if we are dissatisfied with ourselves, we cannot unmake our work at our will. Not even God's grace, which is in itself omnipotent, is omnipotent in us to such an effect.

At last the Sunday came, and William, for the first time, and four or five years later than he might have done, received the Sacrament of the Body and Blood of his Redeemer. The rest of the day he spent, as well he might, in quiet meditation and prayer, according to the rule of the holy Sutton, which Mr. Lee had given him : "That he use much silence, and some solitariness the same day, that he may be private thereunto to God and himself."

And the happiness which William felt in reflecting upon his privilege was not a little increased when the Tuesday's post brought him a most welcome letter from his Ellen, saying, that she was fast recovering, and in a few weeks trusted to return home. This was, indeed, delightful. William's heart overflowed with joy and gratitude as he thought he had passed through all his trials, and that henceforth a happier and a better course was opening out before him. Alas! he knew not himself, nor the self-deception of a heart which he had only so lately endeavoured to examine and improve. The world had not lost its hold on him; and the trials he had endured in his affliction, were less severe than the temptations which awaited him in his joy.

It was arranged that Ellen was to stay some weeks at the Moat House shortly after her return, and many sweet walks and drives were planned by her impatient lover. How would she look? Was she changed? Would she be as pretty as ever? were questions which continually recurred to his mind; and it must be added, that William was in a state of feeling calculated to supersede in her mind, and to allow her to supersede in his, the solemn thoughts and strict resolves of their recent affliction, not intentionally nor consciously; but from allowing his old earthly attachment to come over him as it used, without subjecting it to his higher views and principles, and without being sobered and sanctified by them in this as in other lesser things.

Mr. Blake was much amused at William's ill-concealed impatience and delight, in which he participated to a certain extent. For, though much sobered by the recent commemoration of his departed son, he was not a little glad to see William less grave, and more as young men used to be in his days.

CHAPTER VIII.

𝔗𝔥𝔢 𝔉𝔞𝔩𝔩.

"Said I not so, that I would sin no more?
  Witness my God, I did;
Yet I am run again upon the score:
  My faults cannot be hid.
What shall I do? Make vows and break them still?
  'Twill be but labour lost!
My good cannot prevail against my ill:
  The business will be crost.
O say not so: thou canst not tell what strength
  Thy God may give thee at the length."

GEORGE HERBERT.

SOME ten days after the Sunday upon which William Blake first became a communicant, he had occasion to attend a sale of stock and farming implements in a neighbouring village. He there met many of his old associates, for they could not be called friends, inasmuch, as John was everything to him whilst he lived, and since his death he had associated very little with any one, from grief at first, and afterwards from his engagement to Ellen, and the anxieties and the circumstances which we have already described. He had deserted the club to which he

G

belonged, and which used to meet every fortnight,
at the Anchor, and had seen very little of his equals
in age and station.   On this occasion, however, he
was greeted by many an acquaintance, and rallied
considerably upon his solitary and strict life. He was
not in general wanting in moral courage, nor did he
care as much as most young men do for being laughed
at; but now, partly from his high spirits, and partly
from the excitement of the time, he was off his guard,
and was induced to say that he would attend the
club next evening.   On his return home, he regretted
his rash promise, for the club was not one for quiet
conversation, but for cards and smoking, and had
too often led to drinking to excess. He did not, however, know how to retract: and he half dishonestly,
and half erroneously soothed his conscience by an
old admonition of Mr. Lee not to quit the society of
his equals, nor to show himself indifferent to their
wishes and pursuits, a course which Mr. Lee said
was sure to alienate them and to foster pride and
harshness of spirit in himself.

So he went at eight, the usual hour, and played
a rubber for love, as it is called, and talked, and
joked, and was pleased and agreeable; but soon
one glass was called for after another by his companions; they began to get boisterous, songs were
sung which William did not approve, and ought not
to have remained to hear, and the whole meeting
became most unchristian in its character, and one of
those "revellings" of which it is declared that

"they who do such things shall not inherit the kingdom of God." William left a few minutes before his companions, and went home disgusted with them, and still more with himself. He did not pray: he felt wholly unsettled, and doubted whether he was in a state of mind to address his God. His promises, his resolutions, his solemn act not two Sundays past, all came before him, and he felt struck out, as it were, and no longer worthy or fit to hold the position he had assumed.

Next morning, on his return from the fields, he found one of the village people with his father, asking him to pay for windows which, he said, had been broken the night before, by the club, and by William amongst the rest. This was soon set straight at the Moat House: but not so easily elsewhere. The spite of the Anchor people, and the slanderous tongues of many gossips, had spread it everywhere that William Blake was amongst the rioters, and some were almost ready to swear that they saw him. He now felt the extent of the mischief he had done. It was not himself only whom he had injured, but the whole parish, and through it his kind friend, Mr. Lee. He felt this deeply, and carefully avoided seeing him. The Rector, however, would not suffer this, and sought him out until he found him. When he succeeded, he invited him at once to come down to the Rectory, and, having got him safely into the study, questioned him from first to last upon all the circumstances.

"Then you were not there, you are sure," he said, " when the windows were broken?"

"Yes, quite sure, Sir.   I left before any one else, and went home alone."

" Can you prove this?"

" Only by asking the club."

" It would not do for *you* to do this, but *I* will : stay here."   Mr. Lee got up, and returned in an hour.

" I have been fortunate enough," said he, "to meet young Hodgson, and he has assured me of what you say : so that I now have evidence to go upon. Come down with me into the village, to Mrs. Gardiner's ; and mind, you must hear what I say.   You have brought this on yourself, and if I get you out of some of the blame, you must submit altogether to my guidance."

William looked assent as well as he could, and they proceeded at once to Mrs. Gardiner's cottage.

Mr. Lee knocked at the door.   " Come in," answered a shrill voice.   " It is I," said the Rector. "Oh, come in, Sir, very glad to see you, Sir, I assure ye.   It always does my heart good to see the like o' your blessed face, that it does."

" Stay at the door, William," whispered the Rector, as he entered.

" Come in, Sir, come in, and here's a chair ; and I'm truly thankful to Mrs. Lee for that broth, Sir. It made me feel quite comfortable like inside ; I haven't had such a dinner I don't know when, Sir."

"Well, you can talk about the broth, you know, with Mrs. Lee. I just came down to ask about the windows the other night. I am told you saw the people who did it?"

"Why, yes; I saw them all, Sir, plain enough, out o' here; but I shouldn't like to mention names. I never like to make mischief, no, not I."

"What do you mean, Mrs. Gardiner? take care what you say. You know you have mentioned names already, and it's all over the place that you said William Blake was amongst the party."

"And so I did, and so I will," said the old creature, pretending to be angry, "and I'm not the woman to say what's not true. No, I'm not, Sir. There's my neighbour Goodson there, she tells lies enough, I'm sure; but I speaks truth, Sir, that I do!" she screamed out, as she set a pan down with a jar which made the whole cottage resound.

"And you say you saw William Blake amongst them?"

"Yes, I do say I saw him out of this here window, just as plain as I see you; and he had his grey shooting-coat on, and white hat, as you know as well as I do, and I'm right down positive o' it."

"Come in, Blake. Mrs. Gardiner says she saw you, with your grey shooting-coat on, and white hat. Did you wear them that evening?"

"No, Sir; I was dressed in black."

"Now listen to me, Mrs. Gardiner! I have something to say to you, and your neighbour." Mr. Lee paused a moment, as if in thought, and then, going to the door, beckoned Mrs. Goodson, and three or four others, to the cottage, and waited until they came up before he went on. When they were close, he said, in a clear stern voice—

"I wish you all to hear what I have to say to Mrs. Gardiner here. She has distinctly said, that Mr. Blake was one of those persons who disgraced themselves the other night, by breaking windows, and being drunk in our street. She declares that she saw him, and that he wore a white hat, and grey coat. Now, Mr. Blake was at the meeting, and came away late, and was much to blame, and I tell you so. Perhaps, he will do as much himself."

"Yes, I was; I was much to blame," replied William, colouring as red as fire, and ready to sink into the earth.

"Listen to that. Mr. Blake has done wrong, and he is not ashamed to acknowledge it before you all: remember this. But this woman here has told a slanderous and mischievous lie. Mr. Hodgson, who was at the meeting, has assured me that Mr. Blake left before any riotous act was committed, before any one else left, and that he had nothing to do with the breaking the windows. Besides, he did not wear the grey coat and white hat that evening. Did any other person wear one, William?"

"No, Sir; no one."

"You hear, then, there was nobody in such a

dress, and it is all false from beginning to end.
Now, Mrs. Gardiner, it would only be right that you
should be made to do penance, and to stand in a
sheet at the church-door, for slander. As it is, I
strike you off the coal club, and clothing club, and
I expose you thus before your neighbours as a false
slanderous woman, and I entreat you all who are
here to be warned. Not that I think any of you
have ever been guilty of such a sin, but I entreat you
to beware of ever approaching it. A love of talking
led this woman to say what she was not sure of;
then, having said it, she persisted in it, and invented
lie after lie to back up her slander; and now you
see the disgrace that has come upon her. The sin
which she has incurred, I tremble to think of, for it
is written, 'Whoso privily slandereth his neighbour,
him doth my soul abhor;' 'He that telleth lies
shall not tarry in my sight;' and hell itself is to
be prepared for him who 'loveth and maketh a lie.'
The only course is to stop at the first, to be silent
about our neighbours unless we can praise them;
to overlook and hide their faults, unless we are
cautioning our children against evil example, and
then to be most sure that what we say is true.
Now, William, let us go back to the Rectory."

Mrs. Gardiner looked fiercely at them, and went
on muttering, and scouring a kettle which already
shone like a guinea. The neighbours dispersed.
The news of William's innocence soon spread; but
he had to think still of his fault, and to observe in

Mr. Lee's manner the disappointment and pain which his own conduct had caused.

They were soon seated once more in the study, and Mr. Lee, as a faithful physician, was prepared to probe the wound to the bottom. Though pained himself at the pain he gave, he was firmly resolved to heal the disease thoroughly, and, if possible, to eradicate the cause of it. He, of course, began the conversation. "This is a sad business, William. The club had lost its character too much for you ever to have joined it, after being aroused to thoughtfulness by all the gracious calls and warnings which have been given you, and especially after last Sunday week."

"I feel it indeed, Sir. Pray do not say:——Yes, I deserve anything you can say."

"I know that you are sorry. Your confession just now convinced me of that, and I will say no more except to assist you for the future. Let me ask you now what you think in your heart was the cause of your fall, for such I must call it."

William was silent.

"Have you been unsettled, or thrown off your guard at all, and forgotten the resolutions which you made in the time of sorrow, by the good news of Miss Hilton's return?"

"I think it was that, partly."

"Did you meditate and pray, after receiving the Holy Communion?"

"Yes, Sir; all the rest of the day."

" But not on the Monday, nor afterwards ?"

" No, Sir."

" And you did not make any resolutions? or, if you did, you have not examined yourself by them, since?"

" No, Sir; I made some; but I have not used them as you say."

" Then they have been very useless to you. It may be taken, William, as a fixed rule, that God's grace goes along with our value and use of it; and it is of little efficacy to prepare the soul for solemn days, if you do not sustain it afterwards. It is as if you raised a sick man's health by extraordinary nourishment, and then suddenly withdrew it. He would sink, and so you will, and so you have, under the same treatment. For the future, whatever resolutions you make, (and I would have you make one or more every Communion,) try yourself by your resolves every night, and see whether you have kept them. Add the power of memory to that of expectation, and put to yourself such questions as these :

" I have been pardoned ; am I more wary of sin ?

" I have been strengthened; am I stronger in soul ?

" Christ has given Himself to me ; do I love Him more ?

" I have been made a member incorporate of His mystical body, which is the blessed company of all faithful people; do I value this privilege, and am I more gentle, more loving, as its result?

"I have communicated with a crucified Saviour; do I crucify sin?

"These and such other questions as your particular circumstances and temptations suggest are as necessary after, as their counterparts are before Communion. And now, with reference to the other cause, I would advise you not to see Miss Hilton without solemn prayer to God that you may not be led by any earthly joy to forget Him and His holy works and ways.

"And I would also suggest to you that you should make some sacrifice to punish yourself and remind yourself of your fall. Do you not think you ought?"

"Yes, indeed, Sir; I will try."

"Well, think it over; and whatever you resolve, mind you keep your resolution. There is one point more. If you had a vivid sense of God's presence, you would neither have been weak enough at first to promise to go, nor afterwards to remain hearing and seeing things which your conscience disapproved. It is most important to you to try and gain this incalculable security and consolation. It would be almost impossible for a Christian to commit any conscious sin, or to despair in difficulty, pain, and sorrow, if he could realise his Saviour as close to him, seeing, hearing, reading him through and through. You cannot easily realise the presence of God the

Father, who has no form by which we may picture Him to ourselves; but God the Son took upon Him our nature, partly, I believe, that we might have a lively image of a personal God, whose eye and ear are ever ours. This, however, may be otherwise to you; but at any rate, seek after a sense of the presence of God, a consciousness that you are entirely present to Him, before Him, with Him; and if you cannot gain this sense except by very frequent meditations, then make a rule that every time you rise, or every time you sit down, or every time you enter a house, you will bring this thought before your mind. Only do not charge yourself with a sin if you forget. Memory is innocently frail, and the conversation of others will often prevent your doing what you wish. Keep your conscience clear on this head; but try the rule if you find it desirable. It is very singular, William, how nearly fallen we are when we think ourselves safe. Often after a high privilege, and a much nobler state of mind than is usual to us, we are nearest our ruin. St. Peter, confessing Christ on His way from Mount Tabor, deserved and received the rebuke, 'Get thee behind me, Satan;' and again, after his profession of fidelity and that of the other disciples, he denied, and all forsook their Master. Let these things warn us. You felt as if you had taken a new stand. New ideas of usefulness opened at once before you; ideas fresh to you and strange to your equals. You had been in my society, and so perhaps had religious subjects brought before you until you imagined they were more connected with you than they are : and you had received the inestimable honour and blessing of the Lord's Supper; and then came all that has passed.

"Let me urge you, then, to keep yourself down ; to feel that you have only just begun to wish to do right ; that but for God's grace you would never have wished it ; that you are no better than others ; that you have still a great deal to learn and a great deal to do before you can become that which you might have been years ago; and whilst I bring before you your high privileges and duties as a Churchman, whilst I tell you how honourable and useful a position you occupy as an English farmer ; whilst I make a friend of you and see much of you ; do not let all this wean you from your plain duties, or unsettle you, or make you think yourself *anything ;* but take especial pains to apply your principles to every detail, every most trivial part of your duties. Be more than ever obedient, submissive, gentle, and affectionate to your parents ; more than ever attentive to your business ; and let your religion make you good *in* your calling, not taking you out of it ; but sanctifying it to you and you in it every day more and more. And now ' Let us pray.'"

Mr. Lee read some prayers out of "Kettlewell's Penitent ;" and William left sad and humbled, but wiser, and better, and safer than he was. The sacrifice which he made was to give up shooting for that year. He bestowed the cost of his license in charity, and denied himself his favourite amusement. When questioned as to his motive, he assigned none, but simply answered that he had private reasons, and that he hoped to shoot the following year. His querists were rather troublesome, but he bore it as part of his self-punishment; and a real punishment it was, for he was truly fond of the sport; and as he walked through the stiff, bright stubble and flushed a covey, or raised the fresh scent of the turnips as he crossed them in his evening walks, he often longed to see his pointer dashing across, and not unfrequently raised his stick as a partridge whizzed across his path. A true sportsman will know what William felt, and he will, therefore, see that he was in earnest when he renounced this pleasure.

CHAPTER IX.

The Return.

" A month's sharp conflict only served to prove
The power, as well as truth of Walter's love."
                    BLOOMFIELD: WALTER AND JANE.

How is it possible to describe the first meeting
of William and Ellen? With a confession of in-
ability it shall be passed by; and the reader must
picture to himself, if he wishes it, the words, looks,
and feelings with which, perhaps, experience can
supply him. Be this as it may, Ellen's stay at the
Moat House must be the recommencement of the
narrative; and there we do not hesitate to say how
delightful was the filbert hedge under which the poor
pointer was destroyed, and how romantic seemed the
old moat when they glided along its surface in William's punt, and plucked the bulrush, and watched
the moor-hens, with their downy brood, glide in and
out under the old roots. But there was one portion
of the moat particularly pleasing; that, namely, under
an old postern door, now grown over, and completely
shielded from observation. Why they liked this
place so much, it is hard for a grave author to
imagine—but so it was.

Mr. Lee often came up to the house, for it was William's wish that he should see as much as possible of his intended. He soon won her confidence, in addition to the respect and regard which she entertained for him before; and many were the agreeable and profitable conversations which this intercourse produced.

On one of these occasions, Ellen asked Mr. Lee to tell her some things in which he thought she should alter her habits, and in which she might make herself more useful.

"I am not your clergyman," he replied, looking rather mischievously.

"Yes, Sir; I know; but ——, but ——"

"But you think I shall be soon. Ah! I knew that was it. That's very true; and I shall be very glad to have you for my parishioner."

Ellen coloured up; but Mr. Lee soon put her at ease, and began upon the subject on which she had inquired.

" I never give many hints at a time. I will only mention two points to you; and if you think them important I can hereafter mention some others.

" The first great point is, simplicity in dress, which is incumbent upon you for many weighty reasons."

Ellen looked at her gown, and said, " I did not buy this, Sir. It was given me."

" Well, well, I was not speaking of what you are, but of what you are to be when you are Mrs. Blake,

you know. This is what you asked me about. Now
when you are Mrs. Blake, you will be my parishioner,
then I shall expect you to be remarkably plain in
your dress, for the following reasons :—

"1. For example. The great temptation and
snare to young women of the present day is vanity
in dress, the desire to appear as well dressed, and
dressed in the same style, as those who are richer.
This induces giddiness and extravagance, and leads
to dishonesty and ruin. I see it in my parish every
day. Modest girls are made bold, form evil ac-
quaintances, expose themselves to the most fearful
temptations, all through this love of dress; and are
often brought to ruin of body and soul. Now it
will be your duty steadily to set your face against
this great evil of our day; and you can consistently
and successfully do this in no other way than *by
example*.

"2. For your own sake and for others' also, I
expect this of you, because you cannot have enough
to give away if you spend much in dress; and only
think what a fearful thing it would be if any member
of Christ should suffer want or remain untaught—
suffer, that is, in body and soul—because your love
of finery, or weak yielding to the habits of others,
render you unable to relieve them, or to assist the
good works which are undertaken for the spreading
of Christ's kingdom.

"3. For your own sake I caution you against
dress, because you will find it prevents devotion

in church. It leads people to think of it, to be arranging for fear of its being spoiled; and often induces them not to kneel, or not to go to church at all in bad weather. At any rate, it occupies their thoughts in church, the last place where it should.

"And now, if you are not tired of this string of reasons, I will add one more,—

"4. The incompatibility of finery with humility. We are told to be 'clothed with humility.' But if we are gay and grand we are clothed *with pride*, with that which nourishes pride, with that which makes it almost impossible to be humble and to enter into the poverty of our Lord and His apostles. We are cautioned against gold or apparel as our adorning; and are recommended to deck ourselves with the ornament of a 'meek and quiet spirit.' Now, I do not say that a person cannot have a 'meek and quiet spirit,' who is dressed with ornament; but I say that such things make it much *harder* to be meek and quiet, and that a humble person will by no means *seek* out ornament. A queen may, indeed, endure it as part of her rank; but if she be truly meek and quiet, she would far rather be free from it, and certainly will never seek it. If you wish to be humble and retiring, dress in a humble and retiring manner.

"And now for my other point. I should like to mention it to William as well as to you. Do you think you could find him?"

H

"O yes, Sir; he is only in the yard. I can bring him in a minute."

William was soon found, and was somewhat surprised, on entering, at being made the subject of a series of questions.

"Can you tell me, William, whether Cayling Common is going to be enclosed?"

"Yes, I think so, Sir."

"I am sorry for that."

"Why, Sir, it seems quite a sin it should not be used."

"Are there no cottages near, to which it is serviceable?"

"Very few; and they will have allotments, which will be six times as valuable."

"You think it would be quite a sin to keep it as it is?"

"Yes, I do, Sir."

"Why a sin?"

"Because it would be a waste."

"You mean that we are bound to use whatever is given us in some way or other?"

"Yes; certainly."

"To improve it to the utmost?—Yes, it is a law, a duty; and every one sees this where interest clears the eye; it is a duty to improve God's gifts to the utmost."

"Yes, that is what I mean, Sir, only you express it much better."

"Well, now I have caught you by my little net, I will tell you why I sent for you, William. Miss Hilton asked me to mention some points in which I thought she could improve, and I have come to this, which applies to you quite as much. God has given you both a mind, powers of learning, remembering, comparing, concluding, of growing wiser, and more able to appreciate His glories, in order that you may benefit your fellow-creatures, and occupy your own time and thoughts with purifying and exalting subjects. This mind, and these powers, it is your duty to cultivate to the utmost, that is to say, as far as you can, without sacrificing plainer and nearer duties. It is a great mistake to suppose that it is enough for a farmer, as far as religion is concerned, to know his Catechism, and, in other matters, to be well acquainted with his business. He cannot be so useful a man, and seldom so high-minded a man, as he ought to be, knowing no more than these. He ought to know why he is a member of our Church, why not a Dissenter, and why not a Romanist: he ought to know something of the principles of our constitution, if he uses his vote ; he ought to have a knowledge of English history, in order to appreciate his country, and his own position; he ought to know something of chemistry, mechanics, and similar sciences, for his own occupation. If our farmers would only see this, and use their long winter evenings as they might do, they would occupy a very different position in the public regard. They are now considered an ignorant, obstinate, and prejudiced race, and in many cases with justice. There is a coarseness and common-placeness about their conversation, because they have nothing improving to talk of. They go over and over their profits, and murmur about the weather and crops, and join in much that is wrong and injurious to their souls, from being empty of better and more really interesting and important topics, and they are thus empty simply because they do not use the abundant time and opportunity which they enjoy. Now, if you, William, would ever be useful to me with our schools, or in the vestry; if you would keep yourself out of the way of many a temptation; secure yourself against degrading worldly cares, and trifling conversation; above all, if you would use that gift of God, which you allow it is your duty to improve and perfect to the utmost, simply because it is His gift, you will set to in good earnest this winter, and go through a course of reading; and you, Miss Hilton, will do the same."

"Will you be good enough to tell us what books we should read, Sir?" asked William.

"Yes, certainly; I will make you out a list, rather a long one, and you must not expect to get through it at once. However, I will put them down, and you can then choose, and I will look it over again, if you show it to me next spring. I shall lend you most of them, and will put a mark against those which I have. I am only going to make a list of modern books, however."

The following was the list, enlarged by subsequent alterations.

History.

Merchant and Friar, by Sir F. Palgrave.

Poole's History of England.

Wilberforce's Five Empires.

Churton's History of the Early English Church.

Palmer's History of the Church.

The Histories of Spain and Portugal, published in the Juvenile Englishman's Library.

Tales of my Grandfather.

Strickland's Queens of England.

The Fall of Crœsus.

Historical Parallels. (Family Library.)

Devotional Books.

Blunt's Lectures on the Old Testament.

Bennett's Lectures on the Distinctive Errors of Romanism.

Lectures on the Common Prayer, by the same Author.

Scripture Similitudes, by Trower.

Rectory of Valehead.

Nature and Benefits of Holy Baptism, by the Rev. F. Garden.

Trench's Hulsean Lectures. (First Series.)

Trench on the Parables.

Manning's Sermons.

Sherlock's Practical Christian.

Nelson's Fasts and Festivals.

Law's Serious Call.

Williams on the Passion.

Shadow of the Cross.

General Books.

Englishman's Library.

Livonian Tales.   (Murray's Colonial Library.)

Ivo and Verena.

Lives of Englishwomen of the Seventeenth Century.

Sintram.

Lives of Englishmen, in Cheap Library of Biography.

Memoirs of M. de La Rochejaquelein. (Constable's Miscellany.)

Markland's Observations on English Churches.

Tales for the Bush.

Walton's Lives.

Days and Seasons.

Thoughts in Past Years.

White's Selborne.

Journal of a Naturalist.

By the time Mr. Lee had finished his list, Mr. and Mrs. Blake came in, and the conversation remained, for once, much the same, for Mr. Lee had something to say of much importance.   He, therefore, led their thoughts on gradually, and showed them how that all persons dwelling together in a house are one family, knit together, and subjected to its head, who, as a pastor, or as a father, is always in a pastoral relation to his children, is responsible for guiding, controlling, and instructing them to the best of his power.   He then pointed out, that, as a family, they had need of united worship, not merely because servants often neglect the study of their Bibles, or are unable to read them, and because their prayers are probably very imperfect, but because the whole family being one, should send up one voice to Heaven, and should bind its various members to each other, by bonds of spiritual affection, by together asking for grace to fulfil their mutual as well as their personal duties.

The Blakes were sincerely attached to Mr. Lee, and immediately promised that they would thenceforth have family prayers, morning and evening, and only left it to their Rector to recommend some for their use. He told them that he purposed opening his church for daily service, directly the restoration was completed, and that, therefore, he should not advise the use of the Confession, and other prayers, in the Prayer Book, as he would otherwise have done. But he promised to mark the most applicable passages in Andrewes' Private Devotions, and to insert a collect, and a sentence or two, and recommended them to use these with the collect for the day, a psalm, and a chapter, or part of a chapter, of the Bible.

It was now evening, but Mr. Lee could not be persuaded to stay to tea, as it was a birthday at the Rectory; so the family at the Moat House drank tea together, and afterwards William determined on taking Ellen round the house in his punt.

When they came to the place where it was

moored, they found that it had been used, and fastened up in an unusual manner. This attracted attention; and the farming men declared they had not touched it. William was not satisfied, but he took the paddles and soon forgot all about it. After going round the moat once or twice, they returned to their favourite shelter, and, keeping hold of some ivy which overshadowed the old door, they sat talking, till dusk. Suddenly, they found it was getting late, and William exclaimed that it was time to go in, for fear Ellen should catch cold. He pushed off, but as he did so, he observed that the grass under the door, which was long and rank, had been trodden down: he rowed back, got out, and examined the spot. It was nearly dark under the door, but he could just see that it had been recently cut off its hinges, and that the way down into the cellar was open. He said nothing, but rowed thoughtfully back, and Ellen was silent also. When they had landed, William moored the punt just as he had found it, but fastened a long line, which he chanced to have in his pocket, to the stern, and then to a root, sinking the line under the water. He then left the boat, and went with Ellen. Mr. Blake met them, and William, taking him on to the causeway in front of the house, told him all that he had observed and done. It was clear that the house was to be broken into by the old door, where, as there seemed no danger, there had been no precaution, and where no one could possibly see; for the

causeway was in front of all the windows, and two
pointers always guarded the entrance. It was arranged
that Mr. Blake with three men should sit up, and be
ready to enter the cellar when William blew a horn.
William was to lie in wait in the orchard to give the
signal, and to pull the boat away when the thieves
were safely landed on the other side. They would
then be in a trap of their own making, and, it was
thought, would be easily captured. The arrangements were no sooner made than adopted. William
took his horn, went quietly into the garden, slung
himself up into an old apple-tree, and lay along one
of its branches in quiet expectation.

Time seemed to travel like the snail; so slowly did
dusk pass into darkness, and so long was it between
ten, eleven, and twelve, as the village clock told the
tardy hours to the sleeping country. Soon after
twelve, however, steps were heard nearer and nearer.
William's heart beat, as they approached his tree,
and came quite under it. At last he made out that
it was only one of the cows out of the home-close,
and his breath came more easily. On a minute's
reflection, however, it occurred to him that mischief
was at hand; for the cow could not have opened the
gate of herself; it must have been left open by some
person. He was not mistaken in his conjecture; four
dark figures came softly by him, and went towards the
boat. He heard them push off before he descended,
and then he crept quietly towards the bank. The dogs
barked violently, and he could hear the punt pause,

and then return to the bank as if the project were abandoned. He dared not move. The only chance was to lie still, and this he did. In a few minutes, however, the dogs were silent, and the punt went on. William now listened very carefully, and when he was convinced that the punt was empty he began to draw it slowly towards himself. But here all his plans were destined to fail, for after two or three yards it would come no farther. The robbers had fastened it themselves, and he could draw it up to the length of their line, and no more. This was an unexpected difficulty, and William hesitated what course to adopt. After a moment's thought, however, he drew out a pistol, and, having cocked it, he laid it by him on the ground ; then, holding his line hard round the root, and putting his foot against it, he blew a shrill blast in his other hand.

In a moment he heard voices, and a rush towards the door ; then the sound of fire-arms ; and a second after a man jumped off the bank into the boat, tumbling into it as he could, and recovering, began pulling fast to the bank. William went to meet him, keeping just out of sight. As soon as the punt touched, the fellow jumped from the boat, but was in too great a hurry. The impetus of his spring pushed the boat back, and he fell in between it and the edge. William ran up in a minute and tried to catch hold of him, but could not ; the man struck out boldly, and swam up the moat towards the other end. William doubted for a minute whether he should fire, but he could not bring himself to do so; and well was it that he refrained; for he could scarcely have been happy afterwards. He ran on therefore to meet the man, wherever he should land, but just as he turned he heard another rush through the door, and a splash. The splashing increased, but did not alter its position. Whoever was in the moat was drowning. In another minute he heard his own men shouting to him, " All right, Sir."

"Come round, then, as quickly as you can to the barn end, and help me," was the answer.

"Coming, Sir."

And indeed it was time. The swimmer was no easy foe to deal with. He was out and on his legs in a moment, and grappled directly with William, who presented a pistol to his ear, threatening to fire. Again, however, he could not bring himself to take the life of a fellow-creature. He held on, and feeling himself stabbed in the side, he suddenly left go; and before his opponent was aware of his danger, for he thought he had given William a mortal wound, young Blake struck him heavily on the forehead, and rolled him again into the moat. He never rose again. The men examined in vain, and soon gave up the useless search to carry William, who had fainted, into the house. There might be seen the two other thieves bound hand and foot, and old Blake in his easy chair, having his head bathed after a heavy blow. The doctor was sent for, and the wounds both of father and son were pronounced trifling ; but they occasioned a great disturbance, during which the prisoners managed to escape, not, as was strongly suspected, without the connivance of some one on the premises—a second proof, if any were wanted, how unsafe that man is whose servants and labourers have been long treated as such only, and not brought to fidelity and honesty by the fear of God.

CHAPTER X.

The Lesson of Nature.

" All things speak from Thee,—every sun that shines
Sets forth thine image, and each day's return
Is herald of the morn that ne'er declines ;
The bright recovering year, when all things burn
In glorious beauty round the source of light ;
All are Thy teachers,—grant us to discern
Their heavenly lessons,—cleanse our mortal sight,—
We have enough to preach, did we but hear aright."
THE BAPTISTERY.

WILLIAM's wound appeared, of course, very fright-
ful and interesting to Miss Hilton ; but, in reality, it
was nothing, and a few days restored him and his
father to their full powers.   A coroner's inquest was
held upon the two men who were drowned, and the
usual verdicts of " Accidental Death," and " Justifiable Homicide," were returned in the several cases.
Neither of the men were identified.   They were
entire strangers, and if there had been anything
about them which might have led to recognition, it
was carefully removed by those who found their
bodies.

The inquest gave occasion to a conversation on
juries, upon which Mr. Lee and Mr. Blake could not
agree.   Mr. Blake defended the common verdict of

insanity which juries generally pronounce upon those who die by their own hands.

"I can't believe," said Mr. Blake, "that any man, Sir, would kill himself if he knew what he was about."

"Why not, Mr. Blake?"

"It's such a mad and terrible act."

"Very true, Mr. Blake, but so are all great crimes. Can anything be more terrible and mad than for a man deliberately to kill his own father? and yet such things occur. Can anything be more terrible than to poison a whole family, or burn a whole house, for some slight offence? and yet these are not unheard-of crimes."

"Very true, Sir; but it does not seem like killing oneself."

"No, it does not. Suicide, certainly, requires a different state of mind, and different motives; but it is not more unnatural, or more irrational. You often hear men say of a wasteful spendthrift, 'Poor man! he hurts no one but himself;' and although this is not true, because no man can lead a wasteful life without injuring others in many ways; yet, undoubtedly, generous and rash persons do justify themselves in a course of ruinous expense, by the notion that they are 'nobody's enemies but their own,' and that the burden will fall upon themselves only; and hence they consider that their better counsellors are impertinent intruders, and often tell them as much. Now, this half natural feeling, that a man has a right to injure himself, you may depend upon it, weighs with the suicide. He says to himself, ' I hurt no one ; true, it is a fearful risk, but *I* run it, and *I* shall suffer for it, if there is anything to suffer ;' and, therefore, he has some generous feeling at the bottom to help him on, whereas the murderer has none at all. All nature is against *him*. *His* act is wholly indefensible. He is the maddest, and most terrible venturer of soul and body, for revenge, or gain, or whatever it may be. I give the suicide, then, this credit, although he does not always deserve it. But, in proportion, mind, as I make his case better, I make the murderer's more mad ; so that if you will have all suicides out of their mind, much more must you reckon all murderers insane.''

" Mr. Ravensworth, at Honiton Gore, thinks just as you do, and he will not bury suicides.''

" You remember, I dare say, the words of the Rubric are, ' That the office is not to be used for any that die unbaptized, or excommunicate, or have laid violent hands upon themselves ;' so you see he has ground to go on, although there is a difficulty in the interpretation of the rule.''

" But is not such a rule very hard?''

" No, not at all ; but, on the contrary, very kind. Mad people have great command over themselves, and if they knew that their violent death would bring disgrace upon their interment, they would often refrain ; and sane people would do so still more, and so might live, and repent of their evil purpose. At any rate, the present system is this, that juries and clergymen combine to delude persons in an afflicted and unsettled state of mind, that a desire and intention of self-destruction are states of mind for which they are not responsible, or, in short, that they are madness; and thus they are led to yield themselves up to such a state, without resistance, and, so yielding, pass by an act of sin into the presence of their Judge, not only depriving themselves of all opportunity of obliterating the past, but adding to their condemnation at the very moment in which they come before their God. I wish, then, that juries would weigh this well, and decide according to their oath, and not according to their feelings. Our course is, perhaps, not so clear as theirs, and the sooner it is made clearer the better."

Mr. Blake had been much won of late by his son's dutiful obedience and affection, and by Mr. Lee's kindness to the whole family. Mrs. Lee, too, and the children, had often been up at the Moat House, and this increased intercourse was the source of increased good-will. No one, indeed, except the most prejudiced person, could see the Lee family without loving them. There was such a simple happiness, such a natural, unconscious kindness of feeling, and cheerfulness, in all their ways; and they were so well informed, ready and useful alike in great things and in small, that they were delightful neighbours, not merely to the clergy, but to their parishioners, who were with them always as much as possible. One of

the children, little Agnes, was a particular favourite
with Mr. Blake, who used to take her upon his knee,
and talk to her by the half-hour together. One day
he was playing with her in this manner, and asked
how her garden was thriving; to which she answered
very merrily—

"I have not one now."

"Why not, my dear?"

"Papa has let all the orchard, where our gardens
were, last week, and he says he will give us some in
the kitchen-garden; but we have not got them yet."

"Has your papa really let the orchard?"

"O yes; did not you know?"

"Why, what made him do that?"

"He could not help it, you know."

"No, indeed, I don't know."

"He told us he could not pay Mr. Giles unless
he did, so we all gave up."

Mr. Giles was the schoolmaster, the chief part of
whose salary had fallen upon the Rector, owing to
the backwardness of others to assist. Mr. Blake
was much struck with what he heard. His respect
for Mr. Lee increased still more, but he felt very
uncomfortable himself; and after some consideration,
he took his hat next day and went down to the
Rectory. Mr. Lee was in, and received him directly.
Mr. Blake was a plain man, and he opened his business at once.

"I've been thinking over that pew business, Sir,
and I don't like it at all."

I

Mr. Lee looked alarmed.

"It is not right, Sir, that it is not, and I never half liked it."

"Well, but you should have said so then, Mr. Blake. It's too late now to do anything."

"I only wish I had, Sir. I'm quite vexed with myself, but it's not too late, and that's just what I'm come down for this morning."

Poor Mr. Lee was fairly staggered. He hoped that all the difficulty had passed away, and Mr. Blake was the last person whom he expected to revive it.

However, his fears did not last long, for Mr. Blake pulled out of his pocket a leather bag, and began counting out very carefully.

"You see, Sir, here's £30 towards the new seats, and £3 for the school; and I shall subscribe that every year, Sir, if you please, to help to pay Mr. Giles."

Mr. Lee was as much astonished as delighted. He called his wife, and they both shook hands with Mr. Blake, and all seemed so pleased, that poor Mr. Blake was quite overcome, and began to think he had not done half enough. However, this notion soon subsided, and, after staying to the Lees' early dinner, he returned pleased with them and pleased with himself, and this in a new fashion: for he used to pique himself on his good sense in being careful of his money, but now he was quite happy at his unwonted liberality—a much better sort of satisfaction than his former.

About the same time a parcel of books arrived, which William had ordered from Mr. Lee's list, and, amongst them, Trench on the Parables, which was not intended to have come so early in his course of reading. William looked at it, and began one day to speak of it with his Rector.

"I certainly did not mean you to have read it so soon," replied Mr. Lee, "and I think you will have to ask for assistance, especially in the Introduction; but it is a very important book, and I hope you will master it when you once begin. It is not only important as enabling you to understand and enter into Holy Scripture, but it is calculated to awaken you to a sense of privileges, which you are tempted to neglect, and to save you from the very great injury which that neglect would occasion.

"You will gather from Mr. Trench's book that one great object of our Lord's teaching by parables was to arouse men to a sense of the spiritual teaching of nature, as well as to make use of the resemblance between our eternal and temporal being, in order to convince men of truths, in respect of the former, which they readily admit in regard to the latter. But I fear I am speaking very obscurely after all. Man, you know, has two beings, a temporal and an eternal, an earthly and heavenly, a visible and invisible; and God has from the beginning made these two beings, or states, resemble each other, so that earth should remind us of Heaven, instead of leading us to forget it, and so that we should not be confused and misled, by finding ourselves under two contradictory systems. For if earth undid all that Heaven works in us, and Heaven contradicted all the teaching of earth, it would not only seem as if there had been two creators, or one inconsistent maker of all things, but we should be confused, and, being pulled first one way and then another, could never advance far, nor see our way clearly, nor make any progress to a higher state. But now we see one gracious will for good in everything, and all things working together for good, in harmony and connexion, to them that love God.

"For example, we are taught to regard God as our Father. Now, how do we know what such love should be? By our having an earthly father. The two ordinances correspond : and every one who loves his earthly father will not only know how, but will also be better able to love his heavenly Father; and the more he enters into his Christian Sonship, the more, again, he will reverence his own parent, who is the type and image of our Father which is in heaven. Observe how the Lord uses this truth, when He tells us, on the one hand, to pray, saying, 'our *Father*,' and to confess thus, 'I will arise and go to my *Father*;' and, on the other, founds all the parable of the prodigal son on the fact, that as a human parent rejoices to receive a lost child, so will

God receive us, when we return to Him.   And again, after saying, 'if a *son* shall ask bread of any of you that is a *father*, will he give him a stone?' He adds, 'how much more shall your *Father* which is in heaven give good things to them that ask him!'

"Now men had become blind to these facts, blind to the resemblance between earth and heaven; and our Lord, by bringing one forth to view, threw light upon both. You will see at once that a difference must ever exist between a man who regards his parent as no more than an earthly relative, however dear, and who looks upon God as a mighty King, condescending to show mercy to His slaves, and a man who, regarding God with the affection of a child, and his earthly father with some of the reverence due to God whom he represents, and from whom he derives his authority and influence.   He who has the noblest view, if he acts upon it, will be the best son as well as the best Christian.   Obedience to his parent will train him to obedience to his God.   The state of mind fit for one relation will serve in the other.   He will feel that God's commandments are not grievous, but parental.   He will readily bend to his parent's will, and honour him, to honour his Creator. The thought of God the Father will evermore be to him a revival of affection, and of reverence to his earthly parent; and the society of his earthly father will be a continual memorial of eternal things, a continual exercise of those faculties, thoughts, and habits, which find their perfect use only in love and obedience to God.

"This is only one point. Marriage is not only a figure, but a counterpart of the relation between each soul and the whole Church to the Redeemer, in which each and all forget also our own people and our father's house, and cleave wholly to Christ, who loveth us, and cherisheth us, and rejoiceth over all our obedience and love, as a bridegroom rejoiceth over the bride.

"Our brothers and sisters are to us a type of the heavenly family, and an aid to our loving and realising the whole Church of the first-born. And all nature is, upon the same principle, a second Church, as it were, an unwritten Gospel. In it, the sun is Christ, the stars are saints. Water, so pure, refreshing, cleansing, sustaining, is the washing and renewing of our souls, under the Gospel, and first, and very especially, in the font. Autumn is Death; Spring is the Resurrection. The fertility and sterility of the ground answer to holiness and unholiness. With man, and with earth, care and culture alike avail, under God's blessing, and, without it, fail. Man himself, in his mere body, is a perfect exposition of a great portion of Christian doctrine : growing, by degrees, into a perfect stature; subject to disease and death by negligence and vice; requiring food, like the soul; upright or prostrate, weak or strong; uniting many members in harmony with each other; when one member suffers, all suffering with it; all his portions having their various offices; all in subjection to the Head; requiring clothing to hide his shame, even as the soul cannot appear before God without the robe of righteousness, given by Him; his whole being is a continual admonition to the thoughtful Christian.

"You will see, now, not only the great importance of teaching by parables, but of the figurative language of the Bible. It is no mere Eastern fashion of language; no mere beauty of poetry; but a spiritual lesson, and a sacrament of grace. And, as the facts upon which it is founded come more especially before the farmer, so it is most important he should be awake to them; for, if he is not, he will be injured rather than benefited. You know that the more we are used to things, the more blind we become to them, unless we take a lively interest in them. Think of the soldier. If he is a good man, every battle is a solemn thing to him, and the thought of death is very awful; but his trust in God supports him, and makes him brave. But if he is a bad man, then he gets so hardened, as not to think of death at all, even when his own nearest comrades are shot down at his side. He sees death so often, without thinking of it, that it loses all power over him; it produces no impression whatever.

"And in this way the farmer, who does not endeavour to see God in all His works, to connect outward with inward things, and earthly with heavenly, becomes the most dull, sense-bound, worldly-minded man in the land, and sees God less

than any man, and has a low, degraded spirit.
Indeed, there are many things in his calling calculated to produce this evil. Constant watchfulness
of the progress of crops, attention to details in
economy, bargaining at fairs, and the like, all help
to lower the mind, harden it, and make it worldly.
These lessons of nature are appointed to help him ;
and, if they fail, he is worse off than ever, more
hardened, dead, and earthly than I can describe, or
wish to realise.

"And now let me give you a sort of sketch of a
succession of thoughts, arising from our temporal
condition, and the creation by which we are
surrounded, which might well come into your
mind from morning to evening, and you will then
judge of the power and importance of such considerations.

"You would rise, when accustomed to such meditations, with the thought of the Resurrection,
of the day in which your work must be done,
of the Sun of Righteousness, whose emblem is
lighting up the earth. You would remember, during
your dressing, sin, and the healing waters of Baptism, and the admonition to approach God, having
the heart sprinkled from an evil conscience. You
would think of the shame of sin, that requires to
be hidden ; the clothing of humility, the ornament
of a meek and quiet spirit, of the man who was found
without the marriage garment, and of the white
robes of the saints. You would, after your devotions,

descend to the lower work of earth, and remember
how Christ came down for us, to sanctify earth to
us, and us by the use of it. You would be reminded of
heavenly truths, by your family and household. You
would go forth into the fresh air, and be put in mind
of the freshness and strength of the Spirit blowing
whithersoever He listeth. The dew would be upon the
grass, speaking of the dew of God's blessing. Every
thing would be seen doing its appointed work, and
shall man alone neglect his? Every living thing
receiving its meat from God, appears an admonition of the entire procession and dependence of all
creation. You see the lark rising to Heaven's gate.
It is praising its God, and soaring as near to Heaven
as earth allows. It descends, 'for the corruptible
body presseth down the soul, and the earthly taber-
nacle weigheth down the mind that museth upon
many things; and hardly do we guess aright at
things that are upon earth, and with labour do we
find the things which are before us; but the things
that are in Heaven who hath searched out?' You
go forth into the corn fields, and there, perhaps,
you pass through a longer course of thought. The
wheat is now up, but a few weeks back it was sown
in weakness, even as now it rises in power; it
was sown bare grain, it is now that body that it
should be; and all death, and your dear brother's
death and life, come before you. And whence is
your hope? You return again to the thought,
'Except a corn of wheat fall into the ground

and die, it abideth alone: but if it die, it bringeth forth much fruit.'

"For even thus our Saviour was trodden into earth in death, a single grain, but He arose, bearing the fruit of the whole world into the garner of Heaven. And you may go on to think of Him in his Sacrament as the food of the world, broken, divided, yet one; given, taken, eaten, making all His people one, and preserving their souls and bodies unto everlasting life. And you can meditate upon the parable of the sower, and think of the fruit which you may be expected to present.

"The day draws on with you, just as life does; evening approaches, and all the time the state of the heavens, the flowers, the rain, or drought, have reminded you of some heavenly truth. As the day closes, you see the shepherd gathering the sheep together, and think with deep emotion of the good Shepherd who laid down his life for his sheep, of the lost sheep in the wilderness, even yourself, and of the one fold, and of the unity of the Church, which you will never quit to follow a strange voice; and that now in such blessed peace you 'go in and out, and find pasture.'

"Then the dew falls, quiet and blessed like the Incarnation of our Lord, as it was typified upon the fleece of Gideon, according to the seventy-second Psalm: 'He shall come down like the rain into a fleece of wool, even as the drops that water the earth.' And then night succeeds, night, in which no work may be done, and you review your day as you review your life, and sleep closes all, admonishing you of the sleep of death, but you fear it not; it is peaceful and secure, because you can use the words of your Redeemer, as He spake, by the Psalmist, of His own death and rising, 'I laid me down and slept, and rose up again, for the Lord sustained me.'

"Such are your privileges, William. By them you may become I cannot say how blessed, and for them you will have to give an account; for a Christian man may not be blind to these things, since Christ has anointed the eyes of the blind, and caused us to see. We behold; only let us think, and feel, and live according to, such thoughts and feelings as as our life, explained by the word of God, produces in a simple heart."

CHAPTER XI.

Winter.

"Though night approaching bids for rest prepare,
Still the flail echoes through the frosty air,
Nor stops till deepest shades of darkness come,
Sending at length the weary labourer home:
From him, with bed and nightly food supplied,
Throughout the yard, hous'd round on every side,
Deep-plunging cows their rustling feast enjoy,
And snatch sweet mouthfuls from the passing boy,
Who moves unseen beneath his trailing load,
Fills the tall racks, and leaves a scatter'd road."

BLOOMFIELD'S FARMER'S BOY.

WILLIAM was now quietly and consistently doing his duty, and improving himself. He read a certain time every evening, and often aloud to his father. He formed a school of his men under Mr. Lee's advice, in which he taught several to read and write : and, in spite of the great difficulty and disappointment of his task, he made considerable progress with his scholars. He induced his father to give allotments to the poor; he made arrangements, also, by Mr. Blake's permission, according to which the crow boys, who were set to watch the corn, were no longer allowed, as is culpably and grievously general, to be absent for a long time from school, and altogether from church : but he so alternated one boy with another, that they always went to church once on Sunday, and every other week to the school. He had also previously arranged those who laboured in the potato fields on a new plan. Formerly, men and women used to work together, and the effects of this intercourse were very bad. The men used language which women should not have heard ; and, as might have been expected, the women and girls employed, became very hardened and immoral. He arranged them, therefore, in gangs, so that the women were alone, with the exception of a few respectable married men, who turned up the potatoes, as the women collected them, and put them into the sacks. In fact, his mind was set upon remedying the evils, and improving the opportunities attached to his business, and hence he went on cheerfully and hopefully, with the best of all happiness, that which results from a regular, humble, and trustful discharge of duty.

It was a very dear year, and corn was high ; wages were, indeed, generally raised, but not proportionably to the prices. Mr. Lee was talking one day on this subject with Mr. Blake, and was at length led to say that he really could not pity Hodgson, who had taken down an old stack, and found the profit of the high prices far more than counterbalanced by the waste through rats and mice.

" I really don't see he was to blame, Sir," replied Mr. Blake, " except for being so foolish."

"I am sorry to differ from you, Mr. Blake, but I have very strong views on this point, and, if you like, I will give you them."

"Certainly, Sir, I shall be very glad to hear, though I don't think you'll convince me very easily."

"Perhaps not, but, as you give me leave, I will tell you some of my notions on farming. I hold that, at the very least, no man has a right to make a time of scarcity and suffering a means of private advancement, by withholding that which he can afford to sell. S. Ambrose, if I remember, speaks very strongly upon this, but there is a pretty plain text in the book of Proverbs, which not only states the result of such conduct, but, to my mind, implies that the result is natural and merited. It is there said, 'He that withholdeth corn, the people shall curse him, but blessing shall be upon the head of him that selleth it.'"

"Well, Sir, but you allow the merchant to make the most of his merchandise, why not allow the farmer to make the most of his corn?"

"Because people can do without the merchandise, but men cannot live without bread! You may defer the purchase of clothes, or wear a coarser sort, but you cannot defer the purchase of the means of life, the English labourer cannot do without bread. Supposing, however, that a merchant held a raw material like cotton or flax, and his holding and speculating on it prevented the manufacturer from working his machinery, and his mill people from earning their livelihood, I should no more exempt him from blame, than I do the farmer."

"Well, Sir, that seems very reasonable; but then we lose in one year, and are obliged to make up in another."

"Very true; but a religious man will hardly endeavour to free himself from God's chastisement by adding to the weight of the sufferings of others. A bad year was God's visitation to you; a dear year, in which you have plenty of grain, is His blessing to you that you may have, and not only have, but give. But I would allow you to reimburse yourself, in ordinary times, for previous low prices, unless heavy crops indemnified you at the time for them. You might sell for the fair price and your loss additional, unless prices were very hard on the poor, and you were better able to bear the loss than they."

"What sort of price, then, would you think fair?"

"I will not take on myself to fix a price, for fear of weakening what I say. My principle is sound, and the application of it I leave to an honest man, who knows his business. Honesty and experience will be his guide, and better he cannot have. However, just to take a nominal sum to illustrate, not to measure or fix what I plead for, I should say that 50s. is a fair price for wheat, when the crops are fine. Suppose, then, wheat was 40s. with noble crops, the year preceding, so that you lost 2s. a quarter; then, that this year the crops were thin so that you required 60s. for a remunerating price,

you should then sell at 62s., or, if the wheat had to
pay for other failures, as high as 70s., if you honestly
deduct profits as well as failures, and cannot afford
to lose ; but, for wheat to be above 70s., to be 90s.,
as now, is altogether monstrous."

"Well, Sir, but the wages are higher."

"They did not rise at once, nor universally.
Your neighbours have not all raised them, and some
very inadequately: and you must remember, that farming labourers are not the population of England. The
poor shirtworkers at 9d. per dozen, the almost beg-
gars of Westminster and St. Giles's, the clerk who
has to keep himself in respectable attire, and a
family on £60, have no more to buy with, therefore
they buy less, and feel the scarcity most bitterly.
And even your own labourer, if he has a family,
loses more by the rise in food than he gains by that
of wages, for you must remember all food is dear
when any is.   Take an example.   Suppose a
married man has eleven shillings in ordinary times,
and thirteen now, and that, out of his eleven, seven
go in food.   Well, food is a third dearer when
wheat is at ninety, therefore he ought to have a
third more to spend in food, whereas he has not.
You might find fault with this calculation, but then
there would probably be faults in each direction,
and the result would lead, I believe, to some
similar conclusion; so that I boldly repeat my
text, 'Blessing shall be upon the head of him that
selleth.'"

"You certainly rather puzzle me, Sir, and I do not know exactly what to say to you."

" Never mind what to say, Mr. Blake, only think it well over, and I shall be satisfied. And, besides all this, I would have you consider that such conduct implies a distrust of God's providence, which is a common temptation to men of your calling. Your liberality the other day enables me to speak with comfort when I say, that farmers are for the most part very niggardly, for fear of poverty. I have often been refused, when asking for assistance to most Christian and necessary works, through fear that things should take a turn, and the money given be wanted afterwards; and indeed, this same want of faith is urging many men, who have enough, to hold back their stores in this trying time. Now all the Bible is full of promises to those who trust in God. A man must either believe the promises or give up the Bible, if he is honest with himself: and there are circumstances in the occupations of a farmer which should remind him continually of this, and make him more trustful and liberal. I can hardly imagine a good man going forth into his fields, and seeing the hope of next year laid in the ground, without remembering, at times, such striking passages as these—'There is that scattereth and yet increaseth,'—'He that soweth little shall reap little, but he that soweth plenteously shall reap plenteously.' Moreover, the whole harvest is so evidently the work of God, from first to last. The manu-

K

facturer, if his produce is bad, justly taxes his men or his machinery. The tradesman, if he loses, blames his want of foresight, or his unprincipled customers. But the farmer, having the best land, the best workmen, the best tools, the best seed, the longest experience, is still in the greatest uncertainty, from first to last. Circumstances, which he can neither foresee, nor, foreseeing, control, keep him sensibly in God's hands—and, if he is wise, resigned and trustful, be his fortune what it may. The worm, the caterpillar, the fly, or drought, and rain, cold, and heat, his very friends—if they fail at the prospering moment, render all his labours doubtful to the end. And therefore, being so entirely and manifestly in God's hands, he should rest satisfied, and not neglect his duty, confident that he is more likely, not less likely, to prosper, even though his alms are what the world would consider rash; but not rash, because they are given to Him, and with faith in Him from whom he holds all that he enjoys."

It was by such conversations as these, under God's blessing, and by the influence of those reclaiming circumstances which He had graciously ordered, that the family at the Moat House were gradually more and more conforming their minds and habits to a Christian rule. Mr. Lee could say more to them than he could to their neighbours, for not only were they ready to learn, but they had entirely given up all those flagrant neglects and irreligious habits, which, so long as they continue, make it worse than useless to go on to higher duties: so universally true is it, that "to him that hath shall be given." And it was well that religion had gained so increasing a hold upon Mr. Blake, for a heavy trial still awaited him. His sight had been for some time failing, and at last he resolved to go to London. He did so, and after consulting an eminent oculist, wrote back to his son the following touching letter:—.

My dear Son,

      I have seen Mr. A——, who says that nothing can be done. I shall soon lose my sight entirely, and I know I deserve it. I have been blind to God's works and God's mercies, and may be, He will make me see more of Himself, by this heavy affliction. I have made up my mind about the farm. I shall put you into it, and go and live in my cottage by the church; and I pray God I may have sight to see you married, and settled comfortably, before I am quite blind. Your mother is very low. God bless you, my support and comfort.

We return on Thursday, and you will meet us at Belborough with the phaeton.

               Your affectionate father,
                   JOHN W. BLAKE.

London, Nov. 30.

William accordingly met his parents at Belborough, and Mr. Lee was ready to receive them at Staunton. They felt his kindness more and more, and were comforted to think that they should be so much nearer to him when they lived in the village. For all this, it was a mournful Christmas, and the blindness came on so much faster than was anticipated, that it was plainly impossible that the marriage could take place in time for Mr. Blake to see it. It was, however, arranged that they should give up the farm to William at Lady-day, and that he should be married in Easter week. This was looking a long time forward, yet the lovers liked such looks. They were pleased enough at their own prospects, although it was painful to both, and especially to William, that his marriage should be brought nearer by his father's misfortune, and that his parents should leave their house for him. But the cottage was prepared, and everything gradually cleared up with a view to the completion of this arrangement. Mr. Blake was to live on the income of some cottages and a few acres, with £100 a-year out of the farm: and he left his capital and the implements for William's use. The furniture, however, was removed to some extent to the cottage, which was enlarged by the addition of a very decent sitting-room, with a good bay-window, planned by Mr. Lee, in which Mr. Blake was to sit in his old arm-chair, varying the side according to the wind and sun. There was something very melancholy in all these movements, but the excitement and the labour attendant upon them, diverted the attention; and William's father and mother were daily becoming more resigned, and cheerfully conformed to their prospects, and daily taking more pleasure in looking forward to the happiness which they trusted their son would enjoy.

CHAPTER XII.

The Union.

" Why should we grudge the hour and house of prayer
  To Christ's own blind and lame
  Who come to meet him there?"

LYRA INNOCENTIUM.

WE have passed over the opening of the church, which took place at Advent, because it was not closely connected with our tale or its general bearings. The commencement of the daily service had been postponed until Ash Wednesday, and it began, thenceforth, to continue as a permanent blessing to the parish. Our readers will easily believe that the Blakes were pretty regular attendants, and William took great pains with the apportionment of his time, and generally managed to come off his marshes or the hill fields so as to take his place amongst the worshippers. It is true that, for this and several other things, he was laughed at, and called "serious William," "saint," and many other names: but he remembered the presence of God, and regarded not the laughter of fools, against the light of God's countenance. This was his constant strength : and whenever he was inclined to give way, he felt as if Christ's eye were upon him, as it was upon S. Peter, and thus he was recalled to himself. But his former fall had made him humble, and he no longer thought himself some one, nor imagined that he was doing anything great. He was daily gaining more and more of that humble and unostentatious piety, whose praise is not of men but of God.

By Easter the old Blakes had removed, and William was in full possession—a melancholy privilege. The house was dull and voiceless, and half unfurnished, and the future, at that time, hardly made amends for the loss of the past.

About furnishing, he consulted Mr. Lee, for he had been much struck with the fittings of the Rectory, and with Mr. Lee's opinions upon the subject.

Mr. Lee advised him to furnish very plainly and in character with the house.

"The position of a farmer," he said, "is one which has changed less than that of any person removed from poverty in the whole country. He has more of the old English ways, and, in some respects, of the old English feeling, than his neighbours. The influence of his position too is old-fashioned, parochial, domestic, homely. Its virtues are old-fashioned virtues, hospitality, kindness to the poor placed under him, hardness and simplicity of life. He is not one of those who act in masses, who compete man against man, whose plans are ever varying and accommodating themselves to varying circumstances: and therefore, I cannot but regret when I see him throw off those external circumstances which tend to remind him of this position, to separate him from the citizen and tradesman, and to connect him with the past, which is his strength. I regret even when I see him modernise his old farm-house, cut out the mullioned windows, pull down the panelling, fill up the wide chimney, and still more when I see the veneered mahogany take the place of old English oak, in chairs and tables. If I were you, I would act upon two rules; first—to furnish plainly and inexpensively, in such a manner as is suitable for strong shoes, and a man of early hours and simple habits ; and secondly—whatever you have handsome, should be in character with the old house in which you live; plain wooden chairs, and an oaken table, with the addition of an old bookcase, and a carved old chest, or chair or two, would make your room all that you require, and in good keeping with you and with itself. You will easily pick up some old things in the cottages, if you look about you. I will give you a couple of engravings for your drawing-room out of my portfolio, and you can have them framed after some of mine, by young Thomas, in the village."

William adopted the suggestion, and, by the addition of a little scraping of whitewashed oak, he made the old house look quite nice by the time it was to be completely occupied. Ellen was charmed with it, and wondered at her own former predilection for shabby modern furniture when she saw the quiet and home-like air which her future house had gained, by a simple and old-fashioned style of furnishing.

Mr. Blake had given up his post at the board of guardians, and Mr. Lee took his place for a year, in order to keep out Mann, and hoping that, by the end of the year, the parish would be willing to elect William in his stead. His line of management was to give out-door relief, wherever the paupers were honestly such. He could not bear to break down the independence of a man, nor to sever a family from its parish, and its home ; and he was sure that the most Christian and most truly economical plans coincided, those, namely, which relieved at the least cost of pain, and in a manner which encouraged and assisted men to make up the deficiency by their own exertions, instead of being wholly supported by the public.

But Mr. Lee had a plan very near his heart, and, having taken every means of rendering it successful, he at last brought it forward.

It so happened that a relieving officer and chaplain had to be elected together, owing to a series of disagreements which occasioned the retirement of the latter officer; and the former had absconded in debt. The board proceeded to elect a relieving officer first, because it was known that there would be considerable discussion about the chaplaincy.

The first candidate was a broken coachman, but he was found to be given to drinking, and was, therefore, soon dismissed; many others followed, all liable to some objection or other, and at last the choice lay between Mr. Octavius Snapper, a smart, clever-looking man, and Mr. John Bright, who looked anything but answerable to his name. Mr. Snapper came first, and was introduced after his testimonials had been read.

" In what business have you been, Mr. Snapper?" inquired the chairman.

" I was in the wine way, Sir."

" In what ?"

" The wine way, Sir."

" Wine whey you made, did you ?" said the chairman, with mischievous stupidity.

" The wine connexion, I mean, Sir; I was agent for a gent at Bristol, in a large way of business."

" Well, wine whey is quite in the wine connexion, I should think. But how came you to leave such a pleasing connexion ? Why did you leave Bristol, Mr. Snapper ?"

" Why, Sir, I had a good offer in the cotton line."

" Twist, I suppose, is the cotton line you speak of. You were a spinner, I presume ?"

" No, Sir, I used to sell on commission for various parties, under the principal."

" Why did you leave Manchester ?"

" Why, Sir, I knew a party, in a house in town, and he persuaded me to join him."

" How many were there in the party ?"

" Only my friend, Sir."

" I thought you said a party."

" No, he was a gent, Sir, that I had often met at different places."

" And what line was he in ?"

" The patent corn-restoring line, Sir."

" Corn-restoring line, Sir ?   What ! do you mean that when corn was bad you made it good ?"

" Yes, Sir."

" What sort of corn ?"

" Damaged."

" How ?"

" With bilge-water."

" And what did you do to it ?"

" We restored it with our patent, Sir."

" How ?"

" On hot plates with sulphur."

" And that made it bright, again ?"

" Yes, quite, Sir."

" Inside as well as out ?"

" No, Sir, I can't say it did that."

" Then, how did you sell it ?"

" Oh, there were plenty of buyers, Sir."

" To sell it again ?"

"Yes, they took it, and disposed of it, as they liked."

" In London ?"

" I can't say."

" Do you think it likely ?"

" No, I don't know that it was, or wasn't."

" Well, and what made you leave, Mr. Snapper?

" We were unfortunate, Sir."

" That is, you failed?"

" Why, yes, Sir, we were unfortunate."

" Had you any capital?"

" No, Sir."

" Nor your friend?"

" Very little, Sir."

" You were very clever, to get on without."

" Why, yes, Sir, we are both good men of business, I reckon, and always were."

" Thank you, Sir. I think that will do. Don't you think it will, gentlemen?" said the chairman, when Mr. Snapper had shut the door. "Don't you think he had better not try the relieving line? Perhaps he would be in a bad way soon, and then be in the absconding line. He is not a *capital* fellow by his own confession."

The merry chairman produced roars of laughter. Mr. Snapper was passed over, and honest John Bright chosen, who answered the purpose very well, being regular, active, and respectable : and then they proceeded to the more important business of electing a chaplain, out of *two* candidates ; for the salary was only £60. One of the applicants was a sporting man, who lived six miles off; the other, the curate of Belborough, a place of three thousand inhabitants. After some discussion upon the qualifications of the two candidates, Mr. Lee rose to address the board.

"I have two measures, gentlemen, of the greatest importance to recommend to you to-day, and those such as I shall have great difficulty in representing to you as they appear to me. I have long thought and felt much upon the subject, and am, therefore, naturally more impressed by it than I can expect others to be ; and I trust, therefore, that whilst I am prepared to expect great difference of opinion in some, or an inactive, and only general approval in others, you, on the other hand, will be kind enough to remember that there may be more in my views than appears at first sight ; since they have been reflected upon, and duly weighed, and are old to my mind and heart, although they are new to yours.

"The union house, we all know, is a place of great trial to the feelings, and often to the religion of its inmates. People come here with the loss of all their old places and habits. They leave their friends, their old haunts, their liberty, their independence ; and the sore trial this must be to their feelings, the need of consolation which arises, the necessity of constant warning and comforting under such circumstances, are only too evident.

"And this is not all. Persons have the choice of their own companions out of this house, but not in it. Poor people, whose faith and whose holiness are of a wavering and dependent kind, (and, alas! how much is this the case with all of us !) are here thrown with and upon godless and wicked companions, ready to stifle every effort after good, and to create that desponding spirit of hatred which so often prevails amongst the inhabitants of such places as this. It is our work to counteract these evils, or to see them counteracted, by all possible means. Now, gentlemen, what do we to counteract these evils, and to alleviate these sorrows? We appoint a chaplain, and we have prayers read by the master.

" We appoint a chaplain. One of the candidates lives six miles off. He will be here, and give a service at eight on Sunday, leaving all the rest of the day unsanctified, dull, hopeless, repining, the fruitful source of evil thoughts and words, the very contrary to that resemblance and road to Heaven which it should be. He will be here, also, once or twice in the week, speaking a word to one man, and giving five minutes to another, and adding a lecture, with a few prayers, upon Wednesdays. Or we choose the other, who can more easily attend, so far as distance is concerned, but less easily as regards population. The population of this town is over three thousand, and to this there are only two clergymen, although it is impossible for one to look thoroughly to the welfare of more than a thousand, if of so many. Gentlemen, no man should ever be a party to adding a single office or occupation to that of the curate of one thousand souls. If he is, he injures priest and people alike, however kindly he may mean. I, for one, can never join in sanctioning such a mischievous mistake, or in doing such an injustice to this town. If Belborough contained only two thousand souls, with the same number of curates, or one thousand with one, no additional labours should be either given or allowed.

"But, to return to the hours of service. It is wholly unjustifiable to have an early service here, and to leave the rest of the day empty ; or to have a service in the middle of the day, leaving the first and last parts unoccupied. For here, more, not less, religious care, is required than elsewhere. There is increased leisure, with less opportunity of innocent amusement; and Sunday will, therefore, be a positive mischief if that leisure is unused and unsanctified.

"Then again, we all know that the master is almost invariably disliked, and, in this house, deservedly. We, ourselves, have rebuked him for his ill-temper ; how, then, can we set such a man, or any man, in his unpopular position, to read prayers to the inmates ? Those prayers, however excellent, become, by his reading them, ludicrous or hateful, and, in many cases, had much better be omitted. For these reasons, I intreat you to reject both these candidates, to raise the stipend, and to have a chaplain who will give up his whole time to his duties, and will have services to occupy Sunday as it should be occupied, and to sanctify and bless every morning and evening to our poor brethren in this house. I will pause before I go on to the other point, and will discuss what I have proposed with my brother guardians, if they will do me the favour of stating their opinion."

"I don't see any good in paying any more to the parsons," said Mr. Higgins, a Dissenting grocer in Belborough; "if they don't think things properly done here, why the Rev. Mr. Gordon would attend; or they may subscribe themselves, and make it up to their own chaplain."

"Mr. Gordon can, of course, attend here, Mr. Higgins, when any of his own persuasion desire it," replied the chairman; "but you know that the majority are not Dissenters. But I own, Mr. Lee, there are serious objections to increasing the stipend."

"I think it would be a waste of clergymen," objected one of the most respected of the neighbouring vicars, "to have a chaplain devoted to every union. In these days, clergy and funds are wanted all over the kingdom for places entirely destitute of churches, schools, and clergymen. I should oppose the resolution, on this ground, very strongly."

Mr. Lee rose to reply.

"I am very happy to find that the objections which have been made are so very moderate, and can be so easily met. It is true that a larger outlay is required; but then, gentlemen, remember you were about to expend £60 as it was. If, then, what I have said is true, you were about to give that large sum for almost nothing, and it would be a very poor economy to lay out so much, and then fail in the object for £20 or £40 more, which would hardly be felt in the rates. And I think, indeed I am sure, that if my brother guardians are convinced of the magnitude of evils which I have stated, they would not grudge such additional outlay to their poor brethren, nor shrink from the obloquy which they may incur from a few, and for a very short time.

"And as to the other objection of the waste of men, which the general adoption of my principle is supposed to involve, I cannot but think that it would disappear upon reflection. Our ancestors had domestic chaplains to their manorial halls, and to alms-houses of no great size; and even now noblemen have chaplains, and are not rebuked for it.

"Besides, consider that the wants of many rural populations are not greater than those of the inmates in this house, and that many parishes are not larger even in entire population. I say wants, because I should be glad to inquire, excepting the case of Belborough, Addington, and Mountfichet, which of my brethren here has more old people, more sick people, and larger schools, *that is to say more persons constantly requiring care*, than are now contained within these walls. And, in the winter, we know that the numbers are as large as those of many whole parishes; so that if my brethren are prepared to assert that it is a waste to have a chaplain solely for this house, they also assert that it is a waste for themselves to be where and what they are.

"And now I will pass on to my other point, though I fear I am detaining the board very long this morning. It strikes me, of course more painfully than it does my lay friends here, how sad

L

it is for the poor people of this house to hold their worship, and to celebrate the most solemn rites, in a room which is associated with other and very different actions. We know how much harder it would be for us to be attentive and to preserve a reverent state of mind in a common room than in a church. What is true of one man, is true of another. Our brethren here suffer the disadvantage from which we shrink ourselves. Besides, Sunday and worship should be a total change to them; should take them out of their misfortunes and their pauper routine; should remind them that they will not long be here; and that, hereafter, they may be where there is no poverty, nor suffering. This is what they require to feel, and what they ought to be assisted to feel. But an ordinary room, used on other days of the week for eating and drinking, can never assist them so to think and feel, but the very reverse. And, on this account, I put it before you that it is our duty to find a proper place of worship for our poor brethren in this house."

"Why, you would have us spend all our neighbours' money, Mr. Lee!" said the chairman; "and I don't know what they would say to us, even if it were legal;—but we could not do it."

"I do not ask you to build," replied Mr. Lee, "out of the rates. This should have been done at first; and, whether the fault rests upon the legislature, or the rate-payers, it certainly is a fault: but I ask, now, whether there is any objection to the *principle,* whether the board approves the plan, although unable to adopt it.

"I do not see that this is a practical question, Mr. Lee," said the chairman, "or one which I can put before the board."

"Indeed it is. I wish to ask whether the board would sanction the plan, were a chapel built by subscription, or other means."

"Certainly, certainly, Mr. Lee ; I should conceive there could be no possible objection ; but you would never get the money in these parts."

"Perhaps not : but may I consider this an understood thing, that the board would not object to a chapel, if one could be built ?"

The chairman looked round, and, after some little conversation, replied, "that as private individuals they had no objection, but that as a board they could not come to any resolution so untangible." Mr. Lee then rose.

"I will trespass on you once more, gentlemen, and then I shall have done. I was not putting idle resolutions for curiosity, or merely to establish a principle which could never be acted upon. I have a definite proposition to make, now that I know your opinions. I have long felt very deeply on these points, and knew how unable I was to do anything in this county, to which I am a comparative stranger : but, by God's providence, the means which I so long desired were placed in my hands, only a few weeks since. An old pupil who has a large property, has

given me a sum of money to lay out in good works,
to the best of my judgment. I shall not mention
his name, as he would not wish it; but I will now
state my proposal, which is this, that if the board
will be good enough to raise the stipend to £120,
and to give the appointment to the Bishop, on condition of the chaplain's holding no other cure
whatever, I will, out of the money placed in my
hands, build a house for his residence within the
walls, at the cost of £600, and a chapel at the cost
of £1000. May I consider that you will accept the
proposal?"

The board, and, indeed, the whole neighbourhood,
were astonished. The plans were produced, and at
an adjourned meeting the resolution was adopted,
with only two dissentient voices: and, as if to show
the power of good example, a retired tradesman of
Belborough came forward, and added the donation
of an acre and a half of ground for two flower
gardens for the use of the paupers; and thus
Belborough Union became what it now is—the
happiest and best asylum for the poor which all
England contains, and yet no happier, nor better
than every union in England might by degrees
become; and which, if such institutions are to exist
at all, they are bound to become.

CHAPTER XIII.

Daily Life.

" The trivial round, the common task,
    Would furnish all we ought to ask.
Room to deny ourselves a road,
    To bring us daily nearer God."
                        CHRISTIAN YEAR.

WILLIAM BLAKE was fully occupied with his own affairs, and with those of his men. He visited the cottages, gave the men hints as to their gardens, encouraged economy, and blamed extravagance and neglect. Every little assistance which it was in his power to supply to make the allotment ground successful, was afforded. In a word, he was occupied in doing good ; and, therefore, he was happier than he ever had been in his life, in spite of the loneliness of the Moat House, and calmer in spite of his approaching marriage.

Amongst other changes for the better which he introduced at this time, was the payment of his labourers on Friday, instead of on Saturday, by which means the Sunday shopping and the Saturday night drinking were considerably checked ; and where they were not, the sin did not rest upon him: he had done all that was possible.

Then, again, about holidays he did his best to keep his men at their work, during the neighbouring fairs, and, by mixed kindness and severity, succeeded to a great extent. On the other hand, he gave them holidays at safer times. For instance, upon his birthday, he gave them a holiday and their wages; and again upon Whit-Monday, provided they went to church, and provided that on both these occasions they came up to him in the evening. They did so, and at first expected nothing to please them, and regarded it as a great drawback to their day; but, when they found that William was prepared to amuse and to feed them, their feelings soon changed. The men played at bowls, although it must be confessed that it was early in the year for such amusements; the boys, at cricket and football; and there were races, and wrestling, and smutty faces, and jumping in sacks, and even more fun than at a fair, only without the mischief. The old Blakes were there, and Mr. Lee and his family. Good humour reigned throughout the evening, and when they all sat down, at the close of it, to a good plain supper, they were as happy as could be; and, with that beautiful trust and enjoyment of the present, which so generally belong to the poor, all anxieties and distresses were entirely forgotten. Songs and merriment succeeded; and at last all went home a goodly troop, chatting of their enjoy-

ment, and of their good young master, who was
daily becoming more popular, in spite of some
punishments and dismissals to which he felt it necessary to have recourse.

A few days after the Whit-Monday festivities,
William received a letter from his long absent
cousin. It ran as follows :—

DEAR WILLIAM,

    I am getting on famously here
on my own account, for I find that it is much better
than being only an agent. If I live five years I
shall go home a rich man. But, shall I ever see
you again at Staunton? Can I ever bear to go
there, or can you bear to see me? Even now, I can
scarcely think of that day, or of what I have done.

I meant to have written a full account of myself,
but I cannot after thinking of that—I would tear
this letter up, and begin another, but Captain Dixon,
of the Albatross, is leaving. He has offered to take
a letter free : but I will write again. Give my love
to my uncle and aunt. You see I have changed
countries again ; or rather plans, for I never got so
far as Chili : but I will tell you more, hereafter.

    Your affectionate cousin,

       EDWARD JONES.

Monte Video.

William was still thinking of his cousin's letter,
and of all the sad hours which it recalled, as he

broke open his next letter without looking at the direction : indeed, he had read half through it before a word of the meaning flashed across him, and was at length surprised by the following passage :—

"it is under their wher i left it, jist afore we went to the punt."

William now turned to the direction and found it to be,

Willium Blood,

Mote Hous,

Starnton.

Hence the mistake. William Blood had been turned away some time, and had left the neighbourhood. William now felt quite justified in reading the whole letter, which was this :—

My dere frend,

i ave ad sum werry quere brushes since I seed you, and am quite hincognitoe has thay say now, and werry ard hup, soe i wish youd luke out for mee for a hold jackut which I ad, you knows where, it lies under the rode jist goin into the orchad, in a sort of a loane place on the rite and, and as a pus and one or two thins which mite be usefull, hand I will pay you andsum for yere truble. it is under their wher i left it, jist afore we went to the punt, and youl esy find sum way o' sendin it hup to Tip Bully's, 15 Zin halley Cabage lane 7 diels.

Your hold frend

TOMAS.

William put on his hat and went to the spot, and stooping down he soon pulled out the jacket in question, and found in it the veritable "pus," containing £3. 12s. 6d., a knife, and some chisels, with part of a centre bit, and an old handkerchief. There was nothing, however, by which to identify the owner, and he guessed that Tip Bully was too sharp a fellow to make anything out of, so he locked up his discoveries and said nothing.

Not long after this, a pedlar called at the door, and asked the maid whether she knew a man named William Blood. She said she did, but that he had left. It was not until two days later that William heard of the circumstance. He went down, however, towards the spot, and found the print of fresh steps in the long grass, which could not have been made more than an hour or two. He called out his men, and let the dogs loose. They beat up and down everywhere, but could find nothing. William concluded, rightly, that the man had been and found out his loss, and believed, therefore, that he would probably never return. At the same time, he thought it just worth while to walk quietly about in the evening; and well it was that he did so, for, just before he was about to go in, he heard a sort of hissing sound in the stack-yard, like a squirt, and, on running there, he was guided by the smell to a stack in which he saw a long sort of fusee stuck in and exploded without firing the hay. As he was examining the spot, a shadow moved slowly along the barn-side and turned the corner; William rushed after it, and found nothing; but the next minute after, as he was searching, he received a heavy blow over the head, and was stretched senseless upon the ground. He lay in this state about half-an-hour, and was only aroused by people tumbling over him. He got up confused, and found that all his men were rushing hither and thither to throw water and dung upon some thatch, which had been taken off an old stack, and which lay close under a rick containing about fifty quarters of wheat. They succeeded by great exertions, and the wheat was saved; but the fellow had got clear off, after firing the thatch and disabling his pursuer.

Fifty guineas reward were offered for his apprehension; but in vain. Many persons had seen just such a man, and a few had really seen the man himself; but this was not having him: and so the barn-ends and guide-posts were covered with handbills, which served to amuse the traveller, and pay the poster, and no other purpose whatsoever.

On the Sunday following, William returned thanks in church for the great mercy he had received in respect to his life and property; and very grateful he felt not only for those mercies, but that he had the opportunity of expressing the feelings of a full heart, and of giving open glory to Him who had been so gracious to him. Indeed, so struck was he by the double deliverance, which he and his had

received from the same villain, that he wrote up
in the old style, over his door, the words of the
Psalmist :

"Thou, O Lord, makest us to dwell in safety."

And often and often he said to himself, "Unless
the Lord keep the city, the watchman waketh but
in vain. It is but lost labour that ye haste to rise
up early, and so late take rest, and eat the bread of
carefulness, for so he giveth his beloved sleep."
And again, "The Lord is on my side; I will not
fear what man doeth unto me."

Every day William's course was becoming easier
to him, more habitual, more sure; and yet he was
not the less humble and distrustful of self, but
very much more so; for the more he knew of God,
the weaker and more unworthy he felt himself;
the more desirous he was of progress, the more he
deplored slight faults and hinderances to his cause.
Besides, his self-examination had become very regular and very real : and whenever this is the case, it
is very strange if a man is not humble. He no
longer questioned himself vaguely and irregularly.
Since the backsliding, which had pained Mr. Lee
and him so deeply, he was on the watch, and examined himself periodically, by a full questioning
and searching out of the inner man, and nightly by
the resolutions made at the last Communion. And
in addition to this, he exercised that continual self-
examination, which is habitual to every earnest

Christian. He continually asked himself why he had said and done his last words and acts; and all day long prayed God's pardon and assistance from time to time : and thus, with diligent use of the means of grace, he added one virtue to another, according to the teaching of the Apostle, and increased, by a humble imitation of Christ, in wisdom and spiritual stature, and in favour with God and man.

CHAPTER XIV

The Marriage.

" The bridegroom kneels beside
His bashful loving bride;
Earth in that hour seems showering all her best.
But more than Earth e'er knew
He wins, if hearts be true:—
An Angel friend, to share his everlasting rest."

LYRA INNOCENTIUM.

At length, the day before *the* day arrived, and it
may be well imagined that neither William nor Ellen
was in a very settled state of mind, however steady
they were in general. Mr. Lee thought that this
would be the case, and, therefore, walked up to the
Moat House, in order to have some conversation
with William. He found him, drolly enough, trying
on various portions of his wedding attire, and looking at himself, most intently, in an old glass which
was left in the drawing-room. At last, he became
conscious of two faces in the mirror, and upon that
which was not his own a long smile of intense amusement. He turned round, and saw the good-natured
Rector standing at the door. He was quite astounded,
so Mr. Lee broke the silence, by saying, with a
laugh—

"Well, I hope it is quite satisfactory, William; your general appearance, your dress, and all combined."

"Really, Sir, I'm quite ashamed of myself, but—"

"Oh, you need not apologise. I can quite understand. It is just an occasion in a man's life when he does look in the glass. I remember being in the room with a friend who tried one neck-cloth after another, till I thought I should never get away; he could not get a bow that day, though he wanted to be a beau."

"Well, I really do feel ashamed of myself, for all that, Sir."

"I am sure it is needless; you are not, generally, vain, or particular about your dress, so it does not matter for once. Luckily, people are not married every day, or I do not know what would become of us. But I see you are rather confused and unsettled, and I want you to take a turn with me in the fields, in order to compose yourself."

They then strolled up the hill fields, and sat down under an oak, the shade of which was very acceptable under a June sun. Everything was fresh, and promising, and beautiful; the crops high up; the trees thick, but still bright; the air full of happy insects; the blackbird singing in the hedge, and the nightingale in the bush; all was bright and promising. Pain, and decay, and destruction, presented no memorials of their existence.

For some minutes they sat quietly, and felt what they saw; but soon Mr. Lee began upon the two subjects of their thoughts—the scene before them, and the morrow.

"All that we see, William, and feel here, is in harmony with your present feelings, and immediate prospects. Everything is bright and hopeful. It is all enjoyment, and abundance. Very good of our merciful God is it, that we have these happy, refreshing times to restore our hearts, and to speak to us of more entire and abiding happiness, of the Tree of Life, ever loaded, and the perpetual summer. And this is your summer, William. Health, strength, competence, a peaceful calling, a heart at peace, happiness here, and hope hereafter, and now the society and most inward real and holy union with her whom you love best upon earth,—these are your summer. I know what you feel, for I remember what I felt ten years ago. It is still fresh in my heart. That was my summer; but I have had a winter, and so will you. Some affliction will come upon you, as upon all, to make you feel how fleeting is all earthly good. You may lose property, or health, or a child, or——your Ellen, for you must be set free from earthly affections, that is to say, you must have so many cut away, that those which are in mercy left, do not bind you, and are altogether under your dominion and government. Thus, Ezekiel lost 'the desire of his eyes;' and Jeremiah saw

his people carried away into bondage; and the
Blessed Virgin Mary felt a sword pass through her
heart, as she stood beneath the Cross. You remember the history of Shadrach and his companions.
They were thrown into the fire, bound; and, trust-
ing in God, the fire loosed their earthly bonds, and
touched no more, leaving them free. So, the fire of
sorrow sets us free bond by bond. This is your
summer, William; keep your eye on the Sun of
Righteousness who gives it to you, or you will have
a dreary winter.

" And now you are at peace in your soul. Your
old temptations are weaker; your intentions you
know are sincere; you are living quietly under
your vine, under the Vine of all of us; day by
day receiving nourishment, by our engrafting; and
enabled to bring forth fruit with the wine of glad-
ness, without persecution, with a full enjoyment of
highest privileges. But it is very unlikely that this
summer will continue through life. I do not say
that persecution will come in your time, or mine;
but, somehow or other, you will yet have great spiritual trials, either from within or without. You will
feel your faith fail under the presence of worldly
anxiety or grief, or your heart grow cold, it may be,
from their absence. Your dark and cold hours will
come, your winter of soul, or rather wintry days.
Keep your eye, then, and your heart, beneath the
Sun of Righteousness, and your warmth and light,
your summer, shall return to you.

"But I wished to give you some more particular advice on one or two points connected with your marriage.

"You find this time, as you said, an unsettling time. It is natural that it should be so, and very mercifully, therefore, the Church has ordered, and wisely and dutifully you have resolved, that your marriage shall be sanctified and confirmed by the Holy Communion. Nothing will so much allay troubled feelings, banish idle thoughts, strengthen and confirm your vows and resolutions, as that inestimable blessing. But you will require an after strength, as you have an after temptation. I do not mean that the grace of the Sacrament will not be to you that after strength; assuredly it will, but only by subsequent diligent use of it. You should lengthen your devotions, and, as far as you can, avail yourselves of the offices of the Church.

"And to return to the subject of sorrows to come. Your hearts will be full of hope, and of worldly hope. It is true that the words, 'in sickness and in health,' 'till death do us part,' are sobering words, but not so chastening as the remembrance of the death of Christ, the showing forth of His Body and of His Blood, the receiving them, the feeding upon them. This is, indeed, the word of sorrow, the sign of the Cross, but such a word and such a sign as will be the most lively joy to you in the wintry days, because that death will then especially be manifested to you as your life, and that Cross as your crown.

Perhaps you will scarcely believe it, William, but, fond as you are of Ellen, and she of you, yet you will be tempted to anger and mutual offences against love, and will *yield* to that temptation if you rest upon your affection for your only security. Believe me, there are times when it will not suffice to remember that she is your wife, unless you also remember that she is your wife in Christ, His gift. This reflection will be your strength, and will save you from idolatry and from wrath. But if ever you should feel hurt or aggrieved, do not cherish or conceal the feeling. Confess it at once, or, if this be impossible, acknowledge it at night, before your devotions. Humble yourself by the acknowledgment, and confirm your mutual confidence and love, by the affection and unity of heart, which such conduct will produce. Confess to each other, and then pray together in the same words, lifting up holy united hands. And this you should do each morning and night, for you will no longer be two single, separate beings only. True, as respects yourselves, you will stand alone before God, as you were born, and as you will die; but, as respects each other, you will be one, and have common duties, common hopes and fears; for every hope, and fear, and pain, and joy, should be common, and nothing concealed, and on account of these, you must pray *together*, for pardon and grace in your married estate.

All the resolutions which, I doubt not, you have made together—resolutions to live simply, to give largely, to set yourselves against expense and show, and rather to increase your alms than your luxuries, should riches increase, all these and whatever other resolutions God has put it into your hearts to make— let them be the subject of examination on each returning anniversary of your wedding day: always go over them together, and also read the service together. I have here a copy of the 'Christian Year,' which Mrs. Lee has sent for Ellen, and you and she will do well to read the marriage hymn together; and I would advise you to add to your devotions the Collect for the Sixth Sunday after the Epiphany. And now I must go home, and you, I should think, have enough to do. May God bless you both!"

They parted in silence, the Rector to his study, and William to his room, where he was long engaged in earnest prayer.

There could not have been brighter weather than that of the 18th of June, a grand day for the marriage; and many were the jokes upon Waterloo and the wedding, although it is difficult to find two more dissimilar events. But all this did not affect the happy couple. They were too much occupied with their own thoughts to care for the sallies of their friends, especially for such blunt darts as those which were generally launched at them.

Now, if William's and Ellen's had been a common marriage it would have been passed over in silence, and the reader would have been requested to attend the next wedding in his neighbourhood instead of having a conclusion to this chapter. But theirs was not a common wedding, for, generally speaking, the bride cries, and the bridegroom looks constrainedly sober, or sheepish; but here the bride did not cry, and the bridegroom looked calm and thoughtful. Again, in most cases, the families of the happy couple half ruin themselves in gaiety; but here all was sober and quiet. Generally, the service is thought long as it is; but in this case it was lengthened unusually without being thought tedious. Usually, persons in their circumstances of life are married by license, but they were by banns. Generally, the bride is married in her own parish, but here an exception was made in favour of some particular fancies, and Great Staunton Church was the place where they met; and therefore it becomes a sort of duty to describe the ceremony, and the chief persons concerned.

The party, then, met at Mr. Blake's cottage, which was close to the church, and proceeded thence in a body, the bride's friends entering at one door, and the bridegroom's at the other, and so they advanced, according to the rule of the service, into the *body* of the church, where Mr. Lee stood ready to receive them with book in hand. There was some little awkwardness in arranging positions, as is usual, but this was soon set right, and the service commenced. When the time came for the man to answer, William Blake spoke out boldly, 'I will,' so that he was audible through all the church; nor were Ellen's words less distinct, although her voice was lower. But when William came to his second answer, and repeated clearly, 'I, William, take thee, Ellen, to my wedded wife, to have and to hold from this day forward, for better for worse, for richer for poorer, in sickness and in health,' suddenly Mr. Lee's words flashed across him, 'You may lose property, or health, or a child, or——Ellen,' and he paused, and finished in a low and stifled voice,— 'till death do us part, according to God's holy ordinance, and thereto I plight thee my troth.' This was enough to upset poor Ellen utterly. Mr. Lee saw that it was doing so, and, catching her eye, looked with the kindest expression, *upwards.* His meaning flashed through her still more quickly than he was able to express it, and she was calm.

After the Blessing, the Rector led the procession from the nave of the church to the altar, chanting the psalm, as he went, with some of his choir, and the service proceeded as usual; but, when it was concluded, Mr. Lee remained at the Communion table, and many of the party knelt down there, whilst others retired. The Communion Service then commenced, and William and Ellen never entered into it more fully than then. It spoke to them of that higher union between the Church and every member of it with the Head of the Church, of which their marriage was the copy and symbol. It reminded them of the supper of Canaan, and that Christ could still turn the water into wine all their lives long. And never had they realised so fully the presence of their Saviour, invisibly doing everything which is done in His name, through the visible hand of man, as when they remembered the words which Mr. Lee had pointed out—

> " 'Tis He who clasps the marriage band,
> And fits the spousal ring,
> Then leaves ye kneeling, hand in hand,
> Out of his stores to bring
> His Father's dearest blessing."

When the service was completed, and the signatures finished, the communicants retired, peaceful and happy, to the cottage : and there they all mounted their various conveyances and left, amid the congratulations of the village, for Mr. Hilton's ; where one feast succeeded another for the rest of the day, and even Mr. Blake forgot the trial of his blindness which he had felt so strongly that morning, and, amidst the praises which were bestowed upon his absent son, and the congratulations offered to his wife and himself, was perfectly happy.

The newly-married couple, meantime, had left for a fortnight's trip, in which, by Mr. Lee's advice, they saw Winchester, Stone Henge, Salisbury, the New Forest, and the Isle of Wight—a nice little journey, full of sweet recollections and cherished feelings for many a year.

But we must not forget a great portion of the festivities, those, namely, which took place at Great Staunton, where, on the following day, in order that

the Blakes might be present, there were dining,
and supping, and dancing, and all manner of games,
in which the poor who were connected with the
family by past or existing relations were rendered
as happy as might be, and drank long life and prosperity to William and Ellen Blake; the latter of
whom received the following compliment amongst
many others:

"I'm blessed, wife, if our young missus didn't
look just like our Bess for all the world," said an
aged labourer to his partner.

"Your Bess, man!" replied old Blake, who over-
heard the remark, "why she's as fat as a Leicester-
shire sheep."

"I knows that. Missus ain't half so fine a gal
yet; but may be she'll pick up after a bit."

"It will be a good bit first, I hope, Jem."

"Well, Sir, I hope so too; but may be she'll pick
up a good bit, as you say, Sir. Why, our Bess
warn't half as big one time, so there's no 'countin'.
But she's a nice young thing, if I may be so bold,
any how; and I wish our young master health and
happiness." But here the handing round the ale
cut short Jem's eloquence, and poor Ellen's praises.

CHAPTER XV.

The First Trouble.

" Deny me wealth; far, far remove
    The love of power or name;
  Hope thrives in straits, in weakness Love,
    And Faith in this world's shame."

LYRA APOSTOLICA.

WHEN the little tour was over, the happy couple received the congratulations of friends and neighbours, and had quite as much or more visiting than they liked; but this, like everything of the sort, passed away, and William and his wife settled down quietly to their duties.

It would be difficult to invent more perfectly happy circumstances than theirs, with the exception of Mr. Blake's blindness, and the death of John; and to these they had become resigned. Perfect unison, at least as perfect as earthly love may be, competence, a happy, healthy calling, the cottage, and the Rectory, all combined to make them the happiest of the happy. This was their summer, which Mr. Lee had described; and they did not neglect to improve it. Kind to the poor, industrious, regular at the Daily Service, and at the Holy Communion; improving their time and minds by a regular course of reading prescribed by their friend the Rector; they were as much the admiration as the envy of others.

There was, indeed, an under current of uneasiness, but only such as earnest persons are sure to find. They felt grieved at the poverty of their gratitude, at the tardiness of their spiritual progress, and at many lesser slips and failings. William had still to combat with the relics of old habits: for years of self-indulgence and neglect of the soul are not lightly nor quickly erased, and continually a shoot from the old root of bitterness would spring up, although, by God's help, it was promptly nipped before it strengthened. Yet such trials he had; and it were unwise and unkind to conceal it. We must be prepared to strive with sin and with self all our lives, and the more painfully, the longer we have served them, although our strife, if continued aright, is daily more and more successful, and will result in rest and victory.

This, then, was their summer; and winter seemed to fall suddenly upon them, and without an autumn of warning.

It was on the 28th of August that William opened a letter written in a hand which he had never seen. It was from Sir Lionel Celer, his landlord, a man whom he had never seen, but of whom he had heard, as an extravagant and wild fellow, who spent all his time in Paris or Italy. He was now, however, in England, and wrote as follows :—

Mr. Blake,

I intend to be upon my ——shire estates for the first week or two in September. I shall have two or three friends with me, and shall make the Moat House my head quarters. You and your family will remain in the house, and prepare for us on the 30th.

Yours, &c.

L. Celer.

Mivart's, Aug. 27.

The fuss which this communication occasioned may be more easily imagined than described, especially by any good housewife, who makes much of her guests, if such there be amongst the readers of this tale. Now the Blakes were not so foolish as some people are. They did not turn everything upside down, and rack their brains day and night, and buy things which they could not afford, nor make the most of appearance by little cheats and deceptions ; but still, to turn themselves out into the attics, and to prepare all the rooms, and find bedding enough, caused abundance of trouble, and they were well sick of the job before their landlord arrived.

At last the day came, and first a curricle drove up containing Sir Lionel and his two guests, and then a drag with two men and luggage and dogs, wine-hampers, shot, guns, &c. &c.

Sir Lionel threw the reins to his groom and alighted. He was a good-natured looking man, but coarse; and gave one the impression of a hard drinker. He shook hands with William and his wife, looked round the room, declared that every-thing was very comfortable, and then introduced his companions, the Honourable Augustus Dyce and Colonel Marlborough Leech.

The first of these men was smooth and elegant, but had a most forbidding expression of counte-nance; the second blustering, and forwardly friendly, with a sort of over-done good humour and heartiness, which gave the idea that it was neither natural nor sincere.

On that day the three strangers and the Blakes dined together upon William's fare, to which the landlord added champagne. The conversation was upon the game and state of the land, and, with the exception of some oaths, which appeared acci-dental, not offensive. After dinner, however, when Mrs. Blake had retired, the face of things changed, and, with much that William could not understand, there was so much of a disgusting and shocking character, that he was glad to retire to give his farm-ing orders. He was now sadly perplexed what to do, and especially as the next day was Sunday. All he could determine was to keep his own servant-maid from waiting in the parlour as much as possible, and to restrict his own attendance upon his guests to the utmost. The two servants also made him equally uncomfortable. They not only gave themselves the greatest airs, but conducted themselves in a very improper manner. One was a foreigner; and the other a regular London groom, who cheated his master at every turn. This soon came out in the kitchen, and reached William's ears, through Mrs. Blake, who was duly informed of everything by her maid.

On the Sunday not one of the guests went to church. William, therefore, left them, whilst they smoked in the garden, examined their guns, and talked over the sport of the next day. His father and mother came up in the evening to pay their respects: for Mr. Blake was still tenant. They found their landlord at dinner, and therefore returned, leaving William to apologise for them. Sunday evening went off without difficulty, for it was so fine that the visitors strolled out and then went to bed early, in order to be in good cue for the morrow. The 'first' was a burning day, and knocked them all up, although they had excellent sport. In the evening they drank long and hard; and Sir Lionel was evidently the worse for it. William was asked in; but he was in the orchard, and was not found for some time. When he went in, the party were engaged at cards, and the groom had been

called in for the fourth. William was immediately
requested to take his place; but he declined, and
said, that he knew so little that he should only spoil
the game, and thus escaped. He stood by, therefore,
and as he looked on, soon saw, although they were
then playing a very harmless game, that Dyce and
Leech were both hangers on—not real friends, and
were probably living on Sir Lionel. But he could
not stay long in the room, for the tone of the conversation was such that he knew he ought not to
sanction it by his presence ; and he therefore withdrew.

Next morning it rained heavily, and ill-humour
prevailed in the house. William went out to give
some directions, and was away for some hours. On
his return, Ellen took him into the attic, which they
were forced to occupy, and told him of conduct, on
the part of Dyce and the two servants, which filled
him with perplexity and pain. He saw that it
would never do to allow the present state of things
to continue ; and yet he knew not how to act.

They knelt down together to ask for guidance,
and rose relieved and calmer.

"This is our first trouble, Ellen," William said
softly, as he took her hand, and looked at her with
affection.

"Yes, and it only unites us more, William."

"True, dearest, but it does more than this."

"I know what you mean."

"I think of Mr. Lee's warning now, Ellen."

" How true it was !"

"Yes, and how little we knew *how* our trouble would come; but he was right, indeed, that it would come."

" Yes, he is always right. Why don't we consult him now ?"

" Strange, I never thought of it; and yet he has always been my adviser and best friend. I have been sadly bewildered ever since Saturday. There is no time, however, to be lost. I will go down at once."

He took his hat and coat, and walked down to the village. He had not, however, walked five minutes, before he came upon Mr. Lee, who was going up to the Moat House.

" I was just coming to your house," he said.

"And I to yours, Sir."

"To me! No bad news, I hope. You look uncomfortable."

" I am, indeed, Sir."

" Well, come in here," replied the Rector, pointing to a cart-shed, which offered some shelter from the driving rain. They went in, and sat down together upon a roller. The air was cold, and a chilling wind rushed through the shed, and drove the splashes of the rain into their faces. Pools of scummy water stood at the entrance, with straws and feathers floating across them; and outside, large-dropped, driving rain swept all the country from their view. It was desolate enough, and the scene had a meaning for William, which he could not but read.

"My winter is come, Sir."

"What do you mean?"

"I think I must do something, which may lose my father and me this farm; and I was coming to ask you to advise me and help me."

"That will I do, William, to the uttermost. But explain to me."

It did not take long to unfold the state of things which William had to describe. Mr. Lee sat in silence for some minutes, without speaking. After he had heard everything, he said—

"I would go up myself, William, and remonstrate, were I not sure to bring down upon you the obloquy of having told me all this. You have, indeed, a difficult course to *act*, but, I think, not so difficult to *choose*. I would simply remove out of the house. It is your landlord's house, you know, and he may do what he likes in it and with it; but, whilst you are there, you are responsible to the poor, and, indeed, to all your neighbours, for allowing such things to go on. You must have nothing to do with it. You must remove, you and yours, away from it, and then the responsibility rests on others. This is your course: the difficulty is, so to follow it as not to give unnecessary offence. It would, perhaps, be best for you, first to make your arrangements, and then to see Sir Lionel, and say, that you think it better to give up the whole house to him during his stay, and that you are going down to your father's for the time. You need not give any reason; and, if he asks one, you can say that you have thought it over, and have found it much the best plan. But you must first see your father, for he ought to have the offer of changing places with you, as you risk his interest as well as your own."

They went down together, and soon found that Mr. Blake was as desirous as William that Mr. Lee's advice should be adopted: so much good had been done, through misfortune, through his son, and through Mr. Lee's teaching.

William went quietly home, and made his arrangements. He sent out his two maid-servants, replacing them with some old women from the village, and went in with Ellen, who was dressed in bonnet and cloak, to announce his resolution, and to take his leave. His heart was full, when he thought of the risk which he was running; but he entered calmly, and said—.

"We are come, Sir, to bid you good evening. We are going down to stay at my father's for a few days. I shall be at your service, and will wait upon you whenever you wish, and everything in the house will be managed as well as we could do it."

"Oh, that will never do," answered Sir Lionel. What! you are going to take Mrs. Blake away too. I can't allow that; why, we should be as dull—as dull as your knives here."

"We are none of us very sharp down here, Sir," said William, glad to turn the conversation; "but I will see about these knives directly."

"Oh, hang the knives! I don't care a pin about them. But I can't let you go—I can't, indeed. You can pay your father a visit just as well when I am gone."

"I am afraid I cannot oblige you in this instance, as I really am obliged to go down."

"Obliged! pooh! pooh! What obliges you? He need not go, now need he, Mrs. Blake?"

"Yes, Sir," answered Ellen, "I think he must, and I hope you will excuse us."

"Well, well, if you must, you must, so good evening to you. I am the last person to cross a lady's wishes," said Sir Lionel, bowing to Ellen.

So they left the room, twice as happy as they entered it, and went down to the cottage; but they had not been gone half-an-hour, before the face of affairs was entirely changed. Colonel Leech came in, fuming and swearing, to his patron, and said—

"I say, Celer, this sneaking, hypocritical fellow of yours has played us a pretty trick!"

"Well, what's the matter, Colonel?"

"What's the matter, indeed! why, he has taken away his servants, and left us some old hags here; and Robert says he knows all about it. Blake has left the house because we are too fast for him, and he does not approve of your goings on."

"I'd soon settle his business," interposed Dyce;

N

"it is close to Michaelmas, and you know his lease is out then."

"Why, what a bit of luck!" exclaimed the Colonel. "It would have been renewed but for me, and I begged you to put it off till you came down, and saw whether it would bear screwing up a peg. I declare that is lucky. I'm your best friend after all, Celer. I got you through that Paris business, and then there was Naples too. There's nothing like a friend."

"There's nothing like praising oneself, Leech," replied the landlord, "especially when no one else will do it for you; but I think you are right for once, and I will send down for Blake directly." He rang the bell, and Robert was despatched.

Less than an hour brought William into the presence of the trio.

"They tell me, Mr. Blake," began Sir Lionel, "that you have moved your servants as well as yourself. May I ask you your reason for this?"

"I'm afraid I cannot state the reason, Sir, but I assure you it was a very good one, and I will take care that you shall not suffer the slightest inconvenience from the change."

"I am the best judge of that. It looks very strange, Sir. It is natural for me to think, and I am sure your neighbours will believe, that you are leaving because you do not like to be in the same house with me."

William was silent.

" Was that your reason or not?" exclaimed Dyce. "Speak out at once."

" That is not a fair question, Dyce," interposed Sir Lionel, "and I do not think mine was either, for it is contrary to our English principle to make a man criminate himself. What I will say, is this, Mr. Blake. You can either explain your leaving, or come back, which you like best."

" I am very sorry, Sir, I really cannot do either."

" Then you cease to be my tenant at Michaelmas."

" We have had this farm for three generations, Sir, and never failed in rent, and you will find the premises in excellent order."

" I know that, I know that; but I can't help it, Mr. Blake, if you persist in such conduct. At least, I do not see——"

"No 'at leasts,' Celer," said Leech, " you must be firmer. It will never do to tolerate such insolence. I would kick the scoundrel out of the room. Will you go or stay, Sir?"

" Do you hear what I say, Sir?" repeated Leech, when he saw that William paid no attention to what he said.

" My business is with Sir Lionel Celer, Sir, not with you. You have no right to speak as you did, and I take no notice of what you say."

" Hear him, hear him, Celer! Come, settle this matter as soon as you can, and let us have a game," said the Colonel, rubbing the cards back till they whirred in his hand.

"Blake is right, Leech. You have no right to speak to him, and I have a great mind——"

Dyce went up, and whispered earnestly into his ear for a few minutes, and Sir Lionel then turned to Blake, and told him to leave the farm at Michaelmas. William bowed, and retired.

It was no fear which made him take so gloomy a view of what the reader may think a very trivial matter. He felt almost sure, from the first, that the business would end as it did.

When William arrived at his father's house, he found Mr. Lee there, and when he had told his sad tale, he sat down exhausted and dispirited.

"We must remember our principles," said his kind friend, "when the time for proving them is come. Your principles are those of trust and submission, and this trial is not testing your principles, but you; is proving how far they have entered into you, and become part of yourself. You must now bring into use the stores which you have laid up in happier days, I was going to say better, but 'Blessed are they that mourn,' and 'Count it all joy when ye fall into temptation:' for, if this anxiety and loss wean you from earth, and, by making you wholly dependent upon God's extraordinary providence, render your soul more dependent upon Him, then you will ever after find it a blessing; and you will understand what that meaneth, 'the trial of your faith being much more precious than of gold.'"

"Yes, cheer up, William," said Mr. Blake, "you

must not be cast down. I know you feel for your mother and me, as if you had done it all; but I should have acted just the same, or I ought to have done. We must come and see you wherever you settle, and by God's blessing you will make up in time the loss of changing farms."

"We can do on £50 instead of the £100," added Mrs. Blake; "we do not spend all we have now."

"And I," said Ellen, "can take some pupils if we are short, for I know music, and Mr. Lee has made me read more than I ever did before."

"This is that which I spoke of," said Mr. Lee, with tears in his eyes; "your affliction is calling forth self-denial and generosity, and love more precious than gold. Only *keep* to them. Now you are excited; by-and-by the loss will appear heavier, your feelings will be more dull and worn, and oppressed; pray together, and read such parts of Scripture, and of your devotional books, as you know will help you. God forbid that I should cease to pray for you!"

The news soon spread, and the dissatisfaction it occasioned was great and ill-concealed. "What do we owe Sir Lionel?" said one; "he never gives anything away, and he is turning out the only people that do, except the parson." "I wish Master Blake was the owner of the Moat House," cried another; "we should have very different doings then, I warrant." Some of these observations reached the ears of the landlord, and he could see by the altered looks of the labourers on the farm that they hated him for what he had done. He was too proud to unsay his word, and his companions also urged him to be firm; but still he was so uncomfortable that he shortened his visit, and left Great Staunton before the week was over, after a long and fruitless conversation with the Rector.

CHAPTER XVI.

A Sunday well spent,

" Haply down some opening glade
Now the old grey tower we see,
Underneath whose solemn shade
Jesus risen hath sworn to be."

LYRA INNOCENTIUM.

AFTER some deliberation, William resolved to spend the little time that was left in the old house, and they returned to it for Sunday. But they had scarcely sat down to tea, when a gig drove up, and a young man of a foreign look jumped out, and, after paying his driver, walked with his carpet-bag into the old hall where they were sitting. It was Edward Jones, who had come back an invalid, but the possessor of £5000. His tale was soon told, and William's in exchange; and then it appeared, that the home-man was strong, and blessed with a good wife whom he dearly loved, but in altered worldly circumstances; whilst the wanderer had returned with broken health, and a full purse—a solitary. No sensible person would have hesitated in choosing William's lot, in preference to his cousin's, bad as some of his prospects then were.

Next day, Edward was surprised to see the change in William and the Moat House. At half-past seven they met at prayers; at eight they breakfasted. From half-past nine until church-time William and Ellen taught in the new schools, under Mr. Lee. At a quarter to eleven the school marched out by two and two towards the church; behind it the choir boys, eight in number, chanting Psalm lxxxiv.; after them the teachers, who joined in the chant; and last of all the Rector, in his cassock and cap and gown.

The church, too, was a changed building, and so were the services. All was very plain and simple still, but strictly correct and in harmony with sacred objects. The font stood at the entrance. The altar caught the eye in passing up the nave. The singing and chanting were very fair; and, what is more, quite natural, simple, and heartfelt. The majority of the congregation knelt and rose at the proper times. The responses were deep and musical, following the tone of the choir. The earnest sermon was listened to with great attention. The offertory was responded to cheerfully, and as much as £2 collected from that small flock; and when the service was over the people left the church very slowly, and quietly dispersed.

Edward was much struck. Two or three years ago he would have objected to much which he witnessed as formalism, and as connected with Popery;

but his travels had shown him what Popery really is, and he saw that the heart went with the act throughout the service. After service he expressed his astonishment to his cousin, who explained to him the slow and gradual progress which had been made, and the sacrifices and labours of his friend the Rector.

Between the morning and evening services the Moat House party stayed, as usual, at the cottage, and when the pain of the first meeting was over, bringing as it did with it the memory of their affliction, cheerfulness and Christian happiness prevailed, and it would not have been thought that the family were in the midst of difficulty and disappointment.

After Evensong the old Blakes accompanied William up to the Moat House, and there passed a delightful and well-spent evening in singing psalms and chants to Ellen's playing, in reading Hammond's Life, and in conversation. Towards the close of the evening Edward was sent for, and did not return until supper was over. This excited much curiosity, but all inquiries were fruitless. He was impenetrable, and the questioners were completely foiled. Before they retired, however, he told them that he must leave them next morning on business, but that he hoped to return in a few days. They expressed their surprise and regret, as he had promised them a week upon his first arrival. But it was useless to argue, so William promised to drive him to Belborough to the coach, at five o'clock on Monday morning.

The two cousins went accordingly to Belborough, and there found Mr. Lee was also bound for London. William congratulated Edward on his companion, and, bidding them both farewell, he got through some little business, and turned his horse's head homewards.

And now the trial grew sorer and sorer. Each day that passed was a day less at the Moat House; a day less where William's youth had been spent; a day less where John had played, and walked, and lived; a day less where his married life had commenced, where he had planned and prepared for, and received his Ellen. Neither could he hear of any farm except a small one of a hundred-and-twenty acres, which also belonged to Sir Lionel, and was therefore unattainable. There were times, therefore, as may be well believed, in which William's heart sank within him; and whenever this was the case, Ellen rose beyond herself, and cheered him with all the love which a wife can show, by word, and look, and deed. But their chief comfort, their real comfort, was the love of God; the love of God to them which insured all that they really needed, and their love of Him which made them bow to His chastisements, and thank Him, and rely upon Him in the midst of them: and thus in good measure they realised the prophecy, "Thou wilt keep him in perfect peace whose mind is stayed on Thee."

One day William went to the end of the marsh which was attached to his farm, to visit a lad who had worked under his father as bird-boy and plough-boy, and who was now dying of consumption. He lived in the same cottage as the sheep-stealer who had been transported. It was now made weather-tight, and was neat and comfortable within and without, although not proof against the marsh air, which had laid poor Jacob Holmes upon his bed.

"Well, Jacob, my lad," William said, as he entered and sat down by his bed-side, "how are you this evening? I have brought you down some broth, and another book which Mr. Lee recommends, and you will find it very interesting."

"Thank you, Sir," returned the poor lad, lifting himself up, "I am greatly obliged, but I don't feel a-better at all, not at all."

"I am sorry to hear that. I hoped this turn in the weather would have made you more comfortable. It is not so hot as it was."

"It don't matter much, Sir, what the weather is now, I'm a-thinking."

"Indeed! Does Dr. Mayning say so? Well, Jacob, you will find health and rest in heaven, then. You will be free from many troubles when you are there."

"Yes, and from my sins too, Sir, for I feel that I am often very cross like, and not patient as I should be."

"True, Jacob, we shall rest from everything there, and that will be our greatest blessing, as Mr. Lee has often said, to rest from *ourselves*, our restlessness, and our sinfulness. I have thought more of this lately myself, Jacob, for I have been, and am still, in trouble."

"I have heard on't, Sir, and we and all your folk is as sorry as may be; I don't know what they'll do without you, Sir."

"Oh very well, very well. I have not done much good, but I'm sorry to leave them."

"Not done much good, Sir!" said the poor boy, sitting up in bed. "I'll like to tell you before I die what good you've done *me*, just for one. I couldna' read a line of my Bible, Sir, till you taught me last winter, and I never used to go to church till you made me change cow-keeping wi' Jack Hodges. I never said my prayers, that I didn't, and I never thought hardly o' God, or heaven, or hell, till you made me go to the Sunday class, and to church. I should just ha' died like a dog, Sir, hadna' been for you."

William's eyes filled with tears. He took the lad's hand, and said earnestly, "Jacob, if I have done you any good, you must thank Mr. Lee, who taught me, and God, who put it into his heart, and into my heart. Pray for me; and I trust we shall meet again, where your pain will be past, and my cares and infirmities also. Good bye."

"God bless you, Sir. I'll pray for you as long as I have breath, and after that too."

Jacob sank slowly down, and William departed full of joy and sorrow. He rejoiced that he had been the means of good, he grieved that he had lost so much time, and had done so little. All his opportunities came out before him, and he saw in what a high position God had placed him. He desired not to rise above his calling as a farmer, but resolved that he would pray and strive to fulfil more faithfully duties and responsibilities already sufficiently arduous.

At the gate of the last field Ellen met him, and as they walked slowly in, William told all that had passed at the cottage which he had just left, and they felt that if the poor boy was patient, how much more should they be, and how over-blessed William already was, in having been the instrument of making their dying brother as Christian and happy as he was.

"And perhaps he is now praying for us," said Ellen.

"Then let us pray for him," was the answer; and they knelt down together, and repeated earnestly some of the prayers of the Visitation Service. How truly Christian! Nowhere does the communion of saints appear more than in intercessory prayer. One brother prays for another, and the second for the first, and all for all, in an endless chain; and strength descends, and the countless links are kept together in the unity of the whole, each by other. If men only realised more fully the blessedness of love, and of love manifested in prayer, then would the unity of the church become more and more perfect; and also in tribulation and pain, men would receive unspeakable comfort from the knowledge, and unspeakable grace from the effect, of the supplications of their brethren.

To those who have realised this truth in any degree, the Daily Service of the church is a continual and increasing happiness. Praying at the same hour, and in the very words of their brethren, and as fellow-members of the mystical body of Christ, they feel that their many voices rise to Heaven as one, and that the one Spirit descends upon all, and abides in all, because all are one.

CHAPTER XVII.

An Early Spring.

"I would not miss one sigh or tear,
    Heart-pang, or throbbing brow;
Sweet was the chastisement severe,
    And sweet its memory now."

LYRA APOSTOLICA.

THE tendency of a life in towns, is to lead men
to forget natural, and to value revealed, religion only;
or, to speak more accurately, to overlook the simple
virtues and plain laws of right and wrong, which are
evident, to a great extent, without the Gospel,
although included in it, and endued with new
sanctions and blessings; and to attend to that portion of Christianity only, which is generally called
the doctrine of grace, the full and free pardon
offered to sinful man, in Christ; as if this were
the whole of the Gospel, as if that free pardon
were offered to persons who, possessing the Gospel
privileges, lived as careless of justice and truth
as the very heathen, and sometimes more so. The
pardon of the cross of Christ, and faith in that
pardon, are the two great ideas of popular or city
religionists, without the practice of the cross, without attention to the ancient virtues now stamped with

the cross, and consecrated as its fruits, and the evidences of its power in the heart of man.

In the country, however, the very reverse is the case. Most farmers and labourers live by a natural religion, and do not enter into the peculiar doctrine of the Incarnation. Right and wrong, death and judgment, the duty to man and to God, are familiar thoughts with them, but unconnected with that new doctrine of them which our Lord revealed. They learn from things around them, much in which the inhabitants of towns are wanting. On the other hand, they do not feel that all outward things are to be seen now in the light of Gospel truth. They do not feel that the religion of the ancient Jews or pious heathens, was something very different, and short of, that which is expected of the Christian. To state the fact roughly but plainly; the people of towns have more Christianity in doctrine, and no more in practice: the people of the country have less doctrinal Christianity, but are more practical of the religion which they possess.

It was to meet this evil, as well as to prevent that deadness and earthliness which a continual un-thoughtfulness of God's creation is sure to cause, that Mr. Lee was so anxious to explain the objects of nature not only in a religious but in a Gospel spirit. He did not speak of the harvest as an emblem of death, without bringing forward the whole doctrine of the seed-corn as declared by our Lord, and in the first Epistle to the Corinthians.

He did not point out the lily as an emblem of the beauty of simplicity, without adding Who it was Who had called our thoughts to it, Who it was Who exemplified the lesson. And hence the spiritual sense in which he had led William to understand the things around him, always led him at once from any dreamy, unreal moralising spirit to Christian doctrine, and to Christian practice.

The thoughts of William and his wife upon the evening of the 28th of September lead to these reflections. As the farm was not let, he was to stay on for the present, and had moved nothing, but he was threshing out some wheat, to bring things gradually into compass.

They were leaning over the yard-gate, and watching the winnowing, and this significant process soon brought its true lesson to their minds.

"This," said William, "is the winnowing and the sifting which we are now suffering. May the chaff be blown away, and the good corn left, if there be any!"

"The chaff He shall burn up with unquenchable fire," added Ellen; "The wicked are like the chaff which the wind scattereth away before the face of the earth."

"I shall never be thankful enough that I have had my eyes opened to these things. I do not know how worldly I should have become without them. Once they were nothing to me, but now they are a constant comfort and warning."

"Look at that beautiful sunset, William; quick,

in a few minutes it will have sunk behind that bank of clouds."

William looked, but the sun was gone; only bright rays remained, reaching from where they stood to the edge of the burning cloud.

"These call us after it," said William; "the Sun of Righteousness calls us to Him."

"But look there in the east. It is nearly as bright as in the west."

"Have you heard Mr. Lee speak of that?"

"No, never."

"He says two things of it. He sees in it the likeness of the Saints helping each other on,—the highest Saints, the clouds in the west made bright by the light of God's countenance, and reflecting their light upon His holy people till they shine, too, though with less brightness."

"And the other?"

"He says that the last act of the sun is to throw some light on the east, to remind people of his rising, and to keep them looking there, like the words of the Angels at the Ascension, that we might keep 'looking for and hasting to' the second coming 'more than they that watch for the morning.'"

"Heaviness may endure for a night, but joy——"

"Yes, dear Ellen, but do not let us be looking for an earthly joy, or all this trial will be lost upon us."

"No, dearest; but still I hope even here."

"Do; but let us hope more *there*," said William, pointing eastwards.

By this time it was dusk, and as they got into the house they did not see, for a minute, that the hall was full of people. In a minute, however, they recognised Edward, Mr. Lee, and two strangers.

"We are come with good news, William," said Mr. Lee; "so let us sit down, and be comfortable."

Poor William was more excited than comfortable, and his heart and that of Ellen beat fast.

"I will not make a long story of it, William. My brother here had £20,000 to invest for his children, and I knew privately that Sir Lionel was in great difficulties, so I thought from the first we could manage it, although I said nothing for fear of disappointing you. This was my notion, and I called in Edward to help me, because I thought we should be refused if the name of Lee appeared. So Edward settled it all, and bought the Moat House farm for £25,000, £5,000 to remain on mortgage; and the little sheep-farm for himself, where he means to settle, and become my parishioner. I do not know that there is anything more to say, except that my brother, Colonel Lee, will be only too glad to have you for a tenant."

"And do my father and mother know, Sir?"

"Yes, William, we told them as we came up."

"I cannot thank you now, Sir," said William, walking to the window.

"No, you need not; neither now, nor ever."

After a few minutes, William recovered his firmness, and asked them to stay to tea.

"No, we cannot do that, William, for I have much in hand, and so have you. To-morrow, you know, is a great festival, and your father says, he and you must feast all his neighbours. He has sent out right and left, and you are to ask your men and their families."

"But where can we put them all, Sir?"

"Why, in the barn, to be sure; and I shall come, and all my family, and bring a guest."

"You know, Sir, I shall feel it an honour and pleasure."

"Well, well, then set about it. Get the geese strung up, and everything ready; and you must stir yourself, Ellen. Luckily, there is plenty of beef down at the butchers'. And now, good night."

"Will you not do one thing for me first, Sir?" said William.

"Certainly. What do you wish?"

"To thank God, Sir."

The servants were called, and candles brought, and Mr. Lee read from the Bible and the Prayer Book, as suited the occasion. The Blessing was given by the stranger, in a very solemn and affectionate manner, and as the party arose from their knees he said, "I am your Bishop, my brethren: God bless you. Good night."

William had never seen him since the commitment of Thompson, and looked confused and astonished.

"I see you remember me," said the Bishop.

"But I understand things are much changed, and we shall meet with unmixed pleasure now."

"Thank you, my Lord. I shall feel it——"

"We shall all feel it,—we shall all feel it. Do not say any more. Good night. Good night, Mrs. Blake. We really must go, Mr. Lee, for I have many letters to write now, before night."

S. Michael's day came, and as bright and invigorating an autumn day it was, as England is ever blessed with. A clear, keen air, softening almost into a summer breeze, with a cloudless sky, gave a vigour and freshness to the spirits; and almost all the people of Great Staunton were ready to enter into its happiness to the full.

It is not necessary again to describe the services at Great Staunton church. The church was well filled upon the morning of that noble festival, and the Bishop preached. The collection at the offertory was unusually large, as might have been expected after the good news of the preceding evening. After service, the greater part of the people went up to the Moat House, and the dinner began at two. The barn had been fitted up, with an upper table across the top, at which the more distinguished of the guests were placed, and with two other long tables down the sides. The Bishop said grace, and the feast commenced. All the smiles, and jokes, and congratulations, and happy speeches, of that day, together amount to so much, that it is hopeless to give them all, and difficult to select any. We will suppose, then, the dinner over, and the toasts begun.

As usual, " Church and Queen " came first, and the Bishop returned thanks, as follows :—

" I confess that I am glad that it has fallen upon me to answer to this toast, because it gives me the opportunity of saying that which is very much in my heart at this time. It may seem as if I were here as a stranger, a guest invited, because upon the spot. I am not, indeed, insensible to the better and kinder feelings of our host, and Mr. Lee, when I say this; but I speak of what the world would generally imagine. It would view me as a guest and casual witness of rural festivities, and perhaps would censure me for being here. But my views of my position here are very different. I consider myself present among you upon the same grounds as your worthy Rector is. I am here as a father, in the midst of a dear and happy family.

" I am here, too, at festivities connected with a holy day, which we have already hallowed, I trust, and consecrated, in your parish church. I am present at a rejoicing in which I heartily participate, in a rejoicing that our host is to remain in his honourable and most useful position in this parish.

" You have received the toast of ' Church and Queen ' with old English loyalty, and I reply by drawing your attention to the truth which our host shows by his life and conduct, that the Church does

not mean the clergy alone, as is too generally thought.
A few years ago it was my painful introduction to
this part of my diocese, to meet a criminal from this
farm, whose only excuse was the utter neglect under
which he had lain. The state of things then,
could hardly have been worse in a Christian land;
and now I know not whether it is better in any
part of my diocese than in this village. And
what is the cause? The *co-operation* of pastor and
parishioner. Mr. Lee from the Rectory, and Mr.
Blake from this farm, have made this parish a
new place, and as their Bishop I take this opportunity of thanking them, and bidding them God
speed. I take this opportunity, also, of pressing
upon you all that you are every one of you equally
members of the Church, equally interested, and
some, perhaps, equally able to help in the good work
which is going on. I would that all the farmers in
this noble county could see what I see and know
this day. They have the country almost in their
own hands, if they will exercise their influence
aright. There is no saying what knowledge, what
prosperity, what comfort, what goodness, what happiness, they may not be the means of producing.
Hitherto, they have neglected, and been neglected,
and I trust the day of both these sins and evils is
passing away. Year by year, I hope to see them
more and more enlightened, more and more set
upon sharing and communicating the full blessings
which, as Englishmen and Churchmen, they have

received. I thank you, then, for your toast, but in so doing I speak for you. You are the Church, and as you see the happiness of this day, the good upon which I congratulate you arising from the Church, so I hope you will all be more and more thankful for your privileges; and that, availing yourselves of them, your example will spread through all the land, so that many and many a day like this may be the portion of yourselves, your countrymen, and your children."

The choir came in as the speech concluded, and, taking up their place near the high table, sang in excellent style the following verses, which had been written off the night before by the Rector—

> We dwell along the spreading plain,
>   And up the mountain side:
> Ours the green grass, and yellow grain,
>   Through all the country wide.
>
> The squire, the lord, may call them theirs,
>   But lords o' the soil are we;
> At our command the fallow bears,
>   And rests the verdant lea.
>
> We rise at dawn of ruddy day,
>   Fresh light, fresh airs are ours;
> Before the dew has passed away,
>   Or the wintry heaven lowers.
>
> For us the earth, the air, the sky,
>   The poor obey our will;
> And whilst its lords the country fly,
>   Their ancient halls we fill.
>
> What need we more but calm content,
>   To use our blessings well,
> Be born, and live a life well spent,
>   Then lay us where we dwell?

The song was well received, especially when the author was known. Toasts followed. William's health was drunk, and that of the Rector; and both made their speeches in return. That of the former was very short, and attributed all the good that was done to Mr. Lee. The latter dwelt at some length on the parochial system, and concluded thus—

"The Bishop will allow me to say thus much, for I am his representative here always; I am the Curate, who lives here year after year, and am placed in perpetual and close connexion with you. I may be allowed, then, to speak to you as a father, and to say how I feel to you all as my own family. We are all one, my brethren; one household, and our church is our house, where we meet most frequently, and most solemnly; but we meet here also, we meet in festivities, in all lawful enjoyments. Indeed, it does me more good than almost anything, to see your happy faces here to-day. I know that the care-worn countenance, the eye turned down, the dull heavy walk, is no more consistent with goodness than with happiness.

"Whatever has robbed merry England of its mirth, has caused in it that evil which shocked our Bishop when he first came among us; and I delight in seeing its signs vanish away, and innocent mirth spreading amongst us, and connecting itself with such events as those of this day. If we will but be *one* parish, seeking each other's happiness from high to low, instructing and learning, guiding and following, ruling and obeying as all of one family here in this place, rely upon it, we must thrive and be happy. We shall be strong by our unity, whatever comes upon us. One shall help another. One shall weep with another, and rejoice with another, and the weeping will be alleviated, and the rejoicing heightened.

"Let me beg of you to regard each farm as containing a community, a family, a body of brethren bound together by brotherly affection, under one father, and to regard all farms and houses collected together as one larger family; and let this unity be constantly brought before you by the sight of your one church, your one font, your one altar, your one burial-ground, by the observance of holidays like this, holy to all as much as to any; and, if I may again say so, by the sight of me, who desire most earnestly to be your spiritual father, to make you happy, and to be happy with you, in parish unity and love."

The choir struck up again, and the fact that the second song was by the author of the first must be the apology for the similarity of ideas. Mr. Lee could not get away from his ruling feeling on the subject, neither did he pretend to be a poet.

> We live in old manorial halls,
>   A stiff, unchanged, unchanging race;
> The tide of fashion flows and falls,
>   But English farmers hold their place.

Ours were the men of Cressy, men
  Who drew the tough and twanging bow;
And we are still what we were then;
  The English yeoman scorns the foe.

We care not for your city ways,
  Not happier we for endless change.
We are hard men of hardy days;
  Nor heed we though you think us strange.

Our village spires are old and grey :
  But we revere them all the more.
They tell us of the good old way,
  In which our fathers walked before.

And there our parish meets in one,
  At morn and eve, and holiday,
And when the work of life is done,
  Our sons their sires together lay.

The old owl oak, the churchyard yew,
  Shall spread their solemn arms the same ;
Shall bid each yeoman still be true
  To his old boast and ancient name.

And though all else should change and fail,
  Our grandsons still will live to show
The heart which made the Frenchman quail,
  The arm which pulled the twanging bow.

Other songs, and finally "God save the Queen,"
followed, and then the whole party adjourned to the
meadow opposite, where all manner of merry games
and manly exercises succeeded to the feast. The
church bell rang for even-song, and a goodly throng
followed the Bishop and Mr. Lee to church. They
soon returned, and when the light failed, supper was
spread, and the feast renewed. At nine, the Bishop
rose to leave, and, encountering Mr. Mann, was told—

"Not many young men, my Lord, like William
Blake."

"No, indeed; there *are* not many, but there *might* be. You may all do as much good if you will. Set your *heart* on it, and you will accomplish it."

"Come, Mr. Blake, we will see you home," said Mr. Lee.

"Thank you, Sir, I must stay to the last. It is not every father that has such a son."

"No, indeed, Mr. Blake. They say England is over-peopled, but the more sons like yours the better; and, indeed, they are increasing. We shall see the good old times back again yet, Mr. Blake; and perhaps something better. Good night!"

In a few hours all was quiet. The cottagers were in their beds. A light in the study window showed that the Bishop and the Rector were in their places. William and Ellen were kneeling down in prayer and praise. The moon was lighting up the old gables of the Moat House, which threw long shadows behind them. It was the reign of rest and peace; that time to which many hearts are looking, a time when the work of life is over, and there is a tarrying and reposing before the break of the endless day.

J. MASTERS, ALDERSGATE STREET, AND NEW BOND STREET.

April, 1848.

NEW WORKS

PUBLISHED BY

JOSEPH MASTERS,

33, ALDERSGATE STREET,

AND

78, NEW BOND STREET,

LONDON.

In the Press and nearly ready.

A REPRINT OF THE BOOK OF COMMON PRAYER
of 1661, according to the *Sealed Copy* in the Tower of London.
In small 8vo., to be handsomely printed in red and black, with the
old Elzevir type, forming a suitable volume for a Clergyman's use
either in the desk or closet.

THE LIFE OF NICHOLAS FERRAR.

AN ACCOUNT OF THE CHURCHES OF SCAR-
BOROUGH, FILEY, and its neighbourhood. By the Rev. G. A.
POOLE, M.A., and JOHN WEST HUGALL, Architect. In fcp.
8vo., illustrated with numerous Engravings.

PREPARING FOR PUBLICATION.

THE GUIDANCE OF CONSCIENCE. Intended as Hints
for the Use of the Parochial Clergy in the work of Spiritual Direction. By the Rev. EDWARD MONRO.

A HISTORY OF ECCLESIASTICAL ARCHITECTURE
IN ENGLAND. By the Rev. G. A. POOLE, M.A.

ORIGINAL BALLADS. By Living Authors, 1848.
Edited by the Rev. HENRY THOMPSON, M.A., Cantab. In Demy
8vo. Illustrated.

MARTYROLOGY : being an Account of some of the Early
Christian Martyrs, and intended to promote a sympathy in the
minds of Children for the Primitive Church. By the Rev. SAMUEL
FOX, M.A., Rector of Morley, in the Diocese of Lichfield.

Parochial Tracts.—A Classified List sent by Post on application.

NEW WORKS
PUBLISHED BY JOSEPH MASTERS.

ADAMS.—THE FALL OF CRŒSUS.

A Story from Herodotus. With Conversations designed to connect the Study of History with a belief in a Superintending Providence. By the Rev. W. ADAMS, M.A., Author of "The Shadow of the Cross." Foolscap 8vo., cloth, with Map. 3s. 6d.

" We venture to say that the attention of no intelligent child will be found to flag in reading this little volume—and those who read cannot fail to be benefited by the simple earnest tone of the writer."—*Ecclesiastic*, February, 1846.

ADAMS.—CRESSINGHAM; OR, THE MISSIONARY.

By CHARLOTTE PRISCILLA ADAMS. Foolscap 8vo., cloth, 2s.

" It is a very delightful sketch of a very interesting character."—*English Churchman*, Dec. 17.

" Those who have read the twenty-eighth chapter of George Herbert's COUNTRY PARSON, entitled ' The Parson in Contempt,' or Barnabas Oley's ' Apology for the Clergy,' in his preface to it, will feel interested in CRESSINGHAM, as it is calculated to remove the impression against which those writings are directed, but the best refutation of which, after all, is the real exhibition of such characters as this work pourtrays, without exceeding the actual truth."—*Gentleman's Mag.*

ADDRESS TO THE MEMBERS OF THE EPISCOPAL CHURCH IN SCOTLAND. By a LAYMAN. A new edition, revised. Price 1s. 12mo., cloth.

ÆLFRIC.—A SERMON ON THE SACRIFICE ON EASTER DAY. Turned into English from the Anglo-Saxon of Ælfric, sometime Archbishop of Canterbury. Price 2d.

ALLESTREE.—THE LIFE OF DR. RICHARD ALLES- TREE. Price 3d., sewed.

APOSTOLICAL SUCCESSION VINDICATED FROM PRESBYTERIAN MIS-STATEMENTS. A Letter to the Author of a Pamphlet, entitled, " The True Succession : a Sermon preached before the London Missionary Society, May, 1846, by the Rev. JOHN CUMMING, D.D., Minister of the Scottish National Church, Crown Court, Little Russell Street, Covent Garden." By a LAYMAN OF THE ENGLISH CHURCH, Author of "The Church and the Meeting-House." Price 1s.

ANNALS OF VIRGIN SAINTS.

Selected both from Primitive and Mediæval Times. By a PRIEST of the Church of England. In cloth, 7s. 6d. This work is also kept, elegantly bound in morocco by Nichols, for Presents, price 22s. 6d.

ARDEN.—A MANUAL OF CATECHETICAL IN- STRUCTION FOR PUBLIC OR PRIVATE USE. Compiled and arranged by the Rev. G. ARDEN, M.A., Wadham College, Oxford, Chaplain to the Right Hon. the Earl of Devon. 18mo., cloth, 2s. 6d.

BAINES. — CANTICLES FROM THE PSALMS POINTED FOR CHANTING, with Four Chants prefixed ; for the Use of Schools and Families. By the REV. EDWARD BAINES, Rector of Bluntisham. 18mo. sewed, price 6d.

BARON'S LITTLE DAUGHTER, AND OTHER TALES. In Verse and Prose. By the Author of "Verses for Holy Seasons." Edited by the Rev WILLIAM GRESLEY, Prebendary of Lichfield. Price 4s. 6d.

BLUNT.—THE USE AND ABUSE OF CHURCH BELLS. With Practical Suggestions concerning them. By WALTER BLUNT, M.A., a Priest of the English Church. 8vo., price 6d., or 8d. by post.

BLUNT.—ECCLESIASTICAL RESTORATION AND REFORM. Considerations and Practical Suggestions on Church Rates,—Parish Officers,—Education of the Poor,—Cemeteries. By WALTER BLUNT, M.A. In demy 8vo., price 1s. 6d. or 2s. by post.

BLUNT.—CONFIRMATION, OR THE LAYING ON OF HANDS. Catechetically explained according to the Formularies of the English Church. By WALTER BLUNT, M.A. In 12mo., price 3d., or 21s. per 100.

BOOK OF MEDIÆVAL ALPHABETS. Oblong 4to., in paper cover, price 3s.
To Gravestone Cutters, Painters, and Decorators, the above will be found an invaluable *vade mecum*.

BRECHIN. (BISHOP OF).—JESUS OUR WORSHIP. A Sermon preached at the Consecration of St. Columba's Church, Edinburgh. By ALEXANDER, by Divine Permission, Bishop of Brechin. 8vo., price 6d., or 1s. by post.

BUTLER.—SERMONS FOR WORKING MEN. By WILLIAM JOHN BUTLER, M.A., Vicar of Wantage, Berks, late the Perpetual Curate of Wareside, near Ware. In good bold Type, price 6s. 6d.

CARTER.—REMARKS ON CHRISTIAN GRAVE-STONES with Working Drawings. By the Rev. ECCLES J. CARTER, M.A., of Exeter College, Oxford, Minor Canon of Bristol Cathedral. Demy 8vo., price 3s. 6d.

CATECHISM, to be learnt before the CHURCH CATE-CHISM. For Infant Schools. A new edition, carefully revised, price 1d., (2d. by post,) or 6s. 6d. per 100.

CERTIFICATES OF CONFIRMATION AND HOLY COMMUNION, handsomely printed in Red and Black on Cards, price 2d., or 14s. per hundred. Strong Paper Cloth Envelopes 4s. per hundred.
The Type being always kept standing, Clergymen may have them printed expressly for their own parishes, having only to sign their names. Price for 50, 10s.; 100, 15s.

CERTIFICATES OF BAPTISM, CONFIRMATION, AND FIRST COMMUNION, on a Large Card, price 2d, or 14s. per 100.

CHARCOAL BURNERS (THE). 18mo. cloth, price 1s. 6d.

CHARLTON.—THE PRINCIPLES OF ENGLISH GRAMMAR SYSTEMATICALLY AND PRACTICALLY ARRANGED; with Examination Paper and Appendix. By SAMUEL CHARLTON, B.A., of S. John's College, Cambridge. In 18mo. price 1s. 6d. cloth.

CHRISTIAN LOYALTY.
A Sermon. Price 1d.

CHURCHMAN'S COMPANION (THE)
is carefully edited, and adapted for general reading for all classes. It contains a great variety of Instructive and Amusing matter:— Biography, Tales, Essays, Explanations of the Church Services and Seasons, Bible Illustrations, Natural History, Anecdotes, Poetry, &c. Vols. I. and II. are now ready, strongly bound and cut edges, price 2s. 9d., with an allowance to the Clergy for Lending Libraries.

EDITOR'S PREFACE.—"In presenting our readers with the first volume of the CHURCHMAN'S COMPANION, we cannot but express a hope, that we have fulfilled the promises made in our Prospectus. Our object has been to present a magazine free from all controversial bias, and yet firmly maintaining the doctrines of the Church; a magazine devoted to the interest of all, as members of the same Body, and in which rich and poor, young and old, might find rational amusement and instruction. To what extent we have succeeded in this our earnest wish, must be left for our readers to decide. It is our pleasing duty to thank many warm-hearted friends for the kindly interest they have taken, and the strenuous exertions they have made to bring the magazine into notice. But at the same time, we must respectfully but earnestly entreat every one of our readers to use his utmost exertions to obtain at least one additional subscriber. A magazine such as this cannot be established but by a very large circulation; and that circulation cannot be attained but by the greatest efforts. In an age when cheap publications of an irreligious tendency command so extensive a sale, it is much to be hoped, that amongst Churchmen *one* cheap magazine, conducted on sound principles, will be enabled **to** gain a footing. If we have already, in any degree, proved ourselves worthy of confidence and support, we can only say, that for the future nothing shall be wanting on our part to render the **magazine** still more useful and acceptable to those who pray for the peace of Jerusalem."

CHURCHMAN'S DIARY (The); being an Almanack for the Year of Grace 1848, being Leap-year. Price 3d., with the usual Allowance to Clergymen taking a number for distribution.

CHURCHES (The) OF ENGLAND AND ROME briefly tested by the Nicene Creed, as applied by MR. NORTHCOTE. By a MEMBER OF THE CHURCH OF ENGLAND. 8VO. 4s. 6d.

CHURTON.—LAYS OF FAITH AND LOYALTY. By the Ven. Archdeacon CHURTON, M.A., Rector of Crayke Price 2s.

CLARKE.—A COLLECTION OF LETTERS addressed by Prelates and Individuals of High Rank in Scotland, and by Two Bishops of Sodor and Man to Sancroft, Archbishop of Canterbury in the Reigns of Kings Charles II. and James VII. Edited from Originals in the Bodleian Library, Oxford, with Explanatory and Biographical Notices, by WILLIAM NELSON CLARKE, D.C.L., of Christ Church, Oxford. Price 5s.

CODD.—SERMONS PREACHED IN THE PARISH CHURCH OF S. GILES, CAMBRIDGE. By the Rev. EDWARD T. CODD, M.A., S. John's College, Cambridge, Perpetual Curate of S. James, Cotes Heath, Staffordshire. In 12mo., price 6s. 6d. cloth.

COMMENTARY ON THE SEVEN PENITENTIAL PSALMS. Chiefly from Ancient Sources. 18mo., cloth, price 1s.
" Under this modest title we have a most useful and truly religious realization of the Evangelical meaning of the Penitential Psalms. The writer has chosen for illustration the internal acts of penitence, and in a very able and eloquent introduction has placed the use of the Psalms in the Christian Church, and of these especially, as exponents of Evangelical repentance, in a very clear and satisfactory light."—*Ecclesiastic.*

COMPANION TO THE ALTAR.
Adapted to the Office for the Holy Communion, according to the Use of the Scottish Church. 32mo., sewed, 6d. ; cloth. 8d.

CONFESSION, AN EARNEST EXHORTATION TO,
Addressed to all Sinners who having Grievously Offended the Divine Majesty, desire by Penitence to destroy the hated past. In Demy 8vo., price 6d., or 8d. by post.

CONFIRMATION CONSIDERED DOCTRINALLY AND PRACTICALLY, in Four Sermons. The Baptism of the Holy Ghost, the Duties and Privileges of the Confirmed. By a CLERGYMAN. Fcap. 8vo. Price 1s.

CONFIRMATION.
Questions and Answers on Confirmation. Price One Penny, or 5s. per hundred for distribution.

CRESSWELL.—THE CHRISTIAN LIFE.
Twelve Sermons by RICHARD CRESSWELL, B.A. Curate of Salcombe Regis, Devon. 12mo. cloth, price 6s.

DESIGNS FOR GRAVESTONES, ON SHEETS.
No. 1, containing 29 designs, price 3d. No. 2, price 2d.

DUKE.—A SYSTEMATIC ANALYSIS OF BISHOP BUTLER'S TREATISE ON THE ANALOGY OF RELIGION TO THE CONSTITUTION OF NATURE, so far as relates to Natural Religion : to which is added, Some Considerations on Certain Arguments therein advanced. By the Rev. HENRY H. DUKE, B.A., Chaplain to the Infirmary at Salisbury. Demy 8vo., price 4s. 6d. Interleaved, 6s.

DUNSTER.—STORIES FROM THE CHRONICLERS, (FROISSART), illustrating the History, Manners, and Customs of the Reign of Edward III. By the Rev. HENRY P. DUNSTER, M.A. 18mo. cloth. Price 2s. 6d.

EARLY FRIENDSHIP; OR, THE TWO CATECHUMENS. 18mo. cloth, price 1s. 6d.

Published every alternate month, price 1s. 6d.

ECCLESIOLOGIST (THE).
Published under the Superintendence of the ECCLESIOLOGICAL LATE CAMBRIDGE CAMDEN SOCIETY.
Seven Volumes are now published, and may be had at the following prices, in boards:—Vol. I., 5s. 6d.; Vol. II., with Two Engravings, 5s. 6d.; Vol. III., with Seven Engravings, 6s. 6d.; Vol. IV., (New Series, I.) with Four Engravings, 8s.; Vol. V., (N. S. II.) with Three Engravings, 8s. 6d.; Vol. VI. (N. S. III.) with Three Engravings, price 7s. 6d.; Vol. VII. (N. S. IV.) with Three Engravings, 8s.

ECCLESIOLOGIST'S GUIDE (THE) TO THE DEANE- RIES OF BRISLEY, HINGHAM, BRECCLES, AND WAXTON, together with Flegg and Blofield Deaneries, and that part of Cranwicke Deanery comprised in the Hundred of South Greenhoe, all in the County of Norfolk. 12mo. sewed, Part I., 1s. 6d. Part II., price 1s. 4d.

ENGLISH CHURCHMAN'S KALENDAR (THE) FOR THE YEAR OF OUR LORD MDCCCXLVIII., being Leap-year. Compiled from the Book of Common Prayer. Third Year. Price 1s.

ENTHUSIASM NOT RELIGION.
A Tale. By the late M. A. C. Foolscap 8vo., cloth, price 5s.
" This is a remarkable little book, in more points of view than one. It is remarkable as the production of a very young person, whose mind seems to have acquired a growth far beyond its years, and to have seized upon sound religious opinions, even in deep matters, without effort. It is also remarkable for powerful delineation of character, for apt illustration, and for dramatic force. Seldom have we met with a more striking combination of simplicity and wisdom."— *Monmouth Beacon.*

EUCHOLOGION.
A Collection of Prayers, Forms of Intercession, and Thanksgiving, Litanies, &c. For the use of Families. 12mo., cloth, price 3s. 6d.

EVANS.—SACRED MUSIC,
Composed and Dedicated [by permission] to the Worshipful and Reverend George Martin, M.A., Oxon., Chancellor of the Diocese of Exeter. &c. By the REV. WILLIAM SLOANE EVANS, B.A., [Soc. Cam.] Trinity College, Cantab., Curate of S. David's, Exeter. Consisting of Twelve Original Psalm Tunes adapted to the New Metrical Version, Sanctus, Kyrie-Eleeson, and Single Chants. Imperial 8vo., price 4s.

FAMILY PRAYERS adapted to the course of the Ecclesiastical Year. Compiled for the use of the Families of the Clergy or Laity. By a Clergyman. *Nearly ready.*

FAMILY PRAYERS,

Consisting of a Selection of the Collects and Prayers of the Chruch of England. By a Graduate of the University of Cambridge. In royal 18mo., price 1s. ; paper cover, 6d.

" The object of the Compiler has been to supply a Form of Family Prayers, at once short, comprehensive, varied, deeply devotional, and suited to the wants of all classes, whether in the mansions of the rich, or in the dwellings of the poor."—*Preface.*

FLOWER.—A CHRISTIAN VIEW OF THE SCHOOL-MASTER'S OFFICE, considered in an Address to the Teachers of the Moral and Industrial Training Schools of the Manchester Poor Law Union, at Swinton. By the Rev. W. B. FLOWER, B.A., one of the Classical Masters of Christ's Hospital. Price 6d.

"The Works of the Lord are great."

FLOWER.—A SERMON PREACHED ON SUNDAY, the 17th October, being the day appointed for the General Thanksgiving, in the Parish Church of S. Hugh, Harlow, Essex. By the Rev. W. B. FLOWER, B.A., late Scholar of Magdalene College, Cambridge, and one of the Classical Masters at Christ's Hospital. Demy 8vo., price 6d., or 8d. by post.

FLOWER.—READING LESSONS FOR THE HIGHER CLASSES IN GRAMMAR, MIDDLE, AND DIOCESAN SCHOOLS, selected and arranged by the Rev. W. B. FLOWER, B.A., one of the Classical Masters at Christ's Hospital, London. 12mo., cloth, 3s.

This work differs in many respects from those that are already in use, and is especially adapted for use in Church Schools, in which religion is still regarded as the basis of Education. The lessons, which are selected from the best authors, are systematically arranged according to the subjects.

FORD.—THE GOSPEL OF ST. MATTHEW ILLUS-TRATED FROM ANCIENT AND MODERN AUTHORS. By the Rev. JAMES FORD, M.A., late of Oriel College, Oxford. Demy 8vo., cloth, price 10s. 6d.

FORM OF SELF-EXAMINATION.

With Prayers Preparatory to the Holy Communion. A New Edition. 2d.

FORM OF SELF-EXAMINATION, with a Few Directions for Daily Use. By F. H. M, Price 3d., or 21s. per 100.

FOUQUE.—ASLAUGA AND HER KNIGHT.

An Allegory. From the German of the Baron de la Motte Fouqué. A new Translation. In 18mo. cloth, price 1s. 6d.

FOUR-PAGE TRACTS, suited also for Tract Covers.

1. Scripture Rules for Holy Living.—2. Baptism and Registration. —3. George Herbert.—4. Dreamland.—5. Songs for Labourers.— 6. Plain Directions for Prayer, with a few Forms.—7. Reasons for Daily Service.—8. Easter Songs.—9. The Good Shepherd.—10. Morning and Evening Hymns.—11. A Few Reasons for Keeping the Fasts and Festivals.—12. The Church Calendar. Price 2s. 6d. in packets of 50, or the whole done up in a sewed volume, price 9d.

FOURPENNY **REWARD BOOKS.**

The Singers.—The Wake.—Beating the Bounds.—The Bonfire. Hallowmas Eve.—A Sunday Walk and a Sunday Talk.—Legend of S. Dorothea.—Dream of S. Perpetua.—Siege of Nisibis.— Christian Heroism.—The Little Miners.—The Secret.—Little Willie, the Lame Boy.—Try Again. Packets of 13, **4s.**

FOX.—MONKS AND MONASTERIES.

Being an Account of ENGLISH MONACHISM. By the **Rev. SAMUEL** FOX, M.A., F.S.A. 12mo. cloth. Price 5s.

FOX.—A HISTORY OF ROME.

By the Rev. SAMUEL Fox, M.A., F.S.A. 18mo. cloth, 3s.

FREEMAN.—PRINCIPLES OF CHURCH RESTORA-

TION. By EDWARD A. FREEMAN, B.A., Fellow of Trinity Coll., Oxford. 8vo., 1s.

FRENCH.—PRACTICAL REMARKS ON SOME OF

THE MINOR ACCESSORIES TO THE SERVICES OF THE CHURCH, with Hints on the reparation of Altar Cloths, Pede Cloths, and other Ecclesiastical Furniture. Addressed to Ladies and Churchwardens. By GILBERT J. FRENCH. Foolscap 8vo., with Engravings, price 4s. boards.

GRESLEY.—COLTON GREEN,

A Tale of the Black Country. By the Rev. WILLIAM GRESLEY, M.A. 18mo. cloth. Price 2s. 6d.

GRESLEY.—HENRI DE CLERMONT ; or, the

Royalists of La Vendée. A Tale of the French Revolution. By the Rev. WILLIAM GRESLEY, M.A. With cuts, 18mo. cloth, **2s.**

GRESLEY.—PAROCHIAL SERMONS.

By the Rev. W. GRESLEY, M.A. 12mo. cloth. **7s. 6d.**

GRESLEY.—PETER PLATTIN ; OR, THE LITTLE

MINERS. A Fairy Tale. By the Rev. W. GRESLEY, M.A. Cuts. Price 4d., stiff cover.

GRESLEY.—CLEMENT WALTON ; or, the English

Citizen. By the Rev. W. GRESLEY, M.A. 12mo. cloth, 3s. 6d. Cheap edition 1s. 8d.

GRESLEY.—THE SIEGE OF LICHFIELD.

12mo, cloth, 4s. Cheap edition 1s. 8d.

GRESLEY.—CHARLES LEVER; the Man of the

Nineteenth Century. By the Rev. W. GRESLEY, M.A. 12mo. cloth, 3s. 6d. Cheap edition 1s. 8d.

GRESLEY.—THE FOREST OF ARDEN.

A Tale illustrative of the English Reformation. By the **Rev. W.** GRESLEY, M.A. 12mo. cloth, 4s. Cheap edition 2s.

GRESLEY.—CHURCH CLAVERING ; or, the School-

master. By the Rev. W. GRESLEY, M.A. 12mo. cloth, 4s. Cheap edition 2s.

GRESLEY.—CONISTON HALL ; or, the Jacobites.

A Historical Tale. By the Rev. W. GRESLEY, M.A. 12mo. cloth, 4s. 6d.

GRESLEY.—FRANK'S FIRST TRIP TO THE CONTINENT. By the Rev. W. GRESLEY, M.A. 12mo. cloth 4s. 6d. Cheap edition, 3s.

GRESLEY.—BERNARD LESLIE.
A Tale of the Last Ten Years. By the Rev. W. GRESLEY, M.A. 12mo. cloth, 4s. 6d.

GRESLEY.—HOLIDAY TALES.
Cloth 2s. Wrapper, 1s. 6d.

GRESLEY.—TREATISE ON THE ENGLISH CHURCH.
Containing Remarks on its History, Theory, Peculiarities; the Objections of Romanists and Dissenters; its Practical Defects; its Present Position; its Future Prospects; and the Duties of its Members. By the Rev. W. GRESLEY, M.A. 12mo. 1s.

GRESLEY.—THE THEORY OF DEVELOPMENT BRIEFLY CONSIDERED. By the Rev. W. GRESLEY, M.A. 3d.

GRESLEY.—THE REAL DANGER OF THE CHURCH OF ENGLAND. By the Rev. W. GRESLEY, M.A. Sixth edition. 8vo. 9d.

GRESLEY.—A SECOND STATEMENT OF THE REAL DANGER OF THE CHURCH. By the Rev. W. GRESLEY, M.A. Third edition. 8vo. 1s.

GRESLEY.—A THIRD STATEMENT OF THE REAL DANGER OF THE CHURCH. By the Rev. W. GRESLEY, M.A. Second edition. 8vo. 1s. 6d.
The above three pamphlets are now sold in one vol. Price 2s. 6d. in a stiff wrapper.

HAND-BOOK (A) OF ENGLISH ECCLESIOLOGY.
By the Ecclesiological late Cambridge Camden Society. In Demy 18mo., cloth, 7s., or strongly bound in limp Calf and interleaved, 10s. 6d.

HAWKER.—ECHOES FROM OLD CORNWALL.
By the Rev. R. S. HAWKER, M.A., Vicar of Morwenstow. Handsomely printed in Post 8vo., price 4s., bound in cloth.
"These verses bear token of not having been written to order, but for the solace of the author's own feelings; and the reader who takes up the 'Echoes' in search of the same calm temper of mind will, we think, not be disappointed."—*Ecclesiastic.*

HEWETT.—A BRIEF HISTORY AND DESCRIPTION OF THE CATHEDRAL CHURCH OF S. PETER, EXETER. By J. W. HEWETT, Trinity College, Cambridge. Honorary Secretary to the Cambridge Architectural Society. 8vo., Sewed, 1s.
IN PREPARATION.
FOUR APPENDICES to the above, with illustrations.

HEWETT. — THE ARRANGEMENT OF PARISH CHURCHES CONSIDERED, in a Paper read before the Cambridge Architectural Society, on February 19, 1848. By J. W. HEWETT, of Trinity College, one of the Secretaries. 8vo., price 6d.

HEYGATE.—GODFREY DAVENANT ; or, School Life.
By the Rev. WILLIAM E. HEYGATE, M.A. 18mo. cloth. Price
2s. 6d.

HEYGATE.—WILLIAM BLAKE ; OR, THE ENGLISH
FARMER. By the Rev. W. E. HEYGATE. Author of "Probatio
Clerica" and "Godfrey Davenant." *Nearly ready.*

HICKES.—DEVOTIONS IN THE ANCIENT WAY
OF OFFICES, with PSALMS, HYMNS, and PRAYERS, for every Day
of the Week, and every Holy Day in the Year. With a Preface.
By GEORGE HICKES, D.D. Royal 18mo., price 6s. cloth, (reprinted from the edition of 1717.) Morocco, 10s. 6d.

HINTS ON ORNAMENTAL NEEDLEWORK,
as applied to Ecclesiastical Purposes. Printed in square 16mo. with
numerous Engravings. Price 3s.

HISTORY OF PORTUGAL.
From its erection into a separate kingdom to the year 1836.
Price 2s. 6d.

HOPWOOD.—CHRIST IN HIS CHURCH.
A Volume of Plain and Practical Sermons. Preached in the
Parish Church of Worthing, Sussex. By the Rev. HENRY
HOPWOOD, M.A., Rector of Bothal, Durham. Demy 8vo.
Price 5s. 6d.

HOPWOOD.—ELISHA'S STAFF IN THE HAND OF
GEHAZI, and other Sermons. By the Rev. HENRY HOPWOOD,
M.A. 12mo., cloth, price 2s. 6d.

HOPWOOD.—THE CHILD'S GEOGRAPHY.
By the Rev. HENRY HOPWOOD, M.A. This work will be found
to contain in a small compass, all the more interesting and important facts of Geography, in connexion with sound religious
principles. Price 1s. stiff cloth cover.

HOPWOOD.—AN INTRODUCTION TO THE STUDY
OF MODERN GEOGRAPHY. Carefully compiled ; including the
Latest Discoveries, and a Chapter on Ecclesiastical Geography.
By the Rev. HENRY HOPWOOD, M.A. With a Map coloured
to show the Christian, Heathen, and Mahometan Countries,
English Possessions, &c. Price 2s. 6d.

HOLINESS IN THE PRIEST'S HOUSEHOLD ES-
SENTIAL TO THE HOLINESS OF THE PARISH. A Plain
Address to my Household. By a CLERGYMAN. 18mo. Price
6d., or 8d. by post.

HORN BOOK (THE) LESSONS FOR LITTLE CHILDREN,
on Cards, in a case. By a Lady. First Series, 2s. Second
Series, 3s.

HYMNS FOR LITTLE CHILDREN.
By the Author of "The Lord of the Forest," "Verses for Holy
Seasons," &c. Price 1s.

HYMNS ON SCRIPTURE CHARACTERS for the use
of the Young. 18mo. cloth, price 1s.

INGLE.—QUEEN'S LETTERS AND STATE SER-
VICES : THE ONE TO BE OBEYED AND THE OTHER RE-
SISTED. By JOHN INGLE, B.A., Trinity College, Cambridge,
Assistant Curate of S. Olave, Exeter. In Demy 8vo. price 6d.

IRONS.—ON THE WHOLE DOCTRINE OF FINAL
CAUSES. A Dissertation in Three Parts, with an Introductory
Chapter on the Character of Modern Deism. By WILLIAM J.
IRONS, B.D., Incumbent of Holy Trinity Church, Brompton,
Middlesex. Demy 8vo., price 7s. 6d.

IRONS.—ON THE HOLY CATHOLIC CHURCH.
PAROCHIAL LECTURES. By the Rev. W. J. IRONS, B.D. Demy
8vo., price 4s. 6d.

IRONS.— ON THE APOSTOLICAL SUCCESSION.
PAROCHIAL LECTURES. Second Series. By the Rev. W. J. IRONS,
B.D. Price 4s. 6d.

IRONS.—ECCLESIASTICAL JURISDICTION.
Being FOUR LECTURES on the Synod—The Diocese—The Parish
—The Priest. With a Preliminary Essay on the Teaching and
Priestly Offices, and Appendices on the Doctrine of UNITY and
the Royal SUPREMACY. By the Rev. W. J. IRONS, B.D. In Demy
8vo., price 7s. 6d.

⁎ The above Three Series may be had in one volume, price 12s.

IRONS.—SHOULD THE STATE OBLIGE US TO
EDUCATE? A Letter to the Right Hon. Lord John Russell.
By the Rev. W. J. IRONS, B.D. Demy 8vo., price 6d.

IRONS.—A MANUAL FOR UNBAPTIZED CHIL-
DREN, PREPARATORY TO BAPTISM. By Rev. W. J. IRONS,
B.D. Price 2d. or 14s. per 100.

IRONS.—A MANUAL FOR UNBAPTIZED ADULTS,
PREPARATORY TO THEIR BAPTISM. By Rev. W. J. IRONS,
B.D. Price 2d., or 14s. per 100.

IRONS.—A MANUAL FOR CHRISTIANS UNCON-
FIRMED PREPARATORY TO CONFIRMATION AND COM-
MUNION. By the Rev. W. J. IRONS, B.D. Fifth Edition. Price
2d., or 14s. per 100.

IRONS.—AN EPITOME OF THE BAMPTON LEC-
TURES OF THE REV. DR. HAMPDEN. By W. J. IRONS, B.D.
Price 1s., or 1s. 4d. by post.

IRONS.—FIFTY-TWO PROPOSITIONS.—A LETTER
TO THE REV. DR. HAMPDEN, submitting to him certain
Assertions, Assumptions, and Implications in his Bampton Lec-
tures; reduced to the form of Propositions. By W. J. IRONS. B.D.,
Incumbent of Brompton, Middlesex. Price 6d., or 8d. by post.

ISLAND CHOIR (THE); OR, THE CHILDREN OF
THE CHILD JESUS. 18mo., Price 6d.

NOTICE.—"This tale has been written without any direct moral, but still with the hope of exhibiting a faint image of some features worth cultivating in the character of boys. If its publication confers the smallest advantage on any of the young, the Author has so far been fulfilling his peculiar calling; but other circumstances of his life lead him to dedicate it specially to Choristers, with the prayer that as it is the Priest's vocation to set forth in his own life the example of GOD in the form of *man*, so these younger Ministers of the Church may shine like lights among their equals, by conforming themselves to the pattern of the *Child* JESUS."

JENKINS. — SYNCHRONISTICAL OR COTEMPO-
RARY ANNALS OF THE KINGS AND PROPHETS OF ISRAEL AND JUDAH, and of the Kings of Syria, Assyria, Babylon, and Egypt, mentioned in the Scriptures. By W. J. JENKINS, M.A., Fellow of Baliol College, Oxford, Assistant Curate of S. George's, Ramsgate. Demy 4to., price 5s.

"A Tabular View of the Kings of Israel and Judah, and the neighbouring Sovereigns, according as they were contemporary with each other. The Prophets are also included in the Plan. The book seems to have been got up with care, and will, we doubt not, be found very useful in Schools."—*Christian Remembrancer.*

JOHNS, B. G.—THE COLLECTS AND CATECHISING
FOR EVERY SUNDAY AND FESTIVAL THROUGHOUT THE YEAR. By the Rev. B. G. JOHNS, Normal Master of S. Mark's College, Chelsea. 18mo. 3s.

JOHNS, B. G.—EASY DICTATION LESSONS.
In Prose and Verse, Original and Selected. By the Rev. B. G. JOHNS. Price 1s. cloth, or 1s. 6d. by post.

JOHNS, C. A.—EXAMINATION QUESTIONS ON
THE HISTORICAL PARTS OF THE PENTATEUCH. For the Use of Families, National Schools, and the Lower Forms in Grammar Schools. By the Rev. C. A. JOHNS, B.A., F.L.S., Head Master of the Grammar School, Helston, Cornwall. Demy 18mo., price 1s., strongly bound in cloth.

JOLLY, Bp.—THE CHRISTIAN SACRIFICE IN THE
EUCHARIST; considered as it is the doctrine of Holy Scripture, embraced by the Universal Church of the first and purest times, by the Church of England, and by the Episcopal Church in Scotland. By the Right Rev. ALEXANDER JOLLY, D.D., late Bishop of Moray. 12mo., cloth, Second Edition, price 2s. 6d.

JOULE.—A GUIDE TO THE CELEBRATION OF MA-
TINS AND EVEN-SONG, according to the Use of the United Church of England and Ireland, containing *The Order of Daily Service*, *The Litany*, and *the Order for the Administration of the Holy Communion*, with PLAIN-TUNE. By BENJAMIN JOULE, JUN., Honorary Chapel-Master of Holy Trinity Church, Manchester, &c. In royal 8vo., price 2s., in a stiff cover.

KILVERT.—HOME DISCIPLINE ; OR, THOUGHTS ON THE ORIGIN AND EXERCISE OF DOMESTIC AUTHORITY. With an Appendix. By ADELAIDE S. KILVERT. New Edition. 12mo. cloth. 3s. 6d.

LAW OF THE ANGLICAN CHURCH THE LAW OF THE LAND. Foolscap 8vo., price 2d.

This Tract forms a suitable companion to "The Distinctive Tenets of the Church of England. By the REV. W. GRESLEY, M.A."

LAWSON.—PLAIN AND PRACTICAL SERMONS. By G. H. GRAY LAWSON, M.A., Perpetual Curate of Dilton Marsh. 8vo. cloth, price 10s. 6d.

LETHBRIDGE.—TABLES SHOWING THE VALUE OF TITHE RENT-CHARGES for the Year 1848 ; with the Property Tax to be deducted therefrom. Calculated by ROBERT LETHBRIDGE, Accountant. Price 6d.

LETTER ON THE SCOTTISH COMMUNION OF- FICE. (Reprinted from *The English Churchman,* and revised by the author.) With Authorities for the Statements in the Letter, and showing the Principle on which those Statements are founded. By a PRIEST OF THE CHURCH IN SCOTLAND. Price 4d., or 6d. by Post.

LETTER UPON THE SUBJECT OF CONFIRMA- TION, addressed to the "Little Ones" of his Flock. By an English Priest. Price 6d. ; or 5s. per dozen.

LIST OF THE DAYS IN THE YEAR OF OUR LORD 1848, on which it is not seemly for Members of the Church to give or accept invitations to Convivial Parties, the Church having ordered them to "Fast" or "Abstain." On a Sheet, Demy 4to., Rubricated. Price 6d.

LITURGY FOR A VILLAGE SCHOOL, compiled for the use of SHENSTONE NATIONAL SCHOOL, Diocese of Lichfield. In stiff cloth cover, price 6d., or 10d. by post.

LONDON PAROCHIAL TRACTS. Conversion, in Two Parts. Price 2d., 14s. per hundred. Be One Again. An Earnest Entreaty from a Clergyman to his People to Unite in Public Worship. Price 1d., 7s. per hundred. The Church a Family ; or, a Letter from a Clergyman to the Parishioners upon their Blessings and Duties as Members of the Household of God.

LORAINE.—LAYS OF ISRAEL ; or, Tales of the Temple and the Cross. By AMELIA M. LORAINE. In Fcap. 8vo., neatly bound in cloth, price 3s. 6d., morocco, 5s.

LORD OF THE FOREST AND HIS VASSALS.

By the author of "Verses for Holy Seasons." With an ornamental border round each page, and beautiful Frontispiece. Small 4to., cloth, elegantly bound, price 4s. 6d.

MANGER OF THE HOLY NIGHT, with the TALES OF THE PRINCE SCHREIMUND AND THE PRINCESS SCHWEIGSTILLA.

From the German of GUIDO GORRES. By C. E. H., Morwenstow. Sixteen Illustrations. 18mo. cloth. Price 2s.

MANUAL FOR COMMUNICANTS.

Being an Assistant to a Devout and Worthy Reception of THE LORD'S SUPPER. Compiled from Catholic Sources. By a Parish Priest. Price 2d. (3d. by post) or 3s. 6d. for 25, gilt edges, suitable for insertion in the small Prayer Books. Also, an enlarged edition, beautifully rubricated and bound, price 1s. 6d., or paper cover, 9d.

MILL.—FIVE SERMONS ON THE NATURE OF

CHRISTIANITY. Preached in Advent and Christmas Tide, 1846, before the University of Cambridge. By W. H. MILL, D.D., late Fellow of Trinity College, and Christian Advocate; Chaplain to the Most Reverend the Lord Archbishop of Canterbury. 8vo., cloth. *Nearly ready.*

MILL.—A LETTER TO A CLERGYMAN IN LONDON

on the Theological Character of Dr. Hampden's Bampton Lectures, and the Extent and Value of Subsequent qualifications to their meaning. By W. H. MILL, D.D., Rector of Brasted, Kent. Domestic Chaplain to the Lord Archbishop of Canterbury. 8vo., sewed, price 1s., or 1s. 4d. by post.

To the Friends of the Scottish Church and Churchmen in general.
Third Edition, Revised and Enlarged.

MONTGOMERY.—THE SCOTTISH CHURCH AND

THE ENGLISH SCHISMATICS: being LETTERS ON THE RECENT SCHISM IN SCOTLAND. With a Dedicatory Epistle to the Right Reverend the Bishop of Glasgow; and a Documentary Appendix. By the Rev. ROBERT MONTGOMERY, M.A., Oxon., Author of "The Gospel in Advance of the Age," "Luther," &c. 3s.

NOTICE.—The attention of Churchmen is respectfully requested to this publication, which all the Scottish Prelates, as well as many of the English and American ones, have pronounced to be the most adequate exponent of the subject there discussed.

"We feel bound to state that the part which MR. MONTGOMERY has taken in this matter reflects the highest lustre both on his character as a Clergyman and gentleman. * * He now stands with a character for a noble and disinterested championship of the truth, for soundness of doctrine, and honesty of purpose, which has met with the approbation and esteem, as well of his former Diocesan, as of every good Churchman in England, Ireland, and Scotland, where his 'LETTERS' have been read, and the facts of the case become known."—*Theologian* for May, pp. 311, 312.

MONRO.—THE DARK RIVER.
An Allegory. By the Rev. EDWARD MONRO, Perpetual Curate of Harrow Weald. 12mo. cloth, 2s. 6d.

MONRO.—THE VAST ARMY.
An Allegory. By the Rev. E. MONRO. 12mo. cloth, 2s. 6d.

MONRO.—THE COMBATANTS.
An Allegory. By the Rev. E. MONRO. 2s. 6d. *Nearly ready.*

MONRO.—STORIES OF COTTAGERS.
By the Rev. E. MONRO. 18mo. cloth, 2s. 6d.; or the Stories separate in a packet, 2s.

MONRO.—DERMOT, THE UNBAPTIZED.
By the Rev. E. MONRO. 3d.

MONRO.—WANDERING WILLIE, THE SPONSOR.
By the Rev. E. MONRO. 2d.

MONRO.—OLD ROBERT GRAY.
By the Rev. E. MONRO. 3d.

MONTAGUE'S, Bp. ARTICLES OF INQUIRY PUT
FORTH AT HIS PRIMARY VISITATION, 1638, with a Memoir. Foolscap 8vo., 124 pp., 1s. 6d.

MORNING AND EVENING EXERCISES FOR BE-
GINNERS. A Form of Daily Prayer: with a Short Form for Daily Examination of the Conscience. Compiled by a Clergyman. Price 2d., or 14s. per hundred.

MORRISON.—THE CREED AS EXTERNALLY SET
FORTH AND ENFORCED BY THE CHURCH CALENDAR. By the Rev. A. J. W. MORRISON, M.A., Curate of S. Illogan, Cornwall. On a large sheet, for the use of Schools, price 4d., or 6d. by post.

NEALE.—A HISTORY OF THE HOLY EASTERN
CHURCH :—A History of the Patriarchate of Alexandria. In Six Books. By the Rev. J. M. NEALE, M.A., of Trinity College, Cambridge, Warden of Sackville College, East Grinsted. 2 Vols. Demy 8vo., price 24s.

Book I. From the Foundation of the Church of Alexandria to the Rise of Nestorianism.—Book II. From the Rise of the Nestorian Heresy to the Deposition of Dioscorus and the Great Schism.—Book III. From the Deposition of Dioscorus to the Capture of Alexandria by the Saracens.—Book IV. From the Capture of Alexandria by the Saracens to the Accession of Saladin as Vizir.—Book V. From the Accession of Saladin as Vizir to the First Interference of the Portuguese.—Book VI. From the First Interference of the Portuguese to the Death of Hierotheus.

NEALE.—LAYS AND LEGENDS OF THE CHURCH
IN ENGLAND. By the Rev. J. M. NEALE, M.A. 12mo., cloth,
3s. 6d.

NEALE.—ON PRIVATE DEVOTION IN CHURCHES.
The Re-introduction of the System of Private Devotion in Churches
considered in a Letter to the Venerable the President of the
Cambridge Camden Society. By the Rev. J. M. NEALE, M.A.
Price 1s.

NEALE.—ENGLISH HISTORY FOR CHILDREN.
From the Invasion of the Romans, to the Accession of Queen
Victoria. By the Rev. J. M. NEALE, M.A. A New Edition,
Revised. 18mo. cloth. Price 2s. 6d.

"We can conscientiously recommend this nice little book, and we
trust that it is the first step towards the banishment from nursery and
school-room of those odious compilations that at present disgrace the
name of 'Histories for the Young,' and which are fraught with eminent
danger to the moral rectitude of those who read them."—*Ecclesiastic*,
Feb. 1846.

NEALE.—TRIUMPHS OF THE CROSS.
Tales and Sketches of Christian Heroism and Christian Endurance.
By the Rev. J. M. NEALE, M.A. 2 Vols. 18mo. cloth. Price
2s. each.

NEALE.—HYMNS FOR THE SICK.
By the Rev. J. M. NEALE, M.A. Large Type. Price 10d., or
1s. 6d. cloth.

NEALE.—HYMNS FOR CHILDREN.
By the Rev. J. M. NEALE, M.A. First and Second Series.
3d. each.

NEALE.—HYMNS FOR THE YOUNG.
By the Rev. J. M. NEALE, M.A. 3d.

₊ These three little works may be had, neatly bound together in
cloth, price 1s.

NEALE.—SONGS AND BALLADS FOR MANUFAC-
TURERS. By the Rev. J. M. NEALE, M.A. Price 3d.

NEALE.—SONGS FOR THE PEOPLE.
By the Rev. J. M. NEALE, M.A. 3d., or 21s. per 100.

₊ These may also be had, stitched together in a neat Wrapper,
price 6d., or 5s. per dozen.

NEALE.—STORIES FROM HEATHEN MYTHOLOGY
AND GREEK HISTORY FOR THE USE OF CHRISTIAN
CHILDREN. By the Rev. J. M. NEALE, M.A. 18mo. cloth.
Price 2s.

NEALE.—STORIES OF THE CRUSADES.

De Hellingley and the Crusade of S. Louis. Comprising a Historical View of the Period. By the Rev. J. M. NEALE, M.A. With Frontispiece by SELOUS, and Two Plans. 12mo. cloth, 3s. 6d.; half bound in morocco, 5s.

NEALE.—DUCHENIER, or the Revolt of La Vendée.

By the Rev. J. M. NEALE, M.A. 12mo. cloth, uniform with the above, price 4s. 6d.; half bound in morocco, 5s.

NEALE.—HIEROLOGUS; OR, THE CHURCH TOURISTS.

By the Rev. J. M. NEALE, M.A. 12mo. cloth. Price 6s. Cheap Edition, in 2 parts, price 1s. 8d. each.

OF THE DUE AND LOWLY REVERENCE TO BE DONE BY ALL AT THE MENTION OF THE HOLY NAME OF JESUS, in time of Divine Service. Price 1d., or 6s. 6d. per 100.

ORDER FOR COMPLINE, or, Prayers before Bed-Time. In post 8vo., price 4d., in a stiff cover, or 6d. by post.

ORGANS, a Short Account of, Erected in England since the Restoration. (Illustrated by numerous Wood-cuts, consisting of drawings of existing examples and designs for Organ Cases, by A. W. PUGIN, ESQ.) By a Member of the University of Cambridge. Fcp. 8vo., price 6s. cloth.

OSMOND.—CHRISTIAN MEMORIALS.

Being a Series of Designs for Headstones, &c., designed and drawn on stone by WILLIAM OSMOND, Jun., Salisbury. In Parts. 4to. Price 2s. 6d. each. To be completed in about six Parts.

PAGET.—THE LIVING AND THE DEAD.

Practical Sermons on the Burial Service. By the Rev. F. E. PAGET, M.A., Rector of Elford. 12mo. cloth, 6s. 6d.

PAGET.—SERMONS ON DUTIES OF DAILY LIFE.

By the Rev. F. E. PAGET, M.A. Second Edition. 12mo. Price 6s. 6d.

PAGET.—SERMONS ON THE SAINTS' DAYS AND FESTIVALS OF THE CHURCH. By the Rev. F. E. PAGET, Rector of Elford. 12mo. cloth, price 7s.

PAGET.—THE CHRISTIAN'S DAY.

By the Rev. F. E. PAGET, M.A. NEW EDITION. *In square 24mo. with bordered pages, and Frontispiece from Overbeck.* Price 3s. 6d. cloth. 6s. morocco. Antique morocco, 21s.

PAGET.—SURSUM CORDA: AIDS TO PRIVATE
DEVOTION. Being a Body of Prayers collected from the Writings
of English Churchmen. Compiled and arranged by FRANCIS
E. PAGET, M.A. In Two Parts, square 24mo., Bordered Pages,
and Beautiful Frontispiece, price 5s., or in Plain Morocco 7s. 6d.;
for presents, Morocco Extra 10s. 6d., or Antique Morocco 22s. 6d.
*** *This is the work announced in the "Christian's Day," under the
title, "A Manual of Devotions," as a Companion to that work.*

PAGET.—MILFORD MALVOISIN; or, PEWS AND
PEWHOLDERS. By the Rev. F. E. PAGET, M.A. 2nd Edition.
12mo. Price 3s.

PAGET.—S. ANTHOLIN'S; or, OLD CHURCHES
AND NEW. By the Rev. F. E. PAGET, M.A. 4th Edition.
12mo. 2s. 6d.

PAGET.—THE PAGEANT; or, PLEASURE AND ITS
PRICE. By the Rev. F. E. PAGET, M.A. 2nd Edition. 12mo.
Price 4s. 6d.

PAGET.—THE WARDEN OF BERKINGHOLT.
By the Rev. F. E. PAGET, M.A. 2nd Edition. 12mo. 5s. Cheap
Edition, in 2 parts, 1s. 4d. each.

PAGET.—LUKE SHARP; or KNOWLEDGE WITHOUT
RELIGION. A Tale of Modern Education. By the Rev. F. E.
PAGET, M.A. 13mo. Price 2s. 6d.

PAGET.—A TRACT UPON TOMBSTONES; or,
Suggestions for the consideration of Persons intending to set up
that kind of Monument to the Memory of Deceased Friends.
By the Rev. F. E. PAGET, M.A. Demy 8vo., with numerous
Illustrations, Second Edition, price 1s., or 1s. 2d. by post.

PAGET.—MEMORANDA PAROCHIALIA; or, THE
PARISH PRIEST'S GUIDE. By the Rev. F. E. PAGET, M.A.
Third Edition, printed on writing paper, bound in leather, with
tuck and pockets, price 3s. 6d. Double size, 5s.

PAGET.—TALES OF THE VILLAGE CHILDREN.
By the Rev. F. E. PAGET, M.A. First Series. 18mo. cloth.
Price 2s. 6d.

PAGET.—TALES OF THE VILLAGE CHILDREN.
By the Rev. F. E. PAGET, M.A. Second Series. 18mo. cloth.
Price 2s. 6d.

PAGET.—THE HOPE OF THE KATZEKOPFS.
A Fairy Tale. By the Rev. F. E. PAGET, M.A. Illustrated by
Scott. 18mo. cloth, 2s. 6d. Second Edition. With a Preface by
the Author.

PAGET.—PRAYERS ON BEHALF OF THE CHURCH
AND HER CHILDREN in time of TROUBLE. By the Rev.
F. E. PAGET, M.A. 1s.

PAGET.—THE IDOLATRY OF COVETOUSNESS.
By the Rev. F. E. PAGET, M.A. 1s.

PAGET.—A FEW PRAYERS, AND A FEW WORDS
ABOUT PRAYER. By the Rev. F. E. PAGET, M.A. 2d. A
Packet of 13, 2s.

PAGET.—HOW TO BE USEFUL AND HAPPY.
By the Rev. F. E. PAGET, M.A. 2d. A Packet of 13, 2s.

PAGET.—HOW TO SPEND SUNDAY WELL AND
HAPPILY. By the Rev. F. E. PAGET, M.A. On a card, 1d.

PALEY.—THE ECCLESIOLOGIST'S GUIDE to the
Churches within a Circuit of Seven Miles round Cambridge.
With Introductory Remarks. By F. A. PALEY, M.A. Price 2s.

PEARSALL.—HYMNS OF THE CHURCH,
Pointed as they are to be Chanted ; together with the VERSICLES,
LITANY, ATHANASIAN CREED, RESPONSES after the COMMAND-
MENTS, &c. Set to Music by T. TALLIS. Revised and arranged
by Mr. PEARSALL, of Lichfield Cathedral. Small 8vo., cloth.
Price 2s., with a reduction to clergymen introducing it into
their churches.

PEOPLE'S LIBRARY OF THE FATHERS.
A series of Select Treatises from the Patristic Writings. Translated
by Priests of the English Church. In Parts 6d. each.

" The PEOPLE'S LIBRARY OF THE FATHERS has our hearty approval.
A judicious selection from the writings of the Fathers must be eminently serviceable. And we sincerely hope that this cheap and well-
arranged edition may secure for them such a circulation as their own
merits deserve, and the circumstances of our Church require."—
Ecclesiastic, October.

PEREIRA.—TENTATIVA THEOLOGICA.
Por P. ANTONIO PEREIRA DE FIGUEREDO. Translated from the
Original Portuguese, by the Rev. EDWARD H. LANDON, M.A.,
late of C.C.C., Camb. This celebrated work, written about the
year 1760, by the most learned divine whom the Portuguese Church
has produced, is a general defence of Episcopal Rights against
Ultra-Montane usurpations. It has been translated into almost
every European language, except English, though publicly burnt
in Rome. In demy 8vo., cloth, price 9s.

" We think the translation of this work is good service done to the
Church of England at the present time. MR. NEALE has prefixed a
useful and interesting Introduction to this work, sketching the circumstances of PEREIRA'S Life, and those which led to this publication,
which he says excited the greatest interest in Europe, and was publicly burnt in Rome."—*Christian Remembrancer, April*, 1847.

POOLE.—TWELVE PRACTICAL SERMONS on the
HOLY COMMUNION. By the Rev. G. A. POOLE, M.A., Rector
of Welford. 12mo., 4s. 6d.

POOLE.—A HISTORY OF ENGLAND,
From the First Invasion by the Romans to the Accession of Queen
Victoria. By the Rev. G. A. POOLE, M.A. 2 vols. cloth, 9s.

"The author is not aware of the existence of a single History of
England, adapted in size and pretensions to the use of the upper
classes in schools, in which any approach is made to sound ecclesiastical principles, or in which due reverence is shown to the Church
of England, either before or after the Reformation, as a true and
living member of the Body of CHRIST. He hopes that the present
volumes will supply this deficiency, and furnish for the use of the
learner an abstract of events necessarily short and imperfect, but
sound and true as far as it goes, and of such a character as not to
array all his early impressions against the truth of history, important,
if ever, when it touches the evidences of CHRIST's Presence with His
Church, in the land of all our immediate natural, civil, ecclesiastical,
and spiritual relations."—*Preface.*

POPULAR TALES from the German, including Spindler's
S. SYLVESTER'S NIGHT; Hauff's COLD HEART, &c. With cuts
from Franklin. Cloth, 1s. 6d.

POPULAR TRACTS, Illustrating the Prayer Book of the
Church of England.
Already published :
No. I. THE BAPTISMAL SERVICES. Second
Edition. Price 1d.
No. II. THE DRESS OF THE CLERGY, with an
Illustration. Price 2d.
No. III. THE BURIAL SERVICE. With an Appendix
on Modern Burials, Monuments, and Epitaphs, containing Seven
Designs for Headstones, and an Alphabet for Inscriptions. Price 6d.
No. IV. THE ORDINATION SERVICES. Price 4d.

These Tracts are designed, as their name implies, for THE PEOPLE,
for Clergy and Laity, for rich and poor. They may serve to remind
the learned, as well as to instruct the ignorant. They are written in
a spirit of the utmost attachment and obedience to the Holy English
Church, and to that Catholick Church of which She is a Pure and
Apostolick Branch. Their writers are independent of any *party*, and
regardless of any sectarian comments.
"This promises to be a convenient and useful series, if we may
judge by the first number."—*English Churchman.*

The following are in preparation :
No. V. THE MARRIAGE SERVICE.
No. VI. THE ARRANGEMENT AND DECORATION
OF CHURCHES.
Communications for the Editor to be addressed to the care of MR.
MASTERS, Aldersgate Street, London.

POYNINGS.
A Tale of the Revolution. Price 2s. 6d.

PRACTICAL CHRISTIAN'S LIBRARY.

<table>
<tr><td></td><td></td><td>s.</td><td>d.</td></tr>
<tr><td>1.</td><td>Learn to Die.—[Sutton.]</td><td>1</td><td>0</td></tr>
<tr><td>2.</td><td>Practice of Divine Love.—[Ken.]</td><td>0</td><td>9</td></tr>
<tr><td>3.</td><td>Private Devotions.—[Spinckes.]</td><td>1</td><td>6</td></tr>
<tr><td>4.</td><td>Parable of the Pilgrim.—[Patrick.]</td><td>1</td><td>0</td></tr>
<tr><td>5.</td><td>The Imitation of Christ.—[A Kempis.]</td><td>1</td><td>0</td></tr>
<tr><td>6.</td><td>Manual of Prayer for the Young.—[Ken.]</td><td>0</td><td>6</td></tr>
<tr><td>7.</td><td>Guide to the Holy Communion.—[Nelson.]</td><td>0</td><td>8</td></tr>
<tr><td>8.</td><td>Guide to the Penitent.—[Kettlewell.]</td><td>0</td><td>9</td></tr>
<tr><td>9.</td><td>The Golden Grove.—[Taylor.]</td><td>0</td><td>9</td></tr>
<tr><td>10.</td><td>Daily Exercises.—[Horneck.]</td><td>0</td><td>9</td></tr>
<tr><td>11.</td><td>Life of Ambrose Bonwicke</td><td>1</td><td>0</td></tr>
<tr><td>12.</td><td>Plain Sermons.—[Andrewes.]</td><td>2</td><td>0</td></tr>
<tr><td>13.</td><td>Life of Bishop Bull.—[Nelson.]</td><td>1</td><td>6</td></tr>
<tr><td>14.</td><td>Death, Judgment, Heaven, and Hell.—[Bp. Taylor.]</td><td>0</td><td>9</td></tr>
<tr><td>15.</td><td>Companion to the Prayer Book</td><td>1</td><td>0</td></tr>
<tr><td>16.</td><td>Christian Contentment.—[Sanderson.]</td><td>0</td><td>9</td></tr>
<tr><td>17.</td><td>Steps to the Altar</td><td>1</td><td>0</td></tr>
<tr><td>18.</td><td>Selections from Hooker.—[Keble.]</td><td>1</td><td>6</td></tr>
<tr><td>19.</td><td>Advice to a Friend.—[Patrick.]</td><td>1</td><td>6</td></tr>
<tr><td>20.</td><td>Repentance and Fasting.—[Patrick.]</td><td>1</td><td>6</td></tr>
<tr><td>21.</td><td>On Prayer.—[Patrick.]</td><td>2</td><td>0</td></tr>
<tr><td>22.</td><td>Practical Christian, Part I.—[Sherlock.]</td><td>2</td><td>0</td></tr>
<tr><td>23.</td><td>————————, Part II.—[Sherlock.]</td><td>2</td><td>0</td></tr>
<tr><td>24.</td><td>Meditations on the Eucharist.—[Sutton.]</td><td>2</td><td>0</td></tr>
<tr><td>25.</td><td>Learn to Live.—[Sutton.]</td><td>1</td><td>6</td></tr>
<tr><td>26.</td><td>The Art of Contentment, by author of " Whole Duty of Man"</td><td>1</td><td>6</td></tr>
<tr><td>27.</td><td>Meditations for a Fortnight.—[Gerhard.]</td><td>0</td><td>6</td></tr>
<tr><td>28.</td><td>The Heart's Ease.—[Patrick.]</td><td>1</td><td>6</td></tr>
<tr><td>29.</td><td>Doctrine and Discipline of the Church of England.— [Heylin.]</td><td>0</td><td>8</td></tr>
<tr><td>30.</td><td>Manual for Confirmation and first Communion</td><td>0</td><td>8</td></tr>
<tr><td>31.</td><td>Hymns for Public and Private Use</td><td>2</td><td>0</td></tr>
<tr><td>32.</td><td>The Young Churchman's Manual</td><td>1</td><td>0</td></tr>
<tr><td>33.</td><td>The Seven Penitential Psalms</td><td>1</td><td>0</td></tr>
<tr><td>34.</td><td>Cosin's Devotions</td><td>1</td><td>0</td></tr>
<tr><td>35.</td><td>Bishop Taylor's Holy Living</td><td>2</td><td>0</td></tr>
<tr><td>36.</td><td>Bishop Taylor's Holy Dying</td><td>2</td><td>0</td></tr>
<tr><td>37.</td><td>The Confessions of St. Augustine</td><td>2</td><td>0</td></tr>
</table>

PRAYERS AND SELF-EXAMINATION FOR LITTLE CHILDREN. Price 2d.

PRIVATE DEVOTION,

A Short Form for the Use of Children. **On a sheet for suspension** in bed-rooms, price 1d., or 6s. 6d. per 100. Also in a Book, 1d.

PROGRESS OF THE CHURCH OF ENGLAND SINCE THE REFORMATION (The). Reprinted with corrections from the " Ecclesiastic." Small 8vo., in a neat wrapper 6d., or cloth 9d.

QUESTIONS FOR SELF-EXAMINATION for the Use of the Clergy in what Concerns their Sacred Office. Price 6d., Rubricated.

RAWLINS.—THE FAMINE IN IRELAND.
A Poem. By C. A. RAWLINS. Handsomely printed on large post 8vo., with gilt edges, and in fancy wrapper, price 1s.

REASONS (A FEW PLAIN) FOR REMAINING IN THE ENGLISH CHURCH, in a Letter to a Friend. Price 4d.

RECOLLECTIONS OF A SOLDIER'S WIDOW.
By the author of "Sun setting; or, Old Age in its Glory." 18mo. Price 1s.

RUSSELL.—THE JUDGMENT OF THE ANGLICAN CHURCH (Posterior to the Reformation) on the Sufficiency of Holy Scripture, and the Authority of the Holy Catholic Church in matters of Faith ; as contained in her authorized Formularies, and Illustrated by the Writings of her elder Masters and Doctors. With an Introduction, Notes, and Appendix. By the Rev. J. F. RUSSELL, B.C.L. 8vo., cloth, 10s. 6d.

RUSSELL.—LAYS CONCERNING THE EARLY CHURCH. By the Rev. J. F. RUSSELL, B.C.L. Fcap. 8vo price 2s. 6d. cloth.

RUSSELL.—ANGLICAN ORDINATIONS VALID.
A Refutation of certain Statements in the Second and Third Chapters of "The Validity of Anglican Ordinations Examined. By the Very Reverend Peter Richard Kenrick, V.G." By the Rev. J. F. RUSSELL, B.C.L. Price 1s., or 1s. 4d. post free.

RUSSELL.—OBEDIENCE TO THE CHURCH IN THINGS RITUAL. A Sermon, preached in St. James's Church, Enfield Highway. By the Rev. J. F. RUSSELL, B.C.L. 8vo., price 1s., 12mo., price 6d.

SCOTTISH MAGAZINE AND CHURCHMAN'S RE- VIEW. In Monthly Parts, price 6d. Commenced in January, 1848.

SERMONS FOR SUNDAYS, FESTIVALS, FASTS, AND other Liturgical Occasions. Edited by the REV. ALEXANDER WATSON, M.A., Curate of St. John's, Cheltenham.
The FIRST SERIES, complete in One Volume, contains Thirty-six Original Sermons, and may be had in Six Parts, price One Shilling each, or bound in cloth, price 7s. 6d.
The SECOND SERIES contains SERMONS FOR EVERY SUNDAY AND HOLY DAY IN THE CHURCH'S YEAR. It may be had in Eighteen Parts, price 1s. each, or in 3 vols. cloth, price 7s. 6d. each.
The THIRD SERIES, complete in One Volume, contains Thirty-two Sermons, illustrating some OCCASIONAL OFFICES OF THE BOOK OF COMMON PRAYER, may be had in Six Parts, price 1s. each, or bound in cloth, price 7s. 6d.
All Three Series are also kept, bound uniformly in half-calf, cloth sides, 10s.; whole calf, 11s.; calf extra, 12s. per volume.

A list of the Contributors, Holy Days, Subjects, and Texts, may be had, free by post, on application.

SERMONS FOR THE PEOPLE. Price 1d.

No. I. CHRIST AND THE "COMMON PEOPLE."
II. THE "LOST SHEEP."
III. THE "PIECE OF SILVER."
IV. THE "PRODIGAL'S SIN."

To be continued.

This Series has been commenced with a view of supplying clergymen with discourses which they may place in the hands of those of their parishioners who do not frequent their parish church. Sold in packets of 25 for 1s. 6d.; 50 for 3s. By post 6d. extra.

SCUDAMORE.—STEPS TO THE ALTAR; a Manual of Devotion for the Blessed Eucharist. By W. E. SCUDAMORE, M.A., Rector of Ditchington. Third Edition, carefully revised and enlarged. Price 1s. Fine paper edition in morocco, 3s. 6d.

SMITH, R.—THE CHURCH CATECHISM ILLUS- TRATED BY PASSAGES FROM THE BOOK OF COMMON PRAYER. By the Rev. ROWLAND SMITH, M.A., formerly of S. John's Coll., Oxford. In stiff cover, price 4d., or 6d. by post.

SMITH, C.—SERMONS PREACHED IN HOLY WEEK, and at other Seasons of the Church, by the Rev. CHARLES F. SMITH, Incumbent of S. John's, Pendlebury, near Manchester, and Domestic Chaplain to the Right Hon. Lord Viscount Combermere. 12mo. cloth. Price 6s.

SMITH, C.—GOD'S THREATENINGS FOR OUR SINS. A Sermon preached on Sunday, October 11th, the Eighteenth Sunday after Trinity; with a Preface, on the present Spiritual Condition of the Manufacturing Districts. By the Rev. CHARLES FELTON SMITH, B.A., of Queen's College, Cambridge; Incumbent of Pendlebury, near Manchester, and Domestic Chaplain to the Right Hon. Lord Viscount Combermere. 8vo. Price 1s.

STRETTON.—A SERIES OF SERMONS ON THE ACTS OF MARY MAGDALEN. Preached in the Parish Church of S. Paul, Knightsbridge, by the Rev. HENRY STRETTON, M.A., Oxon., Curate of Chideock, in Whitchurch-Canonicorum, Diocese of Sarum, late Senior Assistant Curate of S. Paul's, Knightsbridge. *Nearly Ready.*

SUN-SETTING; OR, OLD AGE IN ITS GLORY, AND "OLD SIX-O'CLOCK." By the author of "Recollections of a Soldier's Widow." 18mo. 6d.

SWEDISH BROTHERS.

Cuts, price 1s. 6d. 18mo. cloth.

TEALE.—LIVES OF EMINENT ENGLISH DIVINES. Containing Bishop Andrewes, Dr. Hammond, Bishop Bull, Bishop Wilson, and Jones of Nayland. By the Rev. WILLIAM HENRY TEALE, M.A., Vicar of Roystone, Diocese of York. In royal 18mo. with Steel Engravings, price 5s. cloth.

*** This is intended as a Companion to the Author's "Lives of Eminent English Laymen."

THEOLOGIAN AND ECCLESIASTIC.
A Magazine relating to the Affairs of the Church, Education, &c. In Monthly Parts, price 1s. 6d.

The range of subjects which this Magazine is intended to embrace, will appear from the Title chosen ; and the rule on which it is conducted, is that of setting forth the distinctive principles of the Church boldly and uncompromisingly, with as little reference as possible to those who may be supposed to differ.

Vols. I., II., III., and IV., including Parts I. to XXIV. with Titles and Indexes, are now ready, price 10s. 6d. each, bound in cloth.

TRUEFITT.—ARCHITECTURAL SKETCHES ON
THE CONTINENT. By GEORGE TRUEFITT, Architect. Sixty Engraved Subjects in Demy 4to., price 10s. 6d., bound in cloth.

TUTE.—HOLY TIMES AND SCENES.
By the Rev. JOHN STANLEY TUTE, B.A., of S. John's College, Cambridge. In small 8vo., price 3s., cloth.

TUTE.—THE CHAMPION OF THE CROSS.
An Allegory. By the Rev. J. S. TUTE, B.A. 12mo. price 2s. 6d. cloth.

TWOPENNY REWARD BOOKS.
The Two Sheep.—Little Stories for Little Children.—" I am so Happy."—The Brother's Sacrifice.—The Dumb Boy.

VISITATIO INFIRMORUM ; or, Offices for the Clergy
in Directing, Comforting, and Praying with the Sick. Compiled from Approved Sources. With an Introduction. By WILLIAM H. COPE, M.A., Minor Canon and Librarian of S. Peter's, Westminster, and Chaplain to the Westminster Hospital; and HENRY STRETTON, M.A., Curate of Chideock, Diocese of Sarum, late Senior Assistant Curate of S. Paul's, Knightsbridge. 12mo. Calf, price 16s., morocco 20s. Also, with Silver and Gilt clasps, corners, &c.

WALCOTT.—AN ORDER OF ANTHEMS.
Selected from the New Version of the Psalter, that may be followed in Parish Choirs, and places where they sing, on all Sundays and Holy Days and Evens observed in the Church of England. By the Rev. MACKENZIE WALCOTT, M.A., Curate of S. Margaret's, Westminster. On a Sheet, price 2d.

WATSON.—THE PEOPLE, EDUCATION, AND THE
CHURCH. A Letter to the RIGHT REV. THE LORD BISHOP OF EXETER, occasioned by a Letter of the Rev. W. F. HOOK, D.D., to the RIGHT REV. THE LORD BISHOP OF ST. DAVID'S. By the Rev. ALEXANDER WATSON, M.A., Curate of St. John's, Cheltenham. Reduced to 1s.

" An elaborate examination of the whole subject. We recommend it especially to such of our readers who take an active interest in the education of the Poor."—*English Churchman.*

WATSON.—THE DEVOUT CHURCHMAN; or, Daily Meditations from Advent to the Close of the Christian Year. Edited by the Rev. ALEXANDER WATSON. Vol. I., including ADVENT TO ASCENSION, is now ready, price 7s. 6d.

"This work follows the order and arrangement of the Church's year, and is of an eminently practical character. We can cordially recommend it to the Clergy as a most useful book for the private reading and instruction of their parishioners."—*English Churchman.*

WATSON.—SEVEN SAYINGS ON THE CROSS; or, The Dying CHRIST, our Prophet, Priest, and King. Being a Series of Sermons preached in St. John's Church, Cheltenham, in the Holy Week, 1847. By the Rev. ALEXANDER WATSON, M.A., Curate of the Church. 8vo. cloth, price 6s.

WEBB.—SKETCHES OF CONTINENTAL ECCLE- SIOLOGY.—Ecclesiological Notes in Belgium, the Rhenish Provinces, Bavaria, Tyrol, Lombardy, Tuscany, the Papal States, and Piedmont. By the Rev. BENJAMIN WEBB, M.A., of Trinity College, Cambridge. Demy 8vo., price 16s.

WHAT SHALL BE DONE TO REGAIN THE LOST? or, Suggestions for the Working of Populous Parishes. Demy 8vo., price 3d., or by post, 4d.

WHYTEHEAD.—COLLEGE LIFE. Letters to an Under-Graduate. By the Rev. THOMAS WHYTE-HEAD, M.A., late Fellow of S. John's College, Cambridge, and Chaplain to the Bishop of New Zealand. Foolscap 8vo. cloth, 3s. 6d.

"The author of this little volume has left behind him a memory which must be long and dearly cherished by those who knew him, and be a subject of affectionate interest to many more, who are merely acquainted with the chief points of his short, but not unserviceable life. * * * And if the little book before us shall aid in producing among those to whom it is addressed the tone of feeling and the character stamped upon it by its author, it will do no contemptible service to the Church at large."—*Ecclesiastic,* Jan. 1846.

A few copies only of this interesting work remain unsold.

WRAY.—CATHOLIC REASONS FOR REJECTING THE MODERN PRETENSIONS AND DOCTRINES OF THE CHURCH OF ROME. By the Rev. CECIL WRAY, M.A., Incumbent of S. Martin's, Liverpool. Fourth Thousand. Price 2d., or 14s. per 100.

WILLIAMS.—ANCIENT HYMNS FOR CHILDREN. By the Rev. ISAAC WILLIAMS, B.D. 18mo. cloth, price 1s. 6d.

WILLIAMS.—HYMNS ON THE CATECHISM. By the Rev. I. WILLIAMS, B.D. 18mo. cloth, price 2s.

WILLIAMS.—SACRED VERSES WITH PICTURES. By the Rev. I. WILLIAMS, B.D. 8vo. cloth, price 12s.

Congregational and Choir Music,

FOR THE USE OF THE ENGLISH CHURCH.

I. The Psalter; or, Psalms of David,

Pointed as they are to be sung in Churches, and divided and ar
ranged in lines to Sixty-seven of the Ancient Chants or Tones of the
Church, with a view to general congregational singing.   Each Psalm
is preceded by one or more appropriate Chants.   Price 2s.   A specimen
Copy by post, 2s. 6d.

Companion to the Psalter.

II. Sixty-seven Ancient Chants or Tones of the Church,

Arranged in modern notation, and in four parts for the use of Choir,
Congregational, and Accompanyist; with an explanatory dissertation
on the construction, right accent, and proper use of the Ancient
Tones.   Price 1s., or 10s. 6d. per dozen.   A Copy by Post, 1s. 2d.

III. The Canticles, Hymns, and Creed

Used in Morning and Evening Prayer, set forth and divided to the
Ancient Tones of the Church.   Each one preceded by a Chant in four
parts for the use of Choir, Congregation, and Accompanyist.   Price
6d., or £2 per 100.   A Copy by Post, 8d.

IV. Te Deum in Four Parts,

With Organ Accompaniment, founded upon the Ancient Melody in
the Sarum Antiphonal, and used in places where there were Quires
during the time of Elizabeth, and in subsequent reigns.   Price 2s.

V. Anthems and Services for Church Choirs,

Containing Seventy select pieces by the finest Composers, and suited
for every Sunday and Festival throughout the year; with Organ Accompaniment.   In a handsome 4to. volume, 21s. cloth.   The Numbers
may also be had separately.

VI. Anthems and Services.

Second Series, uniform with the above.

This volume contains several fine and scarce compositions, by
Palestrina, Marenzio, Nanino, &c.; suited to the great Church Seasons, commencing with Advent: also a Te Deum, Jubilate, Magnificat,
and Nunc Dimittis, hitherto unknown in this country.   4to. 12s. cloth.

VII. Easy Anthems for the Church Festivals.

Price 4s.

VIII. Introits adapted to the course of the Ecclesiastical Year.

The music selected from Ancient Ritual Sources, and harmonized
either for unison or four voices.   Price 5s.

NEW WORKS PUBLISHED BY

MUSICAL WORKS
For the Use of the English Church.
EDITED AND ARRANGED BY

HENRY JOHN GAUNTLETT, Mus. Doc.

The Church Tune=Book,

Containing upwards of 309 Melodies for Metrical Hymns, suited for Congregational use, with Organ Accompaniments.

THE TUNES ARE ADAPTED TO EVERY MEASURE IN USE.

Introits or Prose Hymns.

Selected from the Authorised Version of the Psalms in the Holy Bible, set to Plain Tunes or Chant Melodies, and arranged in four parts suitable for congregational singing.

Treble, Alto, Tenor, and Bass Parts with words, each 6d., or 40s. per 100. The Organ Part for accompaniment, 2s.

A Selection from the Quire Psalter,

Being the Psalms according to the Use of the Book of Common Prayer, set forth and arranged to upwards of five hundred Chants ; each Psalm having its Chants descriptive of the emotive character of the words, and divided somewhat after the manner suggested by Bishop Horsley.

This work is handsomely printed in large type and bold music note, and is published in separate Psalters, each being complete with words and music.

1. The Psalter with the Treble Part.—2. The Psalter with the Alto Part.—3. The Psalter with the Tenor Part.—4. The Psalter with the Bass Part.—5. The Psalter with the parts compressed for accompaniment.

Any of which may be had singly.

THE SELECTION, 2s. 6d. each Vocal Part. The Organ Part, with words, 5s.

General Literature.

BEZANT.—GEOGRAPHICAL QUESTIONS classed under heads, and interspersed with HISTORY and GENERAL INFORMATION. Adapted for the Use of Classes in LADIES' and GENTLEMEN'S SCHOOLS, and to the purposes of Private Teaching. By J. BEZANT, Teacher of Geography, the Classics, Mathematics, &c. Demy 18mo., strongly bound, price 2s. A KEY to the above, price 2s. bound in Leather.

BLUNDELL.—LECTURES ON THE PRINCIPLES AND PRACTICE OF MIDWIFERY. By JAMES BLUNDELL, M.D., formerly Lecturer on Midwifery and Physiology at Guy's Hospital. Edited by CHARLES SEVERN, M.D., Registrar of the Medical Society of London. Royal 18mo., neatly bound in cloth. Price 5s.

BUNBURY.—EVENINGS IN THE PYRENEES,

Comprising the Stories of Wanderers from many Lands. Edited and arranged by Selina Bunbury, Author of " Rides in the Pyrenees," " Combe Abbey," &c. Post 8vo., with Engravings, price 5s., handsomely bound.

" She writes well, because she thinks correctly ; and there is often as much vigour as of beauty in her descriptions."—*Fraser's Magazine.*
" Every thing that Miss Bunbury says or does is perfectly and gracefully feminine."—*Naval and Military Gazette.*

CLARK.—A HAND-BOOK FOR VISITORS TO THE

KENSAL GREEN CEMETERY. By Benjamin Clark. In royal 18mo., in a neat cover, with Four Engravings, price 1s.

CLAVIS BOTANICA. A Key to the Study of Botany ; on

the System arranged by Linnæus. Fourth Edition, in post 24mo., elegantly printed on tinted paper, with Coloured Frontispiece. 1s.

CURTIS.—THE YOUNG NURSE'S GUIDE ; or, IN-

STRUCTIONS UPON THE GENERAL MANAGEMENT OF THE SICK. By Joseph Curtis, M.R.C.S., F.Z.S., one of the Surgeons of the Parish of St. Pancras. Royal 18mo., cloth boards, price 2s.

CURTIS.—ADVICE TO YOUNG MARRIED WOMEN,

and those who have the Management of the Lying-in Room, upon the General Treatment of Females during Pregnancy and Confinement. Second Edition. Price 1s.

ELECTRO-CHEMICAL COPYING BOOK.

Extra size large post 4to., containing 240 leaves. Price, complete, with Ink, Sponge Box, &c., 10s. 6d.

The attention of the Clergy, Merchants, Bankers, Professors, Authors, and every class of Tradesmen, is called to this unique Article ; the simple construction of which enables any person to take a Copy of his Letters or other Memoranda instantly, without the trouble attending the Copying Press. It will be of peculiar advantage to Principals by enabling them to take their own copies of all *private* Letters and Papers.

HAMILTON.—A TREATISE ON THE CULTIVATION

of the PINE APPLE ; with an account of the various modes adopted by the most Eminent Growers, and also of the Author's Method of Growing the Vine and the Cucumber in the same House ; a Description of the Pine Stove used at Thornfield, and a Plan for the Construction of Hothouses, to combine the Culture of these Plants ; with Receipts for the Destruction of the Insects peculiar to them. By Joseph Hamilton, Gardener to F. A. Philips, Esq., Thornfield, near Stockport. Second edition, revised and corrected, with Drawings of Stoves, &c., price 5s.

HOWE.—LESSONS ON THE GLOBES,

On a Plan entirely new, in which, instead of being separately studied, they are taken together in Illustration of Terrestrial and Celestial Phænomena: with Original Familiar Explanations of the ever-varying circumstances of our Planet and the Solar System generally. Illustrated by Fifty-eight Engravings on Wood. By T. H. HOWE. Demy 12mo., price 6s.

" In regard to the correctness and profundity of its views, the book is vastly superior to the works, upon the same subject, which I have known." * * * " I have no doubt that it is really a very much more correct and learned book than books with the same object usually are."—G. B. AIRY, ESQ., *Astronomer Royal.*

A KEY TO THE LESSONS ON THE GLOBES. Bound in Leather, price 3s. 6d.

LITTLE ANNIE AND HER SISTERS. By E. W. H.

Printed on Tinted Paper, with a beautiful Frontispiece, embossed cloth, gilt edges. Price 1s. 6d.—Watered Coral Paper, 1s.

The incidents of this little work are Facts, and relate to a Family now moving in the highest circle of Society.

"The production of a pure-minded and accomplished woman, this sweet little tome is a fit offering for the young."—*Literary Gazette.*

MEMORIALS OF THE HIGHGATE CEMETERY.

With an Introductory Essay on Epitaphs and Gravestone Poetry. In royal 18mo., with Engravings, price 1s.

INTELLECTUAL AMUSEMENT FOR ALL SEASONS.

PRICE.—THE MUSES' RESPONSE, a Conversational

Game. " A set of Orient Pearls at random strung." Selected by the MISSES PRICE. Price 2s. 6d.

The object of these Cards is to lead to rational amusement and intellectual conversation.

ROBSON.—THE OLD PLAY-GOER.

By WILLIAM ROBSON. Post 8vo., price 7s. 6d. cloth.

" Mr. Robson's admiration of John Kemble and Mrs. Siddons is an echo of our own. In fact, in reading his work, we have lived over again our own play-going days. Interspersed with his reminiscences are many excellent and judicious reflections upon the drama, the stage, and theatrical matters generally. The volume, which is dedicated to Charles Kemble, is written in a spirited and vigorous style." —*John Bull.*

STRANGER'S GUIDE TO PARIS.

SINNETT.—PICTURE OF PARIS & ITS ENVIRONS:

comprising a Description of the Public Buildings, Parks, Churches, &c.; necessary information on starting; and Notices of the various Routes from the Coast. With a New Map, containing bird's eye Views of Public Buildings, and references to the principal Streets, Railway Stations, &c. Price 5s. strongly bound.

A NEW PLAN OF PARIS, with References to all the Streets, Squares, &c., and Engravings of the Public Buildings in their respective situations, by which the Stranger is greatly assisted in travelling through the Suburbs. Price 2s.

TINMOUTH.—AN INQUIRY RELATIVE TO VA-
RIOUS IMPORTANT POINTS OF SEAMANSHIP, considered
as a Branch of Practical Science. By NICHOLAS TINMOUTH,
Master Attendant of Her Majesty's Dock-yard at Woolwich.
8vo., cloth, with Engravings, price 5s. 6d.

WAKEFIELD.—MENTAL EXERCISES FOR JUVE-
NILE MINDS. By ELIZA WAKEFIELD. Demy 18mo., strongly
bound, Second Edition, price 2s. With the Key, 2s. 6d. The
Key separate, 6d.

"The exercise of our powers is ever attended with a degree of pleasure, which, once tasted, usually operates as a sufficient stimulus to a
repetition of the effort. This holds good in an especial manner with
respect to the mental powers; the delight accompanying the discovery
of truth, the legitimate object of their activity, invariably disposes, particularly in children, to renewed search, and imparts a dissatisfaction
with all that is not convincingly true."—*Preface.*

WAKEFIELD.—FIVE HUNDRED CHARADES FROM
HISTORY, GEOGRAPHY, AND BIOGRAPHY. Second Series.
Demy 18mo., bound in cloth. By ELIZA WAKEFIELD. Price
1s. 6d.

The Juvenile Englishman's Library.

I TALES of the VILLAGE CHILDREN. By the Rev. F.
E. PAGET. First Series, including "The Singers," "The Wake,"
"The Bonfire," "Beating the Bounds," "Hallowmas Eve,"
"A Sunday Walk and a Sunday Talk." 2nd Edition. 18mo.,
with numerous cuts, neatly bound in cloth, 2s. 6d.

⁎ For School Rewards, &c., the Tales may be had in a packet,
sorted, price 2s., or 4d. each.

II. THE HOPE of the KATZEKOPFS. A Fairy Tale.
Illustrated by Scott. Cloth, 2s. 6d. Second Edition. With a
Preface by the Author, the Rev. F. E. PAGET.

III. HENRI de CLERMONT; or, the Royalists of La
Vendée. A Tale of the French Revolution. By the Rev.
WILLIAM GRESLEY. With cuts, cloth, 2s.

IV. POPULAR TALES from the German, including
Spindler's S. SYLVESTER'S NIGHT; Hauff's COLD HEART, &c.
With cuts, from Franklin. Cloth, 1s. 6d.

V. TALES of the VILLAGE CHILDREN. By the Rev.
F. E. PAGET. Second Series, containing "Merry Andrew,"
Parts I. and II., "The Pancake Bell," "The April Fool." Second
Edition. With cuts, cloth, 2s. 6d.

VI. THE TRIUMPHS of the CROSS. Tales and Sketches of Christian Heroism. By the Rev. J. M. NEALE. 2nd Edition. Cloth, price 2s.

VII. EARLY FRIENDSHIP; or, the Two Catechumens. Cloth, price 1s. 6d.

VIII. THE SWEDISH BROTHERS. Cuts, price 1s. 6d. cloth.

IX. THE CHARCOAL BURNERS. Cloth, price 1s. 6d.

X. LUKE SHARP; or, KNOWLEDGE WITHOUT RELIGION. A Tale of Modern Education. By the Rev. F. E. PAGET. Price 2s. 6d.

XI. GODFREY DAVENANT; A Tale of SCHOOL LIFE. By the Rev. WILLIAM E. HEYGATE, M.A. Price 2s. 6d.

"We question whether a more healthy, impressive, and earnest work has appeared in that useful series. We do not know one which we could more heartily recommend for senior boys. The admonitions of Dr. Wilson, the head master of the school—an orthodox Dr. Arnold, —and the example and counsel of Barrow, his most exemplary pupil, cannot fail to have a beneficial influence upon all except the positively vicious, debased, and callous."—*English Churchman.*

XII. LAYS OF FAITH AND LOYALTY. By the Ven. Archdeacon CHURTON, M.A., Rector of Crayke. Price 2s.

XIII. TRIUMPHS OF THE CROSS. Part II. CHRISTIAN ENDURANCE. By the Rev. J. M. NEALE, M.A., price 2s.

"Mr. Neale has favoured us with a second part of THE TRIUMPHS OF THE CROSS, and a charming little volume it is. . . . We do think that the service done to the cause of truth by a careful and judicious selection and publication of such stories as the latter ones, especially, of this series is very considerable."—*Ecclesiastic*, June, 1846.

XIV. AN INTRODUCTION TO THE STUDY OF MODERN GEOGRAPHY. Carefully compiled, including the Latest Discoveries, and a Chapter on Ecclesiastical Geography. By the Rev. H. HOPWOOD, M.A. With a Map coloured to show the Christian, Heathen, and Mahometan Countries, English Possessions, &c. Price 2s. 6d.

"We are indebted to Mr. HOPWOOD for an 'Introduction to the study of Modern Geography,' which appears to us far superior to any manual of the kind yet in existence."—*Ecclesiastic*, Sept. 1846.

XV. COLTON GREEN. A Tale of the Black Country,
By the Rev. WILLIAM GRESLEY. Price 2s. 6d.

" The able and excellent author displays the closest intimacy with
the people and the circumstances about which he writes."—*Morning
Post.*

" We admire this little volume greatly ourselves. We know it to
have been admired by others ; and we have no fear but that such of our
readers as procure it will readily fall in with our opinions."—*Theologian.*

XVI. A HISTORY OF PORTUGAL from its erection
into a separate kingdom to the year 1836. Price 2s. 6d.

" Every one who reads it will find himself irresistibly carried on to
the end."—*Ecclesiastic.*

XVII. POYNINGS. A Tale of the Revolution. Price 2s. 6d.
" A spirited and stirring Tale of the Revolution."—*Ecclesiastic.*

XVIII. THE MANGER OF THE HOLY NIGHT,
with the TALE OF THE PRINCE SCHREIMUND AND THE PRINCESS
SCHWEIGSTILLA. From the German of GUIDO GORRES. By
C. E. H., Morwenstow. Sixteen Illustrations. Price 2s.

" This is a nice Christmas Tale, with a good moral. The Introduction is beautifully written."—*English Churchman.*

XIX. STORIES FROM HEATHEN MYTHOLOGY
AND GREEK HISTORY, for the Use of Christian Children. By the
Rev. J. M. NEALE, M.A., Author of "Tales of Christian Heroism,"
" Christian Endurance," &c., Warden of Sackville College, East
Grinsted. 2s.

XX. STORIES FROM THE CHRONICLERS.
(FROISSART). Illustrating the History, Manners, and Customs
of the Reign of Edward III. By the Rev. HENRY P. DUNSTER,
M.A. Price 2s. 6d.

XXI. A HISTORY OF ROME.
By the Rev. SAMUEL FOX, M.A., F.S.A. Price 3s.

The following are in preparation, and nearly ready :

A HISTORY OF SPAIN. By the Rev. BENNETT G. JOHNS,
S. Mark's College, Chelsea.

A HISTORY OF FRANCE. By the Rev. JOSEPH HASKOLL, B.A.

A HISTORY OF GERMANY. By the Rev. A. J. HOWELL, M.A.

A HISTORY OF HOLLAND. By the Rev. E. H. LANDON, M.A.

A HISTORY OF GREECE. By the Rev. J. M. NEALE, M.A.

PUBLICATIONS

OF THE

Ecclesiological late Cambridge Camden Society.

JOSEPH MASTERS, ALDERSGATE STREET,
Publisher to the Society.

A Hand-Book of English Ecclesiology.
In Demy 18mo., 7s., or interleaved and bound in limp calf 10s.

A Few Words to Churchwardens
On Churches and Church Ornaments. No. I. Suited to Country Parishes. Now ready, the Fourteenth Edition, revised. Price 3d., or 21s. per hundred.

A Few Words to Churchwardens
On Churches and Church Ornaments. No. II., Suited to Town or Manufacturing Parishes. Sixth Edition. Price 3d.

A Few Words to Church-Builders.
Third Edition, entirely rewritten. Price 1s.

Appendix to the former Editions of a "Few Words to Church-Builders"; containing Lists of Models for Windows, Fonts, and Rood-screens. Price 6d.

A Few Words to Parish Clerks and Sextons.
Designed for Country Parishes. A Companion to the "Few Words to Churchwardens." Second Edition. Price 2d.

A Few Words to Churchwardens;
Abridged from the Two Tracts so named. Third Edition. On a sheet, for distribution, or suspension in Vestry-Rooms.

Advice to Workmen employed in Restoring a Church. New Edition. On a Sheet, for distribution, or suspension in Vestry-Rooms.

Advice to Workmen employed in Building a Church. New Edition. On a sheet, for distribution, or suspension in Vestry-Rooms.

Church Enlargement and Church Arrangement.
Price 6d.

The History and Statisticks of Pues.
Fourth Edition, corrected, with very many additions. 2s. 6d.

A Supplement to the First and Second Editions
of "The History of Pues," containing the additional matter inserted
in the Third Edition.   Price 1s.

Twenty-four Reasons for getting rid of Church
Pues.   Ninth Edition.   Price 1d. each, or 5s. per 100.

An Argument for the Greek Origin and Meaning
of the Monogram I H S.   Price 1s. 6d.

On the History of Christian Altars.
A Paper read before the Cambridge Camden Society, Nov. 28, 1844.
Price 6d.   Second Edition.

Church Schemes;
Or Forms for the classified description of a Church.   Fourteenth
Edition, Folio : for rough copies, 6d. per score to Members; 1s. per
score to Non-Members.—4to : for transcription, 1s. per score to
Members; 2s. 6d. per score to Non-Members.

The Orientator.
A Simple Contrivance for ascertaining the Orientation of Churches.
In a case, with Directions for use and Catalogue of Saints' Days.
Price 2s.

The Report of the Society for 1846;
Together with a List of the Members, Laws, &c., of the Society.
Price 1s.   (This exhibits a general view of the constitution, objects,
and operations of the Society.)
  [Copies of the Reports for 1840, 1841, 1842, 1843, and 1844, may
still be had.]

The Transactions of the Cambridge Camden Society.
Part I.   A Selection from the Papers read before the Society at the
Meetings 1840-41.   Royal 4to.   Price 5s. 6d.

The Transactions of the Cambridge Camden Society.
Part II.   A Selection from the Papers read before the Society at
the Meetings 1841-42.   Royal 4to.   Plates.   6s.

The Transactions of the Cambridge Camden Society.
Part III.   A Selection from the Papers read at the Ordinary Meetings in 1843-45.   Royal 4to.   Price 7s. 6d.

Working Drawings of the Middle-Pointed Chancel
of All Saints, Hawton, Nottinghamshire.   Engraved in Outline by
Mr. J. Le Keux, Sen.   Atlas folio, £1. 5s.   (To Members, £1. 1s.)
  This work contains Plans, Sections, and Elevations of one of the
finest specimens of Parochial Pointed Architecture in the kingdom.

The Church of the Holy Sepulchre.
Some Account of the Church and its Restoration, with an audited
Statement of the Treasurer's Account.   Price 6d.

An Exterior View of the Same (as restored by the
Cambridge Camden Society.) A Tinted Lithograph, 2s. 6d.

The Interior of S. Sepulchre's, Cambridge:
Taken immediately after its Restoration. A Tinted Lithograph.
Price 1s.

Stalls and Screenwork in S. Mary's, Lancaster.
A Tinted Lithograph. Price 1s.

A Lithograph of the Font and Cover in the Church
of S. Edward the Confessor, Cambridge, (as restored by the Cambridge Camden Society.) 1s. 6d. plain; India paper 2s.

Illustrations of Monumental Brasses.

With accompanying historical descriptions, and many Architectural
Lithographs. Complete in 6 parts.

No. II. 5s. plain; India-paper Proofs, 7s. 6d.

Nos. I., III., IV., V., and VI., 8s. plain; India-paper Proofs, 10s. 6d.

Instrumenta Ecclesiastica.

Edited by the Cambridge Camden Society.

A series of Working Designs for the Furniture, Fittings, and Decora-
tions of Churches and their Precincts. In 12 Parts, price 2s. 6d.
each, or 1 Vol. bound, price £1. 11s. 6d.

Designs approved by the Ecclesiological late Cambridge Camden
Society for Chalices, Patens, Alms Dishes, Altar Crosses, Candlesticks,
and other Altar Furniture may be obtained through the Secretaries of
the Society, or by application to WILLIAM BUTTERFIELD, ESQ., 4, Adam
Street, Adelphi.

Church Grates, (for warming Churches,) and Coronæ Lucis, or
Chandeliers, Padlocks, &c., from MR. POTTER, South Molton Street,
Oxford Street.

Flowered Quarries, from Messrs. Powell, White Friars Glassworks.

London: J. MASTERS, Aldersgate Street, Publisher to the Society.